Praise fo

"Fresh and exciting, humorous and action-packed...urban fantasy at its best."

—Ilona Andrews, #1 New York Times *bestselling author of the Kate Daniels series*

"Makenna Fraser brings Southern sass, smarts, and charm to the mean streets of Manhattan as she battles monsters and other magical beings."

—Jennifer Estep, New York Times *bestselling author of the Elemental Assassin novels*

"Plenty more gasp- and laughter-inducing adventures...this is a thrilling series, so hang on tight, for things are going to get seriously bumpy!"

—RT Book Reviews

"A word of warning, don't start this book unless you have a solid block set aside as you simply will not be able to put it down."

—A Book Obsession

"Shearin has been on my auto-buy list for years. She is able to combine humor, mystery, suspense, slow-burn romance, high stakes, and her own spin on the supernatural into a cohesive whole. I'm addicted to finding out what will happen next in the SPI Files."

—Bookpushers

"There is so much action that you can't put this book down...fun and truly great adventure stories."

—Night Owl Romance

"There are twists, turns, danger, romance, action, but more importantly—lots of fun... Laugh out loud funny... A brilliantly addictive urban fantasy series."

—Terror Tree

Praise for the Raine Benares Novels

"Exceptional…Shearin has proven herself to be an expert storyteller with the enviable ability to provide both humor and jaw-dropping action."

—RT Book Reviews

"The kind of book you hope to find when you go to the bookstore. It takes you away to a world of danger, magic, and adventure, and it does so with dazzling wit and clever humor. It's gritty, funny, and sexy—a wonderful addition to the urban fantasy genre. I absolutely loved it. From now on Lisa Shearin is on my auto-buy list!"

—Ilona Andrews, #1 New York Times *bestselling author*

"A wonderful fantasy tale full of different races and myths and legends [that] are drawn so perfectly readers will believe they actually exist. Raine is a strong female, a leader who wants to do the right thing even when she isn't sure what that is…Lisa Shearin has the magic touch."

—Midwest Book Review

"Tons of action and adventure but it also has a bit of romance and humor…All of the characters are excellent…The complexities of the world that Ms. Shearin has developed are fabulous."

—Night Owl Reviews

"If you're new to Shearin's work, and you enjoy fantasy interspersed with an enticing romance, a little bit of humor, and a whole lot of grade-A action, this is the series for you."

—Lurv a la Mode

"The book reads more like an urban fantasy with pirates and sharp wit and humor. I found the mix quite refreshing. Lisa Shearin's fun, action-packed writing style gives this world life and vibrancy."

—Fresh Fiction

"Lisa Shearin represents that much needed voice in fantasy that combines practiced craft and a wicked sense of humor."

—Bitten by Books

"The brisk pace and increasingly complex character development propel the story on a roller-coaster ride through demons, goblins, elves, and mages while maintaining a satisfying level of romantic attention...that will leave readers chomping at the bit for more."

—Monsters and Critics

THE SOLSTICE COUNTDOWN © 2021 by Lisa Shearin
Published by Murwood Media, LLC

Editor: Betsy Mitchell
Copyeditor: Martha Trachtenberg
Cover artist: Julie Dillon
Book designer: Angie Hodapp

ISBN 978-1-7327226-5-1

THE SOLSTICE COUNTDOWN

A SPI FILES NOVEL

LISA SHEARIN

For a welcome change, I was doing what normal people did for the holidays.

I was going home to visit my family for Christmas and bringing my boyfriend to meet them.

That was where "normal" screeched to a crashing halt.

No one, nowhere, would ever describe me, my family, or my boyfriend as normal.

My name is Makenna Fraser. I'm a seer and agent for SPI (Supernatural Protection & Investigations), based out of their world headquarters in New York. Since joining SPI, I'd helped prevent a horde of grendels from turning Times Square into a midnight buffet on New Year's Eve, played a big part in keeping the tri-state area's undead population from becoming permanently dead, found a literal Hellpit in time to stop a demonic invasion of New York, helped free the delegates of the supernatural world's UN from a dimension populated by monsters picked from their nightmares, and most recently, had kept Las Vegas from becoming ground zero for a supernatural villain's coming-out party.

I loved my job, I was good at it, and lives were saved as a result. There weren't many workplaces where you could get that kind of job satisfaction.

My SPI coworkers and I would've had a much tougher time accomplishing all of the above without the goblin dark mage who was in the passenger seat of our rented Jeep Wrangler—the aforementioned boyfriend who was about to be introduced to my family.

I knew he was nervous, but he wasn't about to show it.

Rake Danescu was a dark mage, spymaster, and recently named duke of the goblin court as well as governor of Earth's goblin colony. Yes, his bank accounts packed a lot of commas and zeros, but that didn't impress me. I loved who he was, not what he had. Rake had previously occupied a place of dishonor on SPI's most-wanted and watched list. He'd redeemed himself, and was now my most-wanted, and I was taking him home to meet my family.

Rake came from an old-world world, and as we Southerners said, "his momma raised him right." Rake was a door opener, he stood when a lady entered the room (even if the woman wasn't much of a lady), and he pulled out chairs. In short, Rake was the perfect gentleman.

Except when he wasn't.

And he was perfect at that, too.

I hid my slow grin by turning my head slightly to glance out the driver's side mirror.

Rake was the consummate bad boy in all the best ways.

Mom had warned me about them. Though to hear my family talk, my dad had been a bad boy, too. Apparently, I took after Mom.

My bad boy and I were way overdue for a vacation.

For now, we'd be having Christmas with my family. An extended vacation would come later. After my SPI partner Ian Byrne's bravery during our last mission in Las Vegas, Rake had sent Ian and his girlfriend, Kylie O'Hara, SPI's director of media and public relations, on an all-expenses-paid trip to Bora Bora. After Christmas, Rake and I would be going to that tropical paradise ourselves.

We'd taken Rake's jet to Asheville and were driving the rest of the way in the rented Jeep. Once off the interstate, there was nothing but twisty mountain roads farther into North Carolina's western corner, and my hometown.

The winter solstice was tonight. We'd made the trip a few days earlier than planned because a storm was due to blow in from the south. Winter storms from the south sent up red flags with North Carolina meteorologists. What we got precipitation-wise could be bad—either snow or ice. Or both in alternating layers with sleet and hailstone sprinkles on top.

That's why we'd decided to fly in rather than drive from New York. Get there quicker, dodge the storm, and spend more time with my family.

I was coming home for the first time in a year, and I was bringing the first serious relationship I'd ever had home with me.

Home was Weird Sisters, a little town nestled in a remote mountain valley. It didn't show up on Google Maps, was named in reference to the three witches in *Macbeth,* and the first word of the town name perfectly described most of its citizens. Weird Sisters was settled by the kind of people that most people didn't want to have living next door. Outsiders passing through instinctively knew whether they belonged here or ought to just keep going. The town was located on ley lines that magnified psychic and paranormal energies. That might have been what attracted people—and non-people—to stop and stay.

SPI kept the human world from finding out about the supernatural world. It wasn't even all that difficult, especially with modern technology. The CGI in *Game of Thrones* made you suspend your disbelief of dragons. Daenerys's kids looked plenty real, but everyone knew it was just Hollywood magic, not the real kind, because there wasn't any such thing as real magic.

Or monsters.

I'd seen it hundreds of times: Humans jump through all kinds of mental hoops and contort themselves into knots, all to deny the existence of what had just scared the bejesus out of them. The truth—in the form of a ghoul—could be staring them in the face, a face about to get bitten off.

Denial was comfortable, even though it didn't make them safe. They were in denial about that, too. People thought that simply not believing in something would keep them safe from it. I had news: a ghoul didn't care if you believed in it or not. In fact, it'd probably rather you didn't. Disbelief made people freeze, or at least hesitate when they should be running for their literal lives. Hesitation merely helped that ghoul get to eating you sooner.

Our little town was filled with the weird, the eccentric, and the otherworldly. But they're the weird, eccentric, and otherworldly I grew up with and was related to. We didn't fear the strange; we welcomed it to the neighborhood and invited it home to dinner. Though in all honesty, some of our nonhuman townsfolk would rather have it *for* dinner.

Our main street is lined with shops, cafés, tearooms, and bookstores populated with psychics, mediums, crystal healers, tarot and palm readers, clairvoyants, and way too much more. Between that and the influx of tourists from all over the place, Weird Sisters has successfully made a booming business from the bizarre.

There was no hiding what Rake was from my family. Most of us were seers. Some were much more. I've had my seer ability from birth. I was a precocious one. The rest of my relatives got their gifts at the same time as their pimples.

Down through the years, the Frasers have taken it on themselves to protect the prey from the predators. Since the town's founding in 1786, there's been a Fraser in the top law enforcement spot.

Agnes Millicent Fraser is the family and town matriarch. Grandma Fraser has three daughters—and psychic visions. My mom, Margaret, is a seer who was a self-described free spirit in her younger days. (Grandma says she was a hippie.) After Mom finished sowing her wild whatever, she came back home pregnant with me, settled down, got civic-minded, and has been elected mayor three times. My aunts Eleanor and Victoria stayed close to home. Aunt Nora is a medium who runs the local B&B and is head of the town chamber of commerce. Aunt Vickie is a seer and the chief of police. Her husband is her second-in-command, and the rest of the department consists of four officers: a vampire, a werewolf, and two humans.

I'd never even known my father. There were photos and stories, but that was it. He'd been a student with Mom at university, and he'd died before I'd been born.

It'd worked out nicely that my grandmother, mom, and aunts Vickie and Nora were the only Frasers in town this year for Christmas. I wouldn't want to overwhelm Rake by subjecting him to the entire clan on the first visit.

The local color didn't stop with my family. The town's volunteer fire chief was a pyrokinetic. He mostly put out fires. Starting them was reserved for quarterly fire department training sessions. Our town doctor was the grandson of a Cherokee medicine man. There was an antique shop run by a psychometrist. Being able to identify cursed objects with a simple touch had come in handy more than once. However, not everyone who lived in Weird Sisters was a supernatural, psychic, or clued in to either one. Then there were the tourists. Business was too good to blow it by excessive PDA (public displays of ability). We kept things on the down low. For example, the local coven met monthly under the guise of a book club.

In short, nothing rattled my family.

But none of us had ever brought home a goblin for Christmas.

My mom and grandmother had both known what Rake was, and we had done the Zoom meeting thing at least once a month since Rake and I had gotten serious. Rake had been glamoured for the beginning of the first conversation, then had dropped the glamour once the two most important women in my life had been prepared. After the first call to Mom and Grandma, Aunt Vickie and Nora had joined in. Rake hadn't said it, but he had to have felt like he was sitting in an interrogation room.

At her first sight of the real Rake, Mom's eyes had gone a little wide, Aunt Vickie raised one eyebrow, Aunt Nora inhaled what had to have been half the air in the room, and Grandma's expression hadn't changed one bit. A cagey one, Grandma Fraser, hard to read and even more difficult to predict.

For the next four calls, Rake had been his usual hot goblin self, and conversation had flowed more or less smoothly. Rake was a charmer. Mom and my aunts had allowed themselves to be charmed. A little. Grandma was as hard as the granite in the mountains she and our ancestors had tamed and called their own.

It didn't mean she didn't like Rake. It meant she was reserving final judgment for a face-to-face meeting. Grandma didn't trust technology to convey what was inside a person.

She needed contact—a long handshake and an even longer stare. That little woman could pierce your soul with her bright blue eyes. "Hunter eyes," the family called them. She was in her eighties and could still shoot the fleas off a bear that made the poor choice to mess with her prized flock of wool sheep.

Grandma always said the measure of a man or woman showed in their eyes. No one, and I do mean no one, was a better judge of character than Agnes Millicent Fraser.

If she accepted Rake, everyone would accept Rake.

If she didn't…well, this would be a short and awkward visit.

All the calls had gone well, though I had to admit, it'd been less nerve-wracking to do that first look at the real Rake online. Now, everything was going to be in the same room, up close and personal. I was gonna be eating Tums like candy to get through the stress of the next few days. I was partial to Tums mints. Acid control *and* fresh breath while I argued with my family.

I'd also need to assure them that I wasn't Rake's toy or human pet. Goblins had a well-earned reputation for arrogance and thinking themselves superior to any other race or species. Rake wasn't like that. I knew it. Now I needed to make sure my family did, too.

If the next few days didn't go well, I'd be needing a prescription for something stronger than Tums.

I took a deep breath and let it out as the blur of snow-covered trees passed in my peripheral vision.

I'd chosen Rake and he'd chosen me. I desperately wanted my family to approve of him, of us. But if they didn't, they didn't. It would hurt and hurt bad because I loved my family, but it wouldn't change how I felt about him.

My family knew I'd made up my mind and given my heart (and other parts) to Rake. They also knew that if I changed my mind, it would come from me and not them.

The next move was theirs and theirs alone.

Rake reached over and rubbed my thigh. I didn't have a hand to spare. For me, driving a Wrangler took both hands, that is, when I wasn't changing gears. Sure, it had power steering, but driving a Jeep was a fully interactive experience, at least it was for me.

"It'll be fine," Rake told me.

"I'd rather it be better than fine."

"That's up to me and them. Your part is done."

"That's the problem. There's really nothing more I can do. I'm a control freak, remember?"

Silence from Rake.

"You're not even going to try to disagree with the control freak part?"

Rake smiled and patted my leg. "That's another thing I love about you. I can always count on you to tell the truth."

"Thanks. I think."

All that apprehension had grown and wadded itself up into a Gordian knot of fight-or-flight. Oh yeah, this was going to be the vacation of my dreams.

I wished we'd gone to Bora Bora with Ian and Kylie.

2

There were no straight roads within twenty miles of Weird Sisters. I knew every curve, which was why I was driving. I knew the depressions in the road where water tended to pool, and in winter, turn to ice. There was enough snow to cover the ground and roads, but not enough to form a safety barrier between tires and the ice lurking just beneath.

I'd thought that my years living in New York and rarely driving might have dulled my instincts, but once we were close to home, it all came back.

The rental Jeep was new and unfamiliar. My Jeep was an old friend that I'd grown up driving on these roads year-round. Most people would complain that they felt every bump in the road. Not me. I called it being at one with my Jeep, and it was a good thing. My Wrangler didn't have any fancy bells and whistles, just the basics needed to get me where I was going. This Jeep was virtually new and seriously loaded. In my opinion, a tricked-out Wrangler was just wrong. And "wrong" had taken a sharp left turn into "obscene" when they'd made this one an automatic.

Jeep Wranglers should have a stick. Period.

"There's a lot of fog around here," Rake noted.

"We've got hot springs running all under the town and surrounding mountains," I said. "It takes a lot of snow to get any kind of coverage. In some places, a foot at one house could be slush at their neighbor's."

Within the next quarter mile, the Jeep became completely encased in fog. The headlights reflected back at us, and I had to slow to a crawl. I knew which way the road was supposed to go, but it would be all too easy to misjudge exactly where the road was. In most places, we'd be stopped by trees. In others, it'd be a freefall off the side of the mountain. I didn't want to experience either one. I'd never run off the road around here myself, but I'd heard descriptions from Aunt Vickie of people who had.

Fortunately, I knew these roads like the proverbial back of my hand.

Rake was scowling and fiddling with his phone.

"Checking my nav skills against Google Maps?" I asked.

"I'd like to, but I can't. My phone's not working. No signal. Is that normal here?"

The tiny knot already in residence in my stomach started growing. "No, it's not. There's a tower about ten miles from here. They tried to make it look like a pine tree. Emphasis on tried."

"How much farther?"

"About seven miles, but all of it's on roads like this."

He raised a brow. "Your tourists come in on—"

"Oh, Lord no. Grandma's house isn't in town. This is the shorter…" I took a quick glance in my side and rearview mirrors at the wall of fog surrounding us. "And usually scenic route. To tell you the truth, I've never seen fog this bad."

The Jeep suddenly stalled, leaving us coasting down a dip in the road. The lights on the dashboard flickered and died. My next few words expressed my displeasure with our piece of crap rental. The Jeep slid to a stop at the bottom of the dip. I hadn't been going fast enough to have any momentum to even get a start up the next hill.

I put the Jeep in park and tried to crank it.

Click.

I tried again even though I knew what I'd get.

Another click.

Something had just sucked the life right out of the battery, or it hadn't had enough juice when we'd left Asheville. Great.

Dead Jeep, equally dead phones.

The knot in my stomach tightened with a jerk.

The horn honked and we both jumped. Then the radio blared, going up and down the line of stations and static. I looked up through the windshield, half expecting one of the UFOs from *Close Encounters of the Third Kind* to be hovering over us.

Nothing but fog above and all around.

The wind picked up, sending the powdery snow swirling as the frozen crystals caught the last of the day's light.

Twilight.

I had several bad feelings about this.

The Jeep's interior glowed red as Rake powered up his defensive magic, and our headlights began to dim along with my hopes.

I froze. "What is it?"

"Don't know, but they're not friendlies."

"They?"

These woods were home to creatures from the mythologies of those who had settled in Weird Sisters, including Scottish, Irish, German, and a smattering of Scandinavian. Then there were the local Cherokee legends. The people had immigrated and the myths they'd believed in had followed. The power inherent beneath and throughout the area had turned those beliefs into reality.

What both Rake and I sensed was all too real as well.

We were being hunted.

That thought popped complete and unbidden into my head. My lizard brain somehow knew what was about to happen and had determined it was best for our continued survival to let me in on the now not-secret.

Warm air burst from the vents that had nothing to do with the Jeep's heater. The air carried the scent of rich, damp soil—a deep forest in summer. Underneath was a sickly sweet odor of decay, and the musty scent of things long buried and recently disturbed. Fetid, rotting.

My stomach recognized it and tried to turn. I forced it down along with my own rising panic. I knew that smell. I'd been in a cemetery vault more than once during my time at SPI. It was death, but not fresh.

It was old, ancient even.

And it was hunting.

Suddenly, the full weight of that focus landed on me.

Not Rake. It was ignoring him.

Me.

I swallowed on a suddenly dry mouth. "I'm ready for Bora Bora."

"Now you tell me." Rake released the spell building around his hands to cover the entire exterior of the Jeep and then some. His dark eyes intently scanned the gloom for our attackers. And yes, that was what I was calling them. They sure as heck weren't the welcome wagon. We hadn't been physically attacked, yet, but they'd totally incapacitated our Jeep, trapping us out in the middle of snowy nowhere. The closest house was Grandma's, seven miles too far to do us a lick of good. I'd experienced strangeness in these woods, but nothing like this.

Sections of the fog darkened and split off, swirling and solidifying into horses with armored men, all impossibly large as if from time primeval. Hounds restlessly circled the horses' legs, so big their heads were visible over the top of the Jeep's hood. My eyes flicked again to the rearview and side mirrors.

We were surrounded.

The horses' hooves, men, and hounds made no sound. I could see the steam from their breathing, but that didn't necessarily mean they were alive. There were plenty of beings on the supernatural most-scary list that could fake breathing.

The armor was a mix of plate and leather, the weapons archaic. Swords hung in scabbards at waists or from saddles. A few of the men held spears at the ready. Others had bows and quivers full of arrows, and one bearded go-getter hefted a double-headed battle ax. I was grateful for Rake's shields. Without them, I didn't believe for one second that any part of the Jeep's body would stand up to the swords, axes, spears, or arrows the various riders were armed with, and appeared all too eager to use.

My guess was that there were a dozen of them. Normally not insurmountable odds, at least not for Rake, but we didn't know what else they were packing. Rake had plenty of battle magic. I prayed they didn't.

The ax wielder and one of the bowmen turned their horses aside, and a thirteenth mounted figure slowly walked his steed between them.

I saw the antlers first. How could I not? They were growing right out of his head. While the others wore helmets, their leader did not. He was taller than the others, even without the antlers, broad of shoulder and narrow of waist, his lean muscles sheathed in leather armor. His hair was blond and brushed his shoulders.

And his eyes were locked on me.

Now I knew who and what they were. Anyone with even the slightest knowledge of myths and legends knew.

The Wild Hunt.

I didn't know much aside from the basics because they were a European problem, not the New World's. There was no riderless horse that I could see. Every horse had a rider, and every rider's attention was on us. That meant the Hunt wasn't recruiting. There would be no "join or die" demand.

If they weren't hiring, they were hunting.

It appeared they had found who they were hunting.

Me.

I had no intention of enlisting or dying.

They made no move to attack. Their not wanting to kill us didn't make me feel any better. When dealing with supernaturals, there were always fates worse than death.

I took a shaky breath. "Plan?"

"We're safe in here," Rake said.

A horse's leg brushed up against the front grill, sending out a shower of red sparks. The horse didn't seem to mind. "Not sharing the confidence."

I felt a push from Rake, doubling his shield. "The Jeep's steel. The Hunt are fae. Fae don't like steel."

Yes, the body was steel, but the windows were glass. Tough glass, but still plenty breakable, especially with the power of a well-aimed ax. Rake's shields were the best, but were they good enough for these guys? From the size of them, one punch backed with serious magic and any window would be history.

"Uh, 'don't like' and 'can't slice through' are way different. Can you hit 'em from in here?" Rake knew I was talking about battlemagic, not fists.

"If I have to."

"It's me they're interested in."

Rake pushed out another surge of power, and two of the hounds yelped when his shield touched them. "Yeah, I got that, too."

"You wouldn't happen to know what kind of interested, would you?"

"No, but I can't imagine it's good. Listen, if they—"

The Jeep flipped.

I must have hit my head and been out for a moment or

minutes. I opened my eyes to snow, trampling hooves, and being choked by my own seatbelt.

I dimly heard Rake shout something in Goblin and the passenger door exploded off its frame as he took the fight to the Hunt. Metal screamed as the windshield was torn from its frame and cold air and snow filled the interior—followed by a pair of leather-gloved hands, with one gripping an entirely too sharp hunting knife.

I tried to pull back, but only succeeded in cutting off more of my air as the knife sliced through my seatbelt, and the other hand and arm easily scooped me out through where the windshield had been, lifting me free of the Jeep's wreckage and putting me face-to-face with the Master of the Wild Hunt.

He stood, lifting me with him as if I weighed nothing.

This was no myth or legend. He was solid and all too real.

His eyes were cat-like, golden green in a sharp-featured face. Those eyes bored into mine as if he couldn't believe what he was seeing.

That made two of us.

I couldn't look away from those eyes even if I wanted to. They invited you to drown and enjoy it while your life slipped away.

"You are mine."

His voice was deep and rich and soft as forest moss. It bypassed my ears and went straight to my brain, the part that could still function.

Show no fear. Don't be prey.

Rake roared a single word and I knew what was coming. I trusted his power and aim. The shockwave slammed into the Master while shielding and holding me in place. The

Master, his Hunt, horses, and hounds were blasted away in all directions, leaving us at the undisturbed ground zero of Rake's spell.

The fog lifted, and in the distance we heard the clear blast of a hunting horn, the shouts of the men, and the baying of the hounds as they rode and ran up the mountainside, where I knew there to be no trails, and into the sky beyond. Gone, but with a promise to return.

We both stared at the wreckage of the poor rental Jeep.

With a weak laugh, Rake pulled me closer. "I'm glad I got the extra insurance."

"Have you needed it before?"

"More often than I'd like."

3

We'd been attacked by the Wild Hunt, and the Master of the Hunt had told me I was his.

For most people, that would be too bizarre for belief.

For me, it was Thursday.

After the Hunt left, our phone service returned, and I phoned home. Grandma's house, not New York. That would come later. No one answered, so I left a message telling Grandma that we'd had a little accident, but we were fine and would be there soon. There was no way I was leaving what had actually happened on her machine.

As to possibly getting help from our people, we were way outside SPI HQ's jurisdiction. The southeast regional field office was in Atlanta, which, as the crow flew, wasn't that far from here, but what had just happened would be for SPI head honcho Vivienne Sagadraco's ears alone. She would determine who to send and from where. That choice was way above my pay grade, and I was grateful. I had more than enough on my plate without going back for seconds.

Rake had sent out magical feelers in every direction. We were alone, which meant we were safe. Hopefully. Using part muscle and part magic, Rake had gotten our Jeep back on its feet, so to speak. The tires and wheels were seemingly the only parts left undamaged. Having a Celtic god flip you like a pancake was hell on a car body. It hadn't done me much good, either. Then there were imprints of horses' hooves all over the Jeep.

I called Aunt Vickie, our chief of police. She was out on a call, but I talked to her husband and second-in-command, Michael Bryant. Uncle Mike was on his way here, and he said he'd call a tow truck for the Jeep.

One thing made what would follow easier. While not everyone in Weird Sisters knew that magic existed and monsters were real, the police department essentially functioned as an itty-bitty SPI. We could tell them everything, which would certainly make filing the police report easier. Rarely was anyone in town accused of seeing things that couldn't possibly exist. Anything anyone saw was all too real.

It wasn't like Aunt Vickie had ever needed a large police force. On the face of it, the biggest problem had always been traffic and parking during the town's annual Psychic Fest. A local farmer had helped solve that problem by leasing the town the field adjacent to his barn for parking. Tourists parked, and shuttles dropped them off in town, two buses running every quarter hour. Problem solved.

But unless I was mistaken, as of tonight Aunt Vickie had

more trouble than she had officers. She had a tough job on the best day. So did Mom. Keep the peace, enforce the rules, and ensure no one—human or supernatural—was resentful about being told to do either one.

The fog had vanished when the Wild Hunt had, but the Jeep still wouldn't crank, and nothing else in it was working, either. Apparently, Celtic god mojo was fatal to car electronics. Rake insisted that I sit in the Jeep while he remained right outside with the window slightly open so we could talk. The emergency flashers weren't working, but Rake had given them an infusion of his magic, so when either Uncle Mike or the tow truck driver showed up, they would see us. He'd also conjured half a dozen "flares" for the road both in front of and behind the Jeep, likewise magic powered.

"If it runs, the Hunt kills it," he was saying. "If it doesn't run, the Hunt simply kills it quicker. Also, they can appear anywhere, but not at any time. It's mostly during the solstices."

"In other words, now."

"It would seem so."

"But why here? As far as I know, we've never had the Wild Hunt in this country before." I was far from an expert on the Wild Hunt, but I did know from my SPI training that they had never been seen on this side of the pond. I remembered one thing in particular, because it was so out there. Some Christmas legends had Santa Claus as the leader of the Wild Hunt. The being that had me locked down body and soul with one arm and a pair of glowing green eyes definitely wasn't Jolly Old St. Nick. My lack of knowledge of the Wild Hunt was due to the sheer impossibility of my ever encountering them in North America, at least according to the SPI manual.

That manual was overdue for an edit. SPI had been wrong. Big-time.

"I would say maybe they got bored with Europe," Rake said, "but I know better. For the Hunt to appear so far from their usual haunts isn't a case of somebody misreading a map."

We were silent for a few moments. Both of us knew I was the reason for the Wild Hunt's side trip. What neither of us knew was why.

"Are you sure you don't have a connection to the Hunt?" Rake asked quietly.

"As positive as I can be. Could someone have sent them after me?"

Rake shook his head. "The Wild Hunt is not for hire." His eyes were on the darkened forest. He wasn't scanning for threats, at least not entirely. He was thinking. "Right before they appeared, did you smell anything funny?"

"I smelled plenty, but none of it was funny."

"Not haha. Strange."

"Besides a summer forest in the middle of a winter forest?"

"Yes, besides that."

I thought for a moment. My brain was still scrambled from being upright one moment, then hanging upside down the next. I shook my head slowly, to minimize the woozies. "No. You?"

"The slightest whiff of brimstone."

"Demons?"

Rake and I had a knack for being in places where all hell breaks loose, once literally.

"Very unlikely," he replied. "I'm referring to black magic."

"I've smelled that before. I should have recognized it, too." Over the years, I'd developed a knack for knowing when any kind of magic was in use or had recently been used.

I hadn't needed my seer vision to recognize the Wild Hunt. They had made no effort to hide who and what they were. When you were one of the supernatural world's apex predators, you didn't need to. As to sensing anything else, I'd been fully focused on the Master of the Hunt.

And he'd been fully focused on me.

Rake had been holding my hand through the open window. He raised it to his lips and kissed it. "Yes, darling, you were busy. Besides, I've had more experience with the darker flavors of magic. I know them instinctively."

"I didn't know the Wild Hunt used black magic."

"They don't. However, if my suspicions are correct, whoever brought them here does."

"Brought them here? Any names come to mind?"

"I know of entirely too many who use black magic, but none are powerful enough to force the Wild Hunt to come from Europe to your North Carolina mountains. The distance isn't the issue; it's the ancient strength of the supernaturals being summoned. The Wild Hunt is a raging, unpredictable, and unspeakably ancient force of nature. The Master of the Hunt is one of the most powerful supernatural entities in existence. One doesn't simply whistle and he appears."

"And then order them to ambush us on our way home." I shivered, and it wasn't entirely due to the cold. "The leader said, 'You are mine.' What the hell was with that?"

"Cernunnos."

"Cernun-what?"

"Cernunnos. According to your folklore, that's the name of the leader of the Wild Hunt."

It was usually good to be able to put a name to that which you feared. Only this time it wasn't.

"Why did he flip us?" I asked, pushing what he'd said to me—and their possible implications—out of my mind. "It's not like they couldn't have taken the Jeep apart with their bare hands."

"Perhaps to distract me enough to get me to drop that shield?"

Duh, Mac. "That would do it."

"That did do it."

I remembered something and stifled a laugh. "I'm not the only one in trouble."

Rake frowned. "How's that?"

"That would be you, and the trouble would be Gethen."

Rake snarled his favorite Goblin cuss word in realization.

Gethen Nazar was Rake's chief of security. Yeah, *chief* of security, meaning there was an entire staff of people charged with keeping Rake alive. My honey had a lot of people and non-people who wanted him not merely dead, but obliterated. Normally, everywhere Rake went he was leading a parade of security folks. For this trip, he'd negotiated an arrangement with Gethen. Gethen would stay in New York and let Rake and me go to North Carolina alone, with the stipulation that Rake check in every day at a certain time. If he didn't, Gethen would be on Rake's other jet with an entire security team, headed to Asheville. He'd been quite clear on that point. He'd even come right out and said, "Don't make me come down there."

We were due to check in once we got to Grandma's house.

"You gonna lie when you talk to him?" I asked.

"If I was the one in danger, I'd think about it. But this is you. Stacking the deck in our favor is the smartest thing we can do." He took his phone out of his coat pocket. "No signal again."

I stuck my head out the window and took a whiff. "No brimstone."

"We're still safe."

"You can call Gethen when we get to Grandma's. She still has a landline."

Less than five minutes later, we heard the rumble of an approaching vehicle, or maybe a tank. What came around the bend was an actual military Hummer. There was a flashing bar light on top, but it was turned off. Ice broke under the vehicle's absurd weight when Uncle Mike stopped less than ten feet away. Jumper cable distance. I had news. The Jeep had flatlined. No cable was going to bring it back from the great automotive beyond.

"Would that be—?" Rake started.

"Yep. Uncle Mike." I opened the door and got out.

Our police department's Hummer wasn't one of those prissified civilian versions. Uncle Mike had scored it from one of his Army buddies at a Fort Benning surplus auction. The thing still had its gun mount on top. No gun now, though. Vickie and Mike didn't see the need for one. Nothing happened in Weird Sisters that a 12-gauge loaded with iron, silver, or rock salt couldn't take care of. The only military purpose the Hummer served was its ability to get over or through inhospitable terrain. The thing's snow tires were scary just to look at. My favorite was the snorkel. No bridge? No problem. Through the river you'd go.

Aunt Vickie had met Michael Bryant nineteen years ago when they were both attending the Atlanta police academy. They were both seers, and had recognized it in each other, immediately giving them something big in common. The rest grew over time. Aunt Vickie had left the Atlanta force after five years to come home. She'd served under our chief at that time. She and Mike had done the long-distance relationship thing until he left Atlanta for Weird Sisters—and Aunt Vickie—a year after that.

Mike hesitated before getting out. He could've been calling in that he'd found us, but I knew better. He was checking out Rake, his little niece's serious boyfriend who was a goblin dark mage. Aunt Vickie had told him everything, but he hadn't been on any of the Zoom calls. This was his first look. Mike was sitting inside the idling Hummer, using his seer vision. He knew how I felt about Rake, but it would be up to Rake to measure up to Mike's expectations. I knew those were going to be some sky-high expectations, but I also knew Rake would meet every last one of them.

But that didn't mean Mike would cut him any slack. I knew he wouldn't.

When Mike got out of the Hummer, Rake stood straighter and squared his shoulders. I pressed my lips together against a smile. Uncle Mike brought out that reaction in guys. It didn't matter if the guy doing the reacting was a badass goblin dark mage. Mike was a bear of a man, tall, broad-shouldered, solid.

If he'd been a meme, he'd be an absolute unit. He looked plenty tough, and he was, but his heart was as big as the rest of him. All of the above came in handy in his line of work.

He started walking over to us. "What happened here, Squirt?"

That was an essay question if ever I'd heard one.

Rake didn't respond. I knew what he was thinking. These were my people. I would know how much to tell—or not tell.

I opted for introductions first.

I'd told Rake who in my family were seers. He knew exactly what my uncle Mike was seeing, he was merely waiting for the reaction.

Mike's curt nod as they shook hands acknowledged Rake's true appearance. What he thought about Rake the man would wait until he'd seen enough of Rake's character to form an opinion. And Uncle Mike would definitely form an opinion.

Rake got a handshake. I got myself a big, bear hug. When Mike set me back on my feet, I dispensed with the essay, and went with a two-word answer.

"Wild Hunt."

Now it was Mike's turn for quiet, not because he didn't believe me, but because he knew what I did for a living, and if I said our Jeep had been assaulted and battered by the Wild Hunt, that was what had happened.

I didn't mention that the Master of the Hunt had said I was his. Yes, Uncle Mike was family and knew all about supernatural criminal shenanigans. But in a situation like this, I was thinking I should only share that detail with my SPI work family. At least for now.

Mike said he had a tow truck on the way to haul the Jeep

to the small police station. While we waited, he did what he needed to do. Write up the "accident" report.

"We'll go with deer," Uncle Mike told us. "We've got some big ones around here."

"How about those?" I indicated the massive dints all over the body from what I assumed to be Wild Hunt horse hoofprints.

"The impact of the Jeep against the side of the mountain caused a small rockslide. A couple of them nailed you."

I snorted. "We got nailed all right."

Mike continued inspecting the Jeep and making notes. "Leave it up to us. Your aunt and I can explain pretty much anything on a report." He glanced at Rake. "You got the extra insurance, right?"

"Always."

Uncle Mike nodded in approval. Rake had just passed the first test—common sense.

4

Uncle Mike pulled the Hummer up in front of Grandma Fraser's house, and while he and Rake got our luggage out, I rang the bell and waited for either my grandmother or mother to let us in.

This wasn't just my grandmother's house. It was the Fraser family home. It was big, like a log cabin on steroids. Though come to think of it, that would be called a lodge. Multiple generations had always lived here together. I'd lived here all my life with my mother until a few years ago when I'd moved to New York. My Aunt Vickie had lived here until she'd married Mike, and Aunt Nora had moved into town when she'd opened her bed-and-breakfast inn. Now it was just Mom and Grandma.

I had a key to let myself in, but since Rake was with me, the proper thing to do was to ring the bell and be invited in.

It was also the safe thing to do.

The Fraser family home was warded out the wazoo and built for the ages. Thanks to those wards and other magical preservation measures, the house would not rot or deteriorate in any way. It was as solid now as the day it'd been completed a little over two hundred years ago.

"It's nothing fancy," I told Rake as he brought our luggage. "And probably not what you're used to."

Rake was smiling as he looked up at the numerous gables. "On the contrary. This reminds me of my family's hunting lodge. I spent a lot of time there as a child. I have nothing but great memories of being there." His gaze went distant. "It was the happiest time of my life."

The house was mostly wood, but the wards that had been layered over the years had sunk into and become part of the massive logs, beams, and native stone foundation. Generations of Weird Sisters practitioners had layered enough protection on our family home to qualify it as a magically impervious fortress. Nothing could get in that wasn't invited, and even then, crossing the threshold could all but strip the magic from anyone who intended us ill.

Uncle Mike and I were family. Rake was not.

Yes, I could cross the threshold and invite Rake in, but it really needed to be my grandmother who did the inviting. Or my mother. They knew this and had told me they'd be here, but it was becoming all too apparent they weren't home.

No one answered the door. I hadn't checked around back for cars, but we should've had a response by now. Normally, I wouldn't be concerned. It was three days before Christmas. There were all kinds of events in town this time of year.

But we'd been met seven miles away by the Wild Hunt.

Someone should be home, and they weren't.

The door was locked, the wards still in place.

Mike set two of my bags on the porch. "I'll check around back."

Rake carefully scanned the interior. "No one's home, and no one has tried to get inside." He repeated that assessment for Mike when he came back to report that both cars were gone.

The area between my shoulder blades, where a bullseye been in residence for the past two years, began to itch. The bullseye was imaginary, the threat I carried constantly was not. My three predecessors at SPI had met with fatal accidents that had turned out to be not accidental. I was next in line for elimination by a shadowy cabal headed up by Vivienne Sagadraco's sister Tiamat. Tonight, Cernunnos had told me I was his.

The lights were on inside, but my mother and grandmother weren't home.

The threats were forming a line. Though first things first. Get inside the house's threshold and wards, then find out where my family was.

I used my key and opened the door.

I stepped over the threshold, the wards brushing me like an enthusiastic horse-sized cat welcoming me home. Uncle Mike was right behind me. I turned around and gave Rake a big smile, though it probably looked like a grimace. "Come on in...and think happy, harmless thoughts."

Rake took a deep breath, let it out, and stepped into the house.

I blew out my breath. "You didn't burst into flames. Yay."

Rake blanched. "That's what would've happened?"

Uncle Mike took that question. "It only happened once. The other times it's like a supersized taser. You're not flopping around on the floor biting your tongue, so you did good." The radio on Mike's gun belt chirped with an incoming call. "Excuse me," he said, stepping back outside to take it.

Second test passed. Huzzah.

The Christmas tree was up and was just as I remembered. We always cut one from our land, and the garlands for the staircase and wreaths on the doors and above the fireplace had all been made from greenery and whatnot gathered from the farm.

It was beautiful.

It was home.

There were antique rifles, pistols, and cavalry swords mounted on the walls. All were family weapons dating back to the early 1700s. Softening the décor somewhat were various needlepoint, cross stitch, quilting, knit, and crochet art that shared the wall space with them.

Yes, they were art, intricate and flawlessly crafted, but most people didn't consider what they'd been crafted with.

Embroidery needles, knitting needles, and crochet hooks.

My grandma could kill you sixty ways to Sunday with a knitting needle, and I got squicked out thinking about what I'd heard she'd once done with a steel crochet hook.

The phone and answering machine were on the table next to Grandma's favorite rocking chair. There were four messages. Mine would be one of them. That told me she hadn't been home in quite a while.

It was official. Worry had jumped over concern and had landed smack dab on scared to death.

Rake had walked over to the wall next to the fireplace to look at the two black-and-white portraits that hung in a place of honor.

I went to stand beside him. "My grandfather, Colin Fraser. He died before I was born, so I only know him through photos and plenty of family stories." I indicated the other portrait. The woman's impish smile and sparkling eyes were set in a delicate face, all framed by a cascade of dark curls.

"Your grandmother?" Rake asked.

"Oh yeah. Grandpa thought Agnes McLeod was the prettiest little thing he'd ever seen, and the fact that she'd scared off every eligible male in ten counties only further raised his admiration of her. Grandma didn't make it easy for him, but in the end, she decided she might as well marry him to get him to quit pestering her." I paused. "I wish I could've known him."

And I wished I knew where Mom and Grandma were.

Rake pulled me to him and gave my shoulders a gentle squeeze. I leaned into him.

Uncle Mike cleared his throat from the other side of the room. "Your Aunt Vickie needs me. We've got a missing tourist."

That happened way more than anyone liked. The ley lines that attracted supernaturals or the psychically inclined to stay also had a tendency to get tourists and hikers turned around and lost. In winter, that wandering could easily be fatal.

"No need to worry about the ladies," he continued. "Vickie said Miss Beatrice took sick last week, and Miss Agnes took her dinner. Your mom just left the station and is on her way home." He glanced at his watch. "I'd say give her another half hour."

I let out the breath I'd been holding. I waved him on. "Go on and help Aunt Vickie. We're good here." While he'd been inspecting the Jeep for the report, I'd told him what Rake had done to scare off the Wild Hunt. Between Rake and the house wards, we were perfectly safe here.

Uncle Mike left and we took our luggage up to my room. There wouldn't be any sneaking around during the night, because we wouldn't be sleeping in separate rooms for the sake of appearances that hadn't been accurate for months. I'd already told Grandma we'd only be needing one room. Mine.

Thankfully, my childhood bedroom wasn't childish. I'd been eighteen when I'd left for college and had moved back in briefly after I'd graduated. It wasn't like there were any boy band posters on the wall, mainly because I'd never gone through a boy band phase. Thank God.

Rake picked up the phone on my bedside table and started pushing buttons.

I tossed my suitcase on the double bed. "Trying Gethen?"

"Yeah."

We stood there, looking at each other, while we waited for Gethen to answer. He didn't.

"Try Ms. Sagadraco," I said.

He did, and she didn't answer.

"Crap, what are we—" Then I remembered. "Duh. Psychic bond with my dragon boss." I closed my eyes and did what was probably the mind equivalent of screaming her name.

Nothing.

I tried again, less shrieky this time, but just as strong.

Still nada.

"Phones and computers aren't all that's not working," I said.

The front door slammed.

"Makenna!" My mother's shout was nearly a scream.

I glanced at Rake. What the hell?

"Upstairs," I yelled back.

Mom ran up the stairs, down the hall, and into my room. Next thing I knew, I was being crushed in a fierce hug.

Oh, now I understood. Uncle Mike had to have told Aunt Vickie about the Wild Hunt. Mom had been with Vickie. Mom found out and freaked out.

"Mom, we're fine." My voice was tight from lack of air. "But I'm not gonna stay that way if you don't let me breathe."

She loosened her hold but didn't let me go. "I'm sorry, honey, I—"

The back door slammed.

"Makenna Anne!"

Grandma. Though she normally reserved using my first and middle names for when I was in trouble.

Mom did the honors this time. "Upstairs!"

Grandma's speed up the stairs was only slightly slower than Mom's. She stopped in the doorway, saw the three of us, and visibly relaxed. "Thank God."

I extracted myself from my mom's arms. "Let me guess. Mike told Vickie, Vickie told you, you called Grandma, and everyone panicked."

"Yes."

"Thought so. By the way, Mom, Grandma, this is Rake. Rake, this is my family overreacting. So, what did Mike say?"

"Wild Hunt." Grandma's eyes were blazing. With rage.

Okaaay.

Mom put her hands on my shoulders. "Tell us what

happened." She was having to force herself to be calm. "Don't leave anything out."

I told them everything. Well, almost. I omitted those three, little words. There was enough panic around here.

Mom's eyes never left mine the entire time. "Describe the leader."

I did.

She took a shaky breath. "Did he say anything to you?"

"Okay, don't get more upset than you already are. I'm sure there's some kind of explanation. I'm gonna call Ms. Sagadraco, and we'll figure it—"

Mom's hands tightened on my shoulders. "What did he say?"

I hesitated. "You are mine."

Grandma spat a word that had I said it as a kid would've gotten my mouth washed out with soap.

That did it. "All due respect, what the hell is going on here?"

Rake stood motionless. "Who is Cernunnos to you?" he asked my mother.

She answered him, her eyes on me. "Makenna's father."

5

Cernunnos, the Master of the Wild Hunt, was my father.

That gave a whole new meaning to "You are mine."

To say I was in shock was putting it mildly. I'd been told my father had died before I was born. "Why didn't you tell me?" I finally managed. Grandma obviously knew. And Vickie had told Mom as soon as she'd heard about the Wild Hunt from Mike. "Am I the only one who *doesn't* know?" I was in shock, and hurt, and getting angrier by the second. My entire family had lied to me all my life.

Mom took that one. "Mother knows, and so do your aunts Vickie and Nora. I keep nothing from my sisters. No one else knows."

"Why didn't you tell me?"

Her eyes flashed. "The Master of the Wild Hunt returns

for any children they sire. If you had known about him, and even *thought* about him being your father, he could use his biological link to you and those thoughts to track you down. Somehow, he found out about you. And now that he's seen and touched you, he can find you no matter where you go or try to hide."

"He returns for his kids?" I was shouting and did nothing to turn down the volume. "Why the hell did you have sex with him?" I stopped, suddenly sick. "Did he—"

"No, he did not rape me." She gave a short, weak laugh. "He didn't need to. I wanted him and he wanted me. I could have resisted him. I could've run. I chose not to do either one. The words 'young' and 'stupid' come to mind. It was my choice." She blew out a shaky breath. "Honey, just let me tell you what happened, and then I will gladly accept your judgment, any judgment, if you still want to give it."

"Will it be the truth this time?"

My mother looked like I'd slapped her. I felt bad for that, but the hurt I felt outweighed any guilt. When people were hurt, they lashed out. At least I guess I was still people… human…whatever. Right now, I wasn't sure of anything.

"I deserved that," she said quietly. "May I continue? I at least deserve to be heard before you condemn me."

I plopped down on the bed I hoped was behind me. Rake joined me. Mom and Grandma found places as well. We'd all felt the need to sit down after the bomb Mom had dropped. "I'm sorry. Tell me."

"I was young…and your father was… Well, you've seen what he is."

Yeah, I had.

My mother was gorgeous. She had been that plus breathtaking in her late teens when I'd been conceived. She was all ivory skin, with blue eyes and nearly black hair.

I was blond and green-eyed.

Just like Cernunnos. Who probably hadn't aged a day in the last century. Breathtaking and gorgeous also applied to him. Add to that a supernatural come-hither he had in spades, and any reluctance my mom had would've been no match.

"You told me you met—the guy who I thought was my dad—in Edinburgh while at university. I take it that's when you and Cernunnos…"

"Yes. Your father is called Cernunnos now as he was then, but he was once a mortal man. After our night together he even told me his true name."

True names held incredible power in the supernatural world. They could be used against you in spells and summonings. Supernatural beings of power often used aliases to protect themselves. After a night of passion with my mother, a Celtic god had told her his true name.

Wow.

"Where did you…meet?"

"A stone circle."

To me, and to any seer, that said it all. We could see what others could not and were attracted to places that were known gateways between the worlds such as stone circles.

"I knew better than to remain inside for any length of time, and I certainly knew better than to fall asleep. It was after final exams, it was a sunny day, the stone was warm against my back. When I woke up, it was dark—and he was there. I can't claim ignorance. I knew he was real, and the antlers told me who he was." She paused, her gaze distant. "He was magnificent. He walked slowly toward me, giving me time to run. I didn't run because I didn't want to. Afterward we talked. I think the stone circle may have lengthened the time that night. He told me he was chosen in 1491 by the previous Cernunnos at the same standing stones where we met. He volunteered as a sacrifice to save his people. Eventually, he took the place of the old Master of the Hunt.

"When I realized I was pregnant, I did the only thing I could do. I left school and came home. I would have a child to take care of, his child. I needed my mother and family. Soon after you were born, I discovered that Cernunnos always returns for his children—and how he could use their knowledge of him to find them."

I swallowed hard. "You knew who and what he was and you still…kept me?"

"I did consider…not having you." Tears began welling in her eyes. "But you're mine, not his. I vowed to fight to my last breath to protect you. The mistake was mine, and you weren't going to pay for it."

I didn't speak. I couldn't.

"I would not let him take you, so when you wanted to go to New York, I encouraged it. Mother has a friend who is close to Vivienne Sagadraco. She put us in touch with her. Ms. Sagadraco looked out for you once you got to New York, and when the time was right, she offered you a job."

Another punch to the gut. "Grandma got me the job?" I thought I'd earned that on my own.

You told her to be honest, Mac.

"No, no, baby. Ms. Sagadraco wouldn't have hired you if

she hadn't thought you were the best seer she had ever met. She would have continued to protect you as long as you were in her city."

Ian wasn't the main one who'd been protecting me. It'd been Vivienne Sagadraco all along.

"But who is the man in your wedding pictures?"

"I staged the photos with a friend of mine."

"So, all the stories y'all told me about my dad were just made up?"

"Yes. We had to make it real so you would never question who your father was. Your stubbornness comes from me. I knew nothing would stop you from searching until you had answers, if you had any doubts as to who your father was."

I huffed a weak laugh. "So much for why I love horses—and why you tried to keep me away from them."

Mom eyes went to Rake. "She wanted riding lessons. Demanded them. Her friends were riding and had horses, so I relented and agreed to lessons. Of course, she was a natural."

I leaned against Rake, and he pulled me close. "I thought she was scared of me falling off. I promised I would never ride without a helmet. All I got for that was a sad little smile, and the worried looks continued. I never understood why, until now."

Rake kept horses at a boarding farm in Westchester County. We went riding every chance we got. I loved it. I'd never felt so free. *Exhilarated.* That was the word. There were trails through the forests there, and I loved to ride fast. I wasn't about to tell Mom that, and I knew Rake would never volunteer the information.

"Was there a riderless horse with the Hunt?" Grandma asked quietly.

"Not that I could see," I told her. "Rake? You were outside the Jeep."

That little fact took their attention off me and onto Rake.

"When Cernunnos flipped the Jeep, Rake kicked the door off and took the fight to them," I explained. "He's got a spell that packs a seriously nasty shockwave. He shielded me and blasted Cernunnos and the entire Wild Hunt into the woods. They decided it was in their best interests to keep going."

Grandma had leaned back in the chair she was sitting in, looking older than she had ten minutes ago. "Mr. Danescu, you have our undying gratitude."

I took Rake's hand. "His name is Rake, Grandma."

"I love your granddaughter more than my own life, Mrs. Fraser. There is nothing I wouldn't do for her."

I looked back to my mom. "Rake, Grandma, would you leave us alone for a few minutes?"

When they left, I patted the bed next to me and took a deep breath. "This isn't exactly what I expected as a Christmas present."

Mom put her arms around my shoulders and held me. We sat in silence for nearly a minute.

"So, what's the verdict?" she asked.

"Excuse me?"

"Verdict. Your judgment."

Oh, that.

"If it hadn't happened, I wouldn't be here. I like being here. Existing is good."

Mom's lips went to my hair, leaving kisses there. "Oh, baby. I didn't want it to be like this. I knew this day would come, but at the same time, I prayed it wouldn't."

I pulled back and looked in her eyes. "Thanks to SPI, I'm better equipped to deal with things like this. My partner, Ian, recently found out his ancestor is an ancient Irish god. And apparently, there are enough agents with that kind of background that they've formed a support group. Looks like I'll be joining them."

"I was so proud when you told me you'd joined SPI. Proud, but scared sick for you." She paused. "She called me, you know. Told me what a great job you were doing. She promised to protect you as much as she was able."

There could only be one "she" Mom was talking about.

Vivienne Sagadraco.

The boss lady. The dragon lady.

"She's told me what you've done for them." Mom pushed a stray piece of hair out of my eyes. "You've found your place in the world. You're making the family proud." Her voice dropped to a whisper. "I'm so proud of you."

I pulled back and looked at her. "Was there anything you asked Ms. Sagadraco about? A certain goblin, by chance?"

Her blue eyes twinkled. "I was going to ask, but Ms. Sagadraco volunteered the information."

"And?"

"You've found yourself a good man, Makenna. I'm so happy for you."

My throat tightened and tears welled in my eyes. Tonight had simply been too much. But now I knew that my mother approved of Rake. I'd wanted her blessing more than anything and had worried myself sick over the past few months imagining how this moment would go, or not go. A massive and overwhelming weight lifted from my shoulders.

I bit my bottom lip against the tears. "Thank you," I managed.

Mom took my face in her hands. "Yes, I lied to you. Only to protect you and keep you safe. You are so precious to me, and I love you more than I can say. Cernunnos Will Not Take You."

I couldn't hold back any longer.

I ugly cried. Mom ugly cried.

It was beautiful.

6

I blew my nose for the umpteenth time. "So now what?"

"I would say you need to leave. Now. But you've been found and marked, and he can find you anywhere, even New York, though at least you'd be better protected there. As little as I like it, it's best that we deal with this here and now."

I nodded in total agreement. "One phone call, and Ms. Sagadraco will send our best team here. Tonight. SPI has experts on every flavor of supernatural there is—including ancient gods and goddesses. We'll find his weakness. If Cernunnos tries to pull a fast one, he'll be getting more than he bargained for, and hopefully, more than he and his boys can handle."

"What a fighter you are." She pulled me close again. "So, so proud."

I sniffed. "Keep that up, and I'll cry again, and I just got my nose clear from the last round." I glanced over at the box on my bedside table. "And we're about out of Puffs."

Rake had closed the door when he and Grandma had gone downstairs. I opened it quietly because I had a feeling about what was going on. I knew Rake heard it the instant I opened the door, probably when I touched the knob. Goblin ears did more than just look good. Come to think of it, Grandma probably knew we were listening, too. I couldn't pull anything over on either one of them.

Yep, I was right as to what was happening.

Grandma had sat Rake down and they were having The Boyfriend Talk.

I'd always been there with Rake when we'd done the Zoom thing with the women in my family. Not that I'd ever needed to run interference, but I was there, just in case. The questions Rake had gotten were always polite. They may have touched on sensitive subjects, but no one had ever gone full-on interrogator with Rake.

Grandma was going there.

At the moment, they were discussing Rake's business interests, and Grandma was demanding an accounting of one business in particular.

Bacchanalia.

The fact that it wasn't a business anymore because it'd fallen into a molten Hellpit didn't interest Grandma. She wanted Rake to "explain himself" as to why he'd felt the need to own a sex club in the first place.

I had not—nor would I *ever*—tell her that was where we'd met.

Rake had seen it as the best way to get information and foreign intelligence from people who would never talk to him otherwise. For certain people, an environment such as Bacchanalia was a powerful lure, and with lowered inhibitions, information flowed more freely. Grandma acknowledged the usefulness of obtaining such information, but saw the way he got it as "flesh peddling."

"I am not a hillbilly, Mr. Danescu. I am computer savvy and have researched you quite thoroughly."

I knew that Rake wanted to say, "Don't believe everything you read online," but in his case, most of it was true, or at least pointed in the right direction. I'd told him how Grandma felt about "sass." Rake also valued everything he'd walked across that threshold with. He didn't want to risk damage to any piece or part.

In her defense, Grandma was adept at separating the online wheat from the chaff. I knew she wasn't singling Rake out because he was a goblin or a goblin spy who'd owned a sex club. Yes, Rake's profession and businesses were a far cry from any of the men who had crossed Agnes Fraser's threshold seeking her approval to court her daughters, and now granddaughter, but she wasn't treating Rake any differently. I'd been told she'd been just as hard on my granddad when he'd come courting. I'd also been told he'd been all the more determined because of the challenges she'd laid down to win her approval.

Rake had never shied from any challenge that stood between him and what he wanted.

He wanted me, and I had no doubt he'd meet each and

every challenge she'd put in front of him. That being said, she was not going to make it easy on him. I also knew better than to interfere in any way, shape, or form.

"I am no longer in that business," Rake was assuring her. "Nor will I be in that business or any of its kind ever again."

"Because Hell opened up and swallowed your den of iniquity?"

"That and recent events have exposed me as an agent for goblin intelligence."

I winced. Potentially poor word choice with "exposed."

"Goblin intelligence—like our CIA?" Grandma asked.

"Yes, ma'am."

"Double-talkin' spies. I wouldn't trust 'em as far as I could throw 'em."

"I can understand that, ma'am."

"And now you're the governor of the goblin colony here."

"Yes, ma'am."

"That makes you a politician, doesn't it?"

I face-palmed. Oh, God.

Mom fought back a snort. As mayor, technically she was a politician, too. But in her three terms, no one had run against her, plus she was blood family. Grandma considered her a unique case.

Rake was sleeping with her granddaughter.

"I consider it protecting my people," Rake countered. "Nor did I seek the appointment, but consider it an opportunity and honor to serve them. I have been assured that it is only temporary until another qualified individual is found. In the meantime, I am committed to doing the job to the best of my ability regardless of how long I am needed."

Point Rake.

He didn't need rescuing, but I decided Grandma had had enough fun, at least for now.

I came down the stairs, Mom right behind me. "Have you called Gethen?" I asked him.

"I tried my cell, the landline here, *and* the satellite phone I brought with me. Nothing. I also tried to call Vivienne on all three devices. Again, nothing. We're being jammed."

Oh crap.

"I called Nora and reached her," Grandma told us. "She said she can't make any calls outside of town. She has two families coming to the inn for Christmas. They were supposed to have been there by this afternoon. She's tried to call, e-mail, and text them. Nothing went through, and she hasn't had any contact from their end. Then I called down to the station and talked to Officer Morris. They can't call out either, and there's no Internet or e-mail."

Oh, this did not sound good.

"I was supposed to call Gethen a little more than an hour ago at seven o'clock," Rake said. "When he didn't hear from me at seven, he would've started calling me at seven-oh-one. He's the one who insisted I take the sat phone. I also gave him the number here."

"And he probably tried to call me when he couldn't reach you." I took out my phone and looked at the incoming call list. "No calls since we left New York."

"I imagine by now he's gathered the team and the jet is warming up," Rake said.

"Think he would've called Ms. Sagadraco?"

"When he couldn't reach you, definitely."

I took a deep breath. "Then we're just a few hours away from being overrun with help. Calls or no calls." I hesitated before asking the elephant-in-the-room question. "Do you think Cernunnos had anything to do with this?"

Rake shook his head. "I wouldn't think so."

"Could it have something to do with the whiff o' brimstone you detected earlier?"

"That's highly likely."

"Crap."

"In spades."

"What do you mean by brimstone?" Mom asked him.

"Black magic. It's highly suspicious that I detected one of the major signs of black magic workings when we were ambushed. I imagine you have thoroughly researched both Cernunnos and the Wild Hunt since Makenna's conception."

"I have."

"In your research, has Cernunnos ever appeared on this continent?"

"No. Are you connecting him with black magic?"

I knew where she was going. She, like many people, equated black magic with evil. She didn't like the idea of Cernunnos, her one-time lover and the father of her child, being evil.

"Not at all," Rake replied. "I'm postulating that he and his Hunt may have been summoned here by a person or persons using black magic."

"Is that possible?"

"With black magic, many things that should not, or ordinarily could not, be done are possible. However, the power outlay would be enormous. Makenna has told me about the ley lines running under these mountains. Are there specific points of power nearby?"

"Entirely too many," Mom told him.

"For tonight, we should stay put. The Hunt rides at night. After sunrise tomorrow, we need to start checking those places of power for signs of recent use. When magic of any kind is worked, it leaves residuals. Hopefully those residuals will give us a clue as to who is behind this. And by morning, when Gethen and company arrive, we'll have plenty of people to divide the work."

7

Sleep was not going to happen.

Over the past few months, I had imagined every possible way the first few hours with my family and Rake could go. The good, the bad, and the ugly.

My imagination and I needed to have a long talk. She'd been slacking off on the job. Never in a million years would I have imagined anything like tonight.

Tonight was the winter solstice. The barriers between the mortal and immortal realms were at their most fragile.

The Wild Hunt had crossed over to come here, and my father, the Master of the Wild Hunt, could take me back with him.

Not only was my father alive, he was a Celtic god and older than my mother by nearly five hundred years.

Everything I knew about the man I thought was my dad

had been a carefully constructed lie. She'd let me believe my entire life that he was dead. I now had ample evidence to the contrary. She'd lied to keep me safe, to keep me from looking for or even thinking of Cernunnos, but it was still a lie, the biggest. All she had done and had sacrificed was to protect me because she loved me more than anything. She had said it herself: I was hers and no one would ever take me from her.

I was definitely gonna need that SPI support group. The other members had godly ancestors. I had a living, breathing father, possibly of the Darth Vader variety.

Rake was warm, lying next to me. We were in my childhood bed in my childhood bedroom. Yet one more thing that felt beyond surreal.

"What is it humans ask?" he murmured. "A penny for your thoughts?"

I snorted. "If I could manage to tell you all that I'm having right now, you'd have another billion in the bank."

Rake's arms slid around me and pulled me close. "I take it you and your mother worked things out?"

I nodded twice against his chest. "She didn't tell me, and I understand why. I don't like it, it hurt, but I understand. I think…no, I know if I had a daughter, I'd have done the same to protect her."

We were quiet for a few moments.

"What does he want?" I whispered. "He said, 'you are mine,' but he looked surprised to see me."

"Did you sense any threat at all from him?"

"No. His eyes…he was…amazed to see me. A sense of wonder, even. I get the feeling he'd just found out about me." I hesitated. "What do you think he wants?"

Rake's arms tightened. "If it involves taking you anywhere, I promise you he's not going to get it."

I scooched up on the pillow so I could see Rake's face and changed the topic. "Guess what? Mom told me that I'd found a good man and that she was so happy for me."

"Really? Who is he?"

I put my cold feet on his legs and Rake yelped.

"Smart-ass. Mom talked to Ms. Sagadraco about you, and the boss reassured her that she had nothing to worry about."

"Vivienne said that?"

"Oh please. You know Ms. Sagadraco likes you. If she didn't, she'd tell you; though knowing the boss, she'd probably show you. Fatally. Speaking of older women liking or not liking you, I'm sorry about Grandma raking you over the coals."

Rake huffed a laugh. "I've been literally raked over coals. There is no comparison."

"There will be if she decides she doesn't like you."

I glanced over at my phone charging on the nightstand. No calls. No texts. No communication with the outside world.

Rake took a quick glance over my head at his phone on the opposite table. "Nada on mine, too."

"Do you think it's the cabal?" I asked quietly.

The cabal was the name we'd given to an international group of mages and supernatural beings who wanted to show the human race it wasn't the apex predator on our world. It was the prey.

Nearly every major case I'd worked at SPI had directly or indirectly involved the cabal: Vivienne Sagadraco's sister Tiamat, Russian dragon/oligarch Viktor Kain, Isidor and

Phaeon Silvanus, Janus, Marek Reigory, and all their various and sundry minions.

With the exception of Phaeon Silvanus, all were still at large.

Cutting off a small mountain town from the outside world was definitely within their capabilities. The question was why?

"Black magic is right up their dark alley," Rake said.

"As is trying to get rid of me. Maybe they decided it was time to bring in the big guns, aka Cernunnos and the Wild Hunt."

"We'll get to the bottom of it tomorrow," Rake murmured against my hair. "What you need is sleep. Nothing more is going to happen tonight."

I snuggled against him and under the quilt and tried to sleep. Within minutes, Rake's breathing was deep and even. His pulse was not. Rake was awake and worried.

If my dark mage, goblin superspy boyfriend was concerned, I should be terrified.

I was. And I was going to need something stronger than Tums.

8

The sun rose, but Grandma didn't need to set any extra places for breakfast.

Gethen wasn't here, neither were Rake's security team, and there were no SPI reinforcements knocking on the back door looking for coffee.

Phones, Internet, satellite, and cable TV were also kaput. No news was getting in or out.

Not a good start to our day.

Though, on the upside, there wasn't a mushroom cloud on the horizon in any direction, which I took to mean our problems were indeed local. To get a handle on our situation, Aunt Vickie had sent an officer out toward Asheville to see how far "local" extended, and once she got beyond that point, to call Gethen and Vivienne Sagadraco. Rake and I had given the officer our code words to certify that the messages were from us.

Mom convinced Grandma to stay at home in case Gethen or Ms. Sagadraco called or— better yet—arrived, while Mom, Rake, and I went to meet Aunt Vickie and Uncle Mike at the parking lot at the base of Widow's Peak. Since our Jeep was incapacitated, we took Mom's old Land Rover Defender.

She had met Cernunnos in a standing stone circle in Scotland. We didn't have stone circles in North Carolina, at least not the ancient kind. A few artsy types had constructed their own, but they weren't places of power. We did, however, have more than our share of bare mountaintops and deep forest clearings. Both were natural centers of magical and earth energies. Some of our local places, like Widow's Peak, were even above intersecting ley lines. That considerably upped the magical mojo.

It'd stopped snowing and the wind had finally died down. Two days before Christmas was a gorgeous, crisp winter day with clear blue skies. Rake was sporting some serious sunglasses. Like arctic-expedition quality, to protect his sensitive goblin eyes from the sun reflecting off the snow.

He gave an impressed whistle when Widow's Peak came into view.

"It's like a mini-me of Devils Tower in Wyoming," I told him. "You know, where the mothership landed in *Close Encounters of the Third Kind*."

"I am familiar with the film."

"Our version's not as tall, and not nearly as big around. A lot of people have climbed it, and surprisingly, only four have died doing it, at least since we've kept records."

"Do I want to ask why it's called Widow's Peak?"

"On a clear day, you can see to Tennessee and Georgia. The name was adapted from the local Cherokee. Women could watch for their men to come back from war—or not come back."

"Just as cheerful as I thought."

"You asked."

"That I did."

Growing up in Weird Sisters, I'd been one of those climbing to the top of Widow's Peak. In a place where I'd always felt small, I could be like the eagles as they coasted in the thermals above the peak. I could see beyond the small town in the valley below, see at least a part of the outside world, far-flung and inviting, filled with excitement. It had to be. I'd believed that anything had to be better than the tiny town where I was stuck. I couldn't wait until I was old enough to leave. I was certain that while I'd come back to visit, it would only remind me of why I'd left.

But what I had learned was that who I was and all I would come to be had been formed in that little town, where I was nurtured and loved by family and friends. It was there that I'd gained the strength that I would need to literally survive in the big, bad world I'd fought so hard to escape into.

Aunt Vickie and Uncle Mike were waiting, along with an officer I didn't know, in the small clearing that functioned as a parking lot to hikers tackling the peak. Mom parked next to them.

According to the legends, the Wild Hunt only appeared at night. In theory, we should be safe on a bright, sunny morning. That didn't mean any of us were going to be letting our guard down for one instant, considering the stench of black magic Rake and I had sensed along with the Wild Hunt.

I reached for the door handle. "Are you getting anything?" I asked Rake.

"Nothing. At least not yet. I'd probably need to be halfway to the summit before much would register." He squinted. "Is that—"

"Steam," Mom finished for him. "Escaping through thermal vents. There are hot springs running under Widow's Peak. The steam vents in two places at the top, with a couple of smaller openings on the sides."

We got out of the Rover.

While Aunt Vickie had met Rake in a Zoom call, it was their first time in person. I took care of the formalities. Rake shook hands with Vickie and again with Mike, then nodded at the big drone taking up most of the Hummer's hood. "Good idea."

"That's one of Jimmy's babies," Vickie told him. "Officer Kennedy, this is Rake Danescu, and Margaret's daughter Makenna."

Rake and I exchanged handshakes with Jimmy.

My seer vision showed me that Jimmy Kennedy was a young man, but an older werewolf.

"I try to keep at least three drones in working order," Jimmy said. "They've paid for themselves a hundred times over in successful search and rescues. We've got some smaller ones for cave use, but this one's best for altitudes with high wind."

"Jimmy will fly it up," Mike told us. "If we see anything suspicious, we'll make the hike. If not, it'll save us the trip."

We all stood back and gave Jimmy and his pride-and-joy plenty of room for takeoff. Within a few minutes the big drone looked like a black dot in the blue sky.

Vickie was peering over Jimmy's shoulder at the control panel's small screen. As the drone cleared the top of the peak, her lips set in a grim line. "There's our missing tourist."

The top of Widow's Peak was completely flat and normally empty.

It wasn't empty now.

There was a dead body. His eyes were wide open and staring, his mouth agape as if he'd died mid-scream. And his face…I'd never seen such terror; and not only terror, but despair. His face and bare hands were pale as if he'd bled out, but there was no sign of blood. Even starved vampires weren't that pale, and they sure as heck wouldn't be sprawled on top of a mountain at high noon on a clear, sunny day.

We also had an ID. According to Aunt Vickie, the newly deceased matched the description of Tavis Haldane, one of Aunt Nora's guests who hadn't returned to the inn when he said he'd be back.

As to how he had died, it wasn't obvious.

"Can you get us closer?" Vickie asked.

Jimmy goosed the joystick. "No problem, ma'am."

No one spoke as the drone descended toward the body and out of our sight from where we stood in the parking lot.

The body came into stark focus.

Then the screen went white with static.

Rake swore. "Get it out. Now."

Jimmy quickly worked the controls. "It's not responding."

We all looked to the top of Widow's Peak. The black dot that was the drone rose sluggishly into the sky.

Jimmy exhaled in relief. "That was clos—"

And it exploded, leaving nothing but a puff of black smoke.

"Wards," Rake said. "Whoever left that body either didn't want it found, or to make anyone who did find it pay dearly." He glanced around at us locals. "So, how do I get up there?"

"One way up," Mike told him. "Two ways down."

Cop humor. One of those two ways was falling. Our victim hadn't been given that choice. Neither had Jimmy's drone.

Climbing Widow's Peak was possible year-round. Note that I didn't say "safe." Getting to the top didn't require rock-climbing gear, but you needed to be in seriously good shape. There was plenty of signage at the base of the trail informing you in no uncertain terms that your next of kin couldn't sue anybody if you fell off. There were no ropes or railings to keep the clumsy from meeting their maker if they took a wrong step going up or got caught in a crosswind at the top that sent them sailing over the side. All the possibilities were covered in the signage.

With hot springs running underneath, when snow or freezing rain fell on Widow's Peak, it didn't stay long. But there were plenty of wet patches and slick rocks to cause trouble.

This morning, we had to contend with all that, plus a

murderous black mage's wards waiting at the top to potentially make us go "poof" like Jimmy's drone.

Rake was already wearing the proper boots for serious hiking but was re-lacing them for maximum stability.

That was his only preparation for going up a mountain called Widow's Peak to destroy the wards put there by somebody who presumably had enough power to summon the Wild Hunt from across the freakin' Atlantic Ocean.

I was explaining this to him to no avail.

I stood over him, not in any misguided attempt to intimidate, but so he was sitting in my shadow, giving his eyes a break from the sun. "Fine. I'm going with you."

He barked a laugh. "Oh no, you're not. And your mother will tell you the same thing."

"I'm a seer," I reminded him, though he was well aware of my qualifications. "You're not. You can snap that ward like dry kindling, but I can see a lot of things you can't—before they can kill you."

Rake finished lacing and rested his elbows on his knees, then his eyes flicked to someone standing behind me. "Margaret, please talk some sense into your daughter."

"Actually, we're both going." She smiled and draped her arm over my shoulder. "Two seers are even better than one."

I put my arm around her waist and we both gave Rake identical—and no doubt, infuriating—smiles. "I've warned him not to argue with Fraser women," I said.

"Then he must not have listened."

I sighed. "Yeah, he's got selective hearing. One of his less-than-dazzling qualities I have to endure."

"You're holding up well, dear."

"Thank you."

Rake started to speak, but Mom held up a hand. "Please, hear me out. This is your area of expertise, not mine. You want to go first. I want to let you. But whatever is up there involves me and Makenna. We've been up that trail to the top many times, we're seers, and we're going. You can sit there and waste time arguing, or we can go now and start ending this."

Rake shook his head and got to his feet. "Yes, ma'am."

9

Aunt Vickie called Frank Peterson and asked him to stand by with his helicopter. We had to get Haldane's body down, and Frank's chopper was the best way to get it done. However, Rake had to do his part first. When it came to black magic wards, size didn't matter. Wards that fried the electronics and mechanics on a drone could easily do the same to a helicopter. Jimmy's drone could be replaced, but Frank Peterson? Not so much.

"I'm leading a parade," Rake muttered.

I had to admit, he was right.

In addition to me and Mom, Vickie was coming too, with Mike bringing up the rear. Jimmy was staying with the vehicles, acting as the base of communications. Phone signals could be wonky on the peak, so both Vickie and Mike had walkie-talkies to keep us connected with Jimmy. While he waited, the officer would contact our local coroner, and coordinate with Frank once Rake had eliminated the threat.

Just before we reached the top, Rake turned and held up a hand, indicating we were to wait while he took a look. My look told him precisely how I felt about that. He sighed, pointed at me, and crooked his finger. He glanced at Mom, Vickie, and Mike, and again raised his hand telling them to stay put, adding a mouthed "please" for diplomacy's sake.

I knew they didn't like it, but they acknowledged Rake's expertise, so they did it. For now.

I felt Rake's magic wrap us in a protective cocoon. He nodded and we both cautiously raised our heads over the ledge and took a quick glance.

Thanks to the steam produced by the hot springs below, there was no snow on the flat, stone expanse that was the top of Widow's Peak.

All that stood between us and Tavis Haldane was what looked like an oily bubble-like dome some ten feet high and across that was directly over the body. Jimmy's drone must have touched that dome, and it had taken extreme offense.

I'd spent some time in New York City's sewer system. Professionally, not recreationally. Most of the tunnels were surprisingly non-gag-inducing. Others? There were no words to describe the stink. This was the same. Except the stench wasn't physical. It was psychic, permeating everything it came in contact with.

Someone had been here very recently and had done some exceedingly bad things. Deep, dark, black-magic bad things. Things bad enough to summon the Wild Hunt.

I could detect it with my seer vision. Rake could see it with his magic. His scowl said loud and clear that he was sensing everything I had.

"Did anybody we know do this?" I asked quietly.

Rake's eyes scanned the oily dome as it glistened in the sun. "I don't know," he murmured.

"What do you mean, you don't know?"

"I mean it's cabal-level work, but there's no recognizable magical signature."

"Someone new?"

"It could be. Part of the skill that was used here is old, as in older than even Vivienne. Much older."

"I won't tell her you implied that she was older than dirt."

"She would agree with me about this."

"How much older?" I asked. Vivienne Sagadraco was thousands of years old.

"A lot. Possibly prehistoric. No one in the cabal is that old."

Great. Merry Christmas to us.

When it came to mage bad guys or gals, it was better to face the enemies you knew, or at least had a dossier on. Ms. Sagadraco had files on every member of the cabal.

Rake knew the cabal members, some of them personally.

He kept his eyes on the shifting ward. "Let me go first. When I say so, bring the others."

"Done. Be careful of the wind, too. It's calm right now, but a strong gust can take you right over the side."

He gave me a quick kiss. "And the fun just keeps coming."

He climbed up to the stone plateau that was Widow's Peak.

I stood silently and waited, looking over the ledge and watching Rake for any sign of trouble. I had abilities of the magically deductive kind. Rake had more, way more. He was gathering and sorting information, letting the vestiges of the black magic that'd been worked here speak to him.

As a dark mage, Rake was best suited to make a final determination. I quieted my own abilities so as not to compete with what he was sensing. He'd tell me what he'd found when he finished.

Rake stopped about a dozen feet away from the bubble, arms raised, palms toward the oily, restlessly shifting surface.

I felt the gentle push, pull, and probe of Rake's magic. Perfectly controlled and nonthreatening. He wasn't physically touching the dome, and judging from its lack of reaction, his examination wasn't setting off the ward. His fingertips briefly glowed red, and then that light flowed outward, stopping mere inches from the dome's surface, spreading over and around it. When the two sides of Rake's counter-ward met, there was the faintest click that I wasn't sure I heard or merely felt.

The dome shifted uneasily, the ward sensing Rake's work, but it still hadn't set it off.

My honey did good work.

Rake drew his fingers and hands back like pulling on a net. The field he'd woven brought the dome out with it, stretching it in every direction. Tighter and tauter and thinner until it simply popped.

It was my turn to give Rake an impressed whistle. Though just because I could no longer see the dome didn't mean the threat was gone. "It's safe?"

He turned and gave me a grin and shrug. "One way to find out."

He sauntered right over to the body.

I squeaked before I could stop myself. "Stop doing that!" I waved Mom, Vickie, and Mike up, then stalked over to where Rake knelt by the body. "You make me weak in the knees, and not in a good way. One of these days, your cockiness is gonna backfire, and if it doesn't get you killed, I'll do it."

"You'll be standing in a long line," he murmured, his entire attention on Haldane.

Fussing at Rake vented the fear I'd felt for him, but it was also an excuse to avoid looking at yet another human being, a living soul, who had possibly been killed for the sake of black magic power.

I stood just behind Rake. Standing guard over him.

Rake knelt and placed his hands, palms down and fingers spread on the rock closest to Haldane. His back was to us, and I knew from past experience that his eyes were closed because he was sensing the residuals of what had been done here—and by whom.

"He's old," he murmured. "Not human, at least not entirely. Definitely ancient."

Mom shot me a glance. I knew what she was thinking.

Cernunnos.

"Not Cernunnos," Rake said.

Her eyes widened. I'd need to tell her later that Rake and I had developed a psychic bond thing. The more sex we had, the better we could read each other's minds. I had yet to decide if it was good, bad, or merely had the potential to be incredibly embarrassing.

Are you sure it's not cabal work? I silently asked.

Rake didn't respond. "An insane amount of power was expended here. Tiamat or Viktor could possibly handle it, but no one else who I'm familiar with."

"And we'd both know if they'd been here."

"Exactly."

When it came to the mages of the cabal, I paid attention to what I considered to be the two most critical items of identification—physical description and what they were capable of if angered or cornered. As to identifying them from the remnants of their magic, that would have to be Rake's department until we could contact SPI HQ and get access to Kenji's database.

If it hadn't been done by a member of the cabal, that meant this black magic powerhouse was someone new. The last thing we needed was a new enemy. It'd be like S.H.I.E.L.D. finding out there was another organization just as powerful as HYDRA. Or that Thanos had a twin brother.

"Would this have had anything to do with the Wild Hunt's arrival?" I asked Rake.

"The level of magic worked when this man was sacrificed makes that a near certainty."

Vickie went utterly still. "Sacrificed?"

"The victim was a practitioner of impressive strength," Rake told her. "This act was committed as a power boost. A huge one. That means the mage who killed him was of even greater skill and strength," he added.

"How about his soul?" I asked quietly.

"Gone."

"On its own or taken?"

"That I don't know." Rake turned to Vickie and Mike. "You wouldn't happen to have a necromancer in town, would you?"

"Dr. Jean Crombie is our county coroner. She's not a necromancer, but she could probably answer your questions."

"Good. It would be helpful to know."

I knew what Rake was thinking, even if my family didn't. Souls could be extracted to power large spells. Whatever evil had been worked here had probably required this poor man's death and soul.

Mike knelt to join Rake in examining the body and surrounding area. He opened the backpack he'd brought with him, took out an evidence collection kit, and went to work. Vickie was taking pictures with her phone. Mom stood silently a few feet away. Light flickered on the edge of my vision and I adjusted my sunglasses to eliminate the glare.

It flickered again, and I turned my head to see what—

I froze.

A faintly shimmering line started at the very edge of the peak and extended into the sky at least a dozen feet, maybe more.

The remains of a portal. The domed ward must have blocked it.

It wasn't any one color. It had all the colors, sparkling like sunlight through a crystal prism.

Keeping my eyes on it, I flailed around with my hand, trying to find Rake's shoulder to get his attention.

"What are you—" He stopped, realizing what I must be seeing. "Portal?"

"Big-ass portal."

"Wild Hunt sized?"

"Oh yeah."

"You can see portals?" Mom blurted.

"Something new I've picked up."

"You didn't tell me."

"You didn't tell me my father was alive," I shot back,

ignoring my mother's hurt look. Then I had a realization. "Who can probably see portals. According to the stories, that's how the Wild Hunt gets around. You can't exactly use a door you can't see." At least now I could stop worrying that my new talent had come from a one-time psychic contact with Viktor Kain. Though I wasn't sure having the Master of the Wild Hunt as a dad was any better than an unwanted psychic connection to an ancient Russian oligarch/dragon.

Rake appeared beside me. "What do you see?"

I told him.

Uncle Mike wasn't getting it. "A portal in the air over the side of a cliff? Even if that's possible, there's no way to get horses down from here."

I remembered the Hunt riding up the side of the mountain with its thick forest and no trails. "I don't think they pay much attention to gravity. Looks like we could use Kitty's help with this one," I told Rake.

"Kitty?" Mike asked.

"My best friend in New York," I told him. "Also, the best portal mage on the planet."

"And several other worlds," Rake added. "She can open, close, detect, and destroy any portal."

Mom had approached the body. "There's something under him." She sounded like she was about to be sick.

Rake and Mike rolled the body slightly to expose what was beneath.

There were two items. One carefully folded, the other meticulously arranged on top.

On top was my blue hairbrush, missing since last month. I thought I'd just misplaced it.

"I thought so," Mom said. "It's my sweater. It went missing from my office a few days ago."

The cardigan was as perfectly folded as if it was displayed on a store shelf, which only added to the skin-crawling creepiness.

That my mother's sweater and my hairbrush had been involved made the scene even worse. Though I was sure Tavis Haldane would've felt differently.

My hairbrush and my mother's sweater had been used to summon the Wild Hunt.

10

I winced. "That'll teach me to clean my brushes."

"And burn the hair," Rake added.

"Uh, Aunt Vickie, I know this is a crime scene, but can you snap some shots so we can take those now?"

"They're evidence, so we'll need to keep them for the time being."

"That's fine. I just want them away from here and locked up, and then destroyed. They were used once; I don't want to risk that happening again."

"Mother made that sweater for me," my mom said. "I kept it in my office." Her anger grew. "Makenna's brush and my sweater were used as bait."

Rake nodded. "The human sacrifice was to gain strength to work the ritual."

I spoke. "My brush has been gone about a month. So, whoever did this knew about Cernunnos being my father at least that long ago."

"At least. I need you to think back to who was in your apartment around the time you noticed the brush missing. That'll give us something to start on until we can reach Kenji and have him get your building's security tapes."

I knew what Rake had to be thinking. If I'd moved into his building, I'd have been under around-the-clock battlemage protection and I wouldn't have had a brush stolen. Just because he didn't say it out loud now, or even think it long enough for our psychic bond thingie to kick in, didn't mean we wouldn't be discussing it later. Now that I knew my father was a Celtic god, that might be a conversation worth having—and a living situation worth reconsidering. But that would only protect me. I wasn't the only one in danger here. My mother was being threatened.

"If the thief was cloaked, I may still be able to see through it and give you a description," I told them both. My attention kept being drawn back to the portal. I took a couple of steps toward it.

"You can see through cloaks?" Mom asked.

"Probably another DNA gift from Dad," I said without thinking, staring at the portal.

I'd never seen one sliced into the air. They'd always been in a wall. Kitty had never mentioned how rare a mid-air portal was in the lessons she'd been giving me. Unfortunately, she wasn't here to ask. I could tell it was closed, so we were safe from anything else coming through. I tried to do what I'd seen Kitty do.

First, I had to push out of my head that I was scared to death. Not of the portal, but of a Celtic god being my father and having been summoned here to presumably carry me away. Then I had to study and listen to the portal. Kitty told me they usually had a lot to say about their maker.

I sensed Rake gesturing to my family to stay still and quiet.

The portal was completely closed, so I was probably seeing its final vestiges. In another couple of hours, there might not have been anything left to find. That told me this portal wasn't going to be used again. It'd been used to get the Wild Hunt here, not for them to leave through it.

Cernunnos was in an unfamiliar country. Could he open a portal to go home from here, wherever home was? Kitty had told me that there were natural portals, but they were keyed to specific locations, at points of power, like the stone circle where I'd been conceived. Cernunnos was a Celtic god who would intimately know the natural portals in Scotland and Ireland. But now he'd been lured to a foreign land. If the purpose of summoning him was that he take me and leave, wouldn't the mage have left this portal operational?

Perhaps the mage didn't want Cernunnos and his Hunt to leave.

Perhaps he wanted Cernunnos.

Some hunters used bait to lure their quarry into their kill zone.

Though maybe he didn't want Cernunnos dead. Perhaps the bait had been to lure him here to trap him, but that clearly hadn't happened, either. Cernunnos and the Hunt had been free to find me and Rake on that road outside of town.

Rake had sensed brimstone when we'd been ambushed.

The mage had been nearby.

Chasing Cernunnos? Overseeing the ambush? Merely watching? Waiting? If so, for what?

Maybe that's all Mom and I were—bait. I didn't know whether to feel insulted or relieved. I went with both. Tentatively. We couldn't know for sure until we found the mage.

Or Cernunnos found me or Mom. Again.

Rake sensed I was finished and came up beside me. "What did you get?"

"This was a one-way portal," I said. "The Hunt came through and it closed behind them."

Mom froze. "A trap?"

"I think so."

"It doesn't clarify his ultimate motive," I said, "but if I had to choose, I'd rather this mage think of me and Mom as just bait rather than being his main target."

Rake indicated Tavis Haldane, who Mike had covered with a thin blanket from his backpack. "What can you tell me about him?"

"He checked into Nora's inn last week," Vickie said. "He told her he was a nature photographer and would be doing some hiking in the area. He was passing through on his way to visit family in Atlanta for Christmas. Nora saw him go out several times with his camera bag. We found his phone in his room, but we assumed he'd taken the camera with him. It's not here, so it's still unaccounted for. Colton is getting into the phone to find out more." Vickie shook her head sadly. "There's no sign of restraint. Was he drugged or unconscious when he was killed? Or—"

"I believe he was awake and fully aware," Rake said.

"So, whoever did this had accomplices waiting up here?" Mike asked.

Rake shook his head. "Unnecessary. Restraint can be done with a spell. Mr. Haldane was a powerful mage in his own right. In all probability, he was the apprentice of the mage we're looking for."

"He killed his own apprentice?" Mike asked in disbelief.

"To call beings as powerful as the Wild Hunt, that mage would've needed a sacrifice that mirrored his own abilities. What easier way to obtain the qualities he needed than to use his own student? The ritual worked here was the blackest of black magic and required a delicate balance between summoner and sacrifice," Rake continued. "The victim would have to have had the same skills, but the strength level doesn't have to be the same. No doubt the mage was grateful for that part. It made subduing his apprentice easier. One life must fade as the other draws power from it to complete the ritual. I've been told it has to do with proving your commitment. In essence, you must sacrifice yourself. When a mage teaches an apprentice, the mage is giving away his knowledge. Properly applied, that knowledge increases the student's power. The ritual wouldn't work unless the mage sacrificed part of himself. An apprentice would fill that requirement."

Mom looked nauseated. "The mage killed someone he loved?"

"Love has nothing to do with it," Rake told her. "The apprentice could have been led to believe that he was loved, but it would have been merely another lie the mage told to get what he wanted."

"He got the Hunt here," I said. "Now what?"

The Hunt was nocturnal. I had a feeling our megamage was not.

"We might be able to ask him ourselves," Rake said. "If he was nearby last night, he saw what I did to get the Hunt to leave. And I probably just sent him a wake-up call by popping his ward bubble."

Oh good.

"Also, that dome was strong enough to keep me from sensing what he'd done here until we saw it thanks to Officer Kennedy's drone."

"Meaning what?"

"Meaning this man can keep any work-in-progress hidden unless we get close enough to actually see it."

Hundreds of square miles of mountains and wilderness. Not good.

Mike and Vickie's walkie-talkies beeped. Mike answered. "Go ahead, Jimmy."

"Sir, Georgina couldn't get out of town. She tried both Lead Mine and Troll Den Ridge Roads, as well as Cameron Gap. She said there was some kind of shadow blocking the road. She drove through it the first time and ended up turned around going in the direction she just came from. She tried again and the same thing happened. It seems we can't get out, sir."

No communication, no way out.

We were cut off from the rest of the world.

11

"I need to see those shadows," Rake told Mike, his expression grim. "Take me there."

I stepped up next to him. "Take *us* there."

Rake had declared the top of Widow's Peak to be flight-safe. When we got back to the parking lot, Vickie called Frank Peterson to come bring Tavis Haldane's body down. She and Jimmy would take him to Dr. Crombie's for an autopsy. We were going to investigate the shadow on Troll Den Ridge Road, less than four miles away.

Mom went with us.

The citizens of Weird Sisters were self-sufficient and proud of it. Being cut off from the outside world was no biggie for our folks. Usually. Our "usually" didn't involve an ancient mage who'd lured in a marginally less ancient Celtic god and his posse, then locked all of us in together for an unknown—at least to us—purpose.

A couple of years back, there'd been a combo snow and ice storm that had paralyzed western North Carolina. Many small communities had gotten supplies airlifted in from the National Guard. Our people had voted to tell the guardsmen to give ours to another town on their list. We had everything we needed.

Mom was driving her Defender. Mike was in the passenger seat, with me and Rake in the back.

Mike was recounting telling Vickie that Rake and I had been ambushed by Cernunnos and the Wild Hunt. To hear him tell it, Aunt Vickie had had quite the reaction. "I thought *I* was in trouble. Though as usual, I had no idea what I'd done."

Troll Den Ridge Road was just as winding as the road where Cernunnos and his Hunt had ambushed us.

Where my father had ambushed us.

My father wasn't dead. At least I assumed the Master of the Wild Hunt wasn't dead or undead. The undead were people, too. Some of the best people I knew were undead.

I had a dad.

Though somehow, I couldn't imagine playing catch or going fishing with Cernunnos. Hunting was something entirely different. I could certainly imagine that, and I didn't want to.

My dad.

Master of the Wild Hunt.

I just sat there doing a thousand-yard-stare out the side window.

Dang, Mom. I thought I was the Fraser with the thing for bad boys. She had me beat bigtime.

Mom started to slow the Defender. I leaned forward to look out the windshield.

Sure enough, there was a shadow blocking the road.

Rake and I exchange a quick glance. This looked entirely too familiar.

It was closing in on noon, and the sun was high in a clear sky. Without any leaves on the trees, the sun was filtering down to the snow-covered roadway. Directly ahead, what covered the road from one side to the other and extended up through the canopy wasn't merely a shadow, it was darkness. And from the sides of the road, it extended up into the tree line both up and down the mountain.

"Georgina didn't mention that it extended off the road in both directions," Mike said.

"Perhaps it didn't when she saw it," Rake said. "It could be growing." He opened his door. "Let me make sure it's safe before anyone else gets out."

He stood just beyond the open door and sent out feelers, and when the obstruction didn't react, he walked over to it, stopping halfway between it and the Defender. "It's safe," he called back.

Mom, Mike, and I followed. "You think this is Isidor's work?" I asked Rake when I got close enough not to have to yell. This had more than a passing resemblance to the roadblock Isidor had thrown up between us and the Hellpit under Bacchanalia, as well as the pocket dimension Isidor and his brother Phaeon had used to cut off the Regor Regency Hotel from the rest of New York.

"Similar in composition to both, but this isn't his work."

"Who's Isidor?" Mom asked.

I took that one. "Elf mage who has a permanent place on SPI's most-wanted list," I told her. What I didn't tell her was that Isidor Silvanus was from Rake's home world and hated him with the seething intensity of a thousand suns. But if Rake said this wasn't Isidor's work, I wasn't about to open the can of worms that was the cabal in front of my mom and uncle.

"Do you know where he is?" I asked Rake.

"On his home world. I get a daily report of his whereabouts."

I drew breath to ask—

"And yes, my source is *very* reliable. He has one job. Track Isidor. Isidor's brother Phaeon is still in SPI custody."

Snow crunched beneath his boots as Mike joined us. "So, what are we dealing with here?" he asked Rake.

"A cage of the black magic kind."

"And if we tried to drive through it, it'd turn us around?"

"If we're lucky. Your officer was."

"And if not?"

"It could take us to a very bad place."

Mike indicated the shadow. "Can you do to that what you did up on Widow?"

"Unlikely. This is much bigger—and it appears to be still growing. Do you think Officer Kennedy would be willing to risk another drone?"

Mike flashed a grin. "I think our budget can handle it."

"If it can get us out of here to bring help, the town will replace both drones," Mom said.

I knew Rake would gladly buy Jimmy a whole new squadron if it'd get Gethen and a SPI team in here.

Rake was studying the sky directly overhead. "Have him send up whichever one can go the highest. Get video in every direction. We need to know how far up this extends."

"Will video be able to see it?"

I took that one. "Probably not, but I can. It'll show up on video as wavy lines or static."

Mike called Vickie, told her what we'd found and what Rake needed Jimmy to do.

I'd stepped to the side of the road to give myself a better view of the trees beyond the darkness. I removed my sunglasses. It lightened what I was looking at, but only slightly. It was like seeing the world beyond through those safety glasses you could wear to look at an eclipse.

"You've seen one of those before?" Mom asked quietly.

"Kind of." I squinted to see if the tree branches on the other side seemed to be moving in slow motion, like had happened with the pocket dimension at the Regor Regency.

"Where?"

I blinked and squinted again. "A hotel and Hell," I said absently.

"Did you just say Hell?"

Oh crap.

"Uh, yes, ma'am. Technically, it was just an anteroom of Hell. I've never been in Hell itself," I hurried to add.

The anteroom had been in a pocket dimension beyond the wine cellar of my boyfriend's sex club. If Rake hadn't jumped into that draining Hellpit after me, *then* I would have been in Hell.

Mom definitely didn't need to know any of that.

I waved at Rake. "Sweetie, can you step over here a minute?" And save me from myself. "I need those goblin eyes of yours."

"What is it?"

"Those two trees," I pointed to a pair of hemlocks that

appeared to be outside the barrier. Their evergreen branches were shifting in what appeared to be slow motion. "Are you thinking what I'm thinking?"

Rake nodded. "Pocket dimension. If it is, it's the largest one I've ever seen or heard of."

"I'll need you to explain that one to me," Mom said.

"We can see out, but no one can see in," I told her. "Well, they might *think* they can. Anyone trying to drive in would experience what Georgina did. They'd be turned around and going right back in the other direction."

"We can't get out, and no one can get in."

"Afraid so. Gethen was in Rake's hotel when we were trapped inside one, along with Vivienne Sagadraco and half the agents and all the commandos at SPI. All communication was down, too. If they've sent teams down here—and I'm sure they have by now—they know exactly what's happened."

"What can they do about it?"

"Nothing."

"Then how did you get out?"

"We destroyed the magetech generator that was powering it," Rake told her.

"A magetec—"

"That's the name we gave it. A devilish combination of magic and technology."

"Do you think that's what's doing this?"

Rake shook his head. "I'd know immediately if it was. How extensive are the ley lines in the area?"

"They're everywhere."

"Is there a map of—"

"Oh, yes."

"I need it. If we can get the dimensions on this thing from drone footage, we can compare that to the ley lines and locate the central point of power."

"You might not need to do that," Mom said. "Weird Sisters has five major ley line intersections. If you draw lines from one to the next, you get a pentagram roughly seven miles in diameter."

Rake whistled. "I'll bet those five points mark the outermost edges of the barrier. Jimmy's drone can confirm it. If so, our adversary has done his homework."

"Can you shut it down?"

"If the power points are at those ley line intersections, probably not." Rake flashed his fangs in a distinctly unfriendly smile. "The mage constructed it; he'll know how to deconstruct it. Seven miles isn't all that big of an area when you're packing that kind of mojo. When I find him, I'll convince him to cooperate."

Mom smiled back at him. "I like the sound of that. We have a map at home, and others at the police station and my office." She gazed out at the trees just on the other side of our invisible prison wall. "Cernunnos and the Hunt are inside with us, as is this mage who brought them here. Is there a time limit on how long he can keep this going?"

"It'll last until we can separate him from his power source," Rake told her. "Or until he gets what he came for and no longer needs it. I don't think any of us want him to get what he came for."

Mom gave him a sharp nod. "Then let's pull the plug on this bastard."

12

"We can't bring down the pocket dimension from here," Rake was telling Mike. "We need to find the mage who made it. Good news is, he'd need to be inside."

"Bad news?" I asked.

"We're inside with him."

As we were getting back in the Defender, Mike's phone rang. He listened, said "got it" a couple of times, and ended with, "I'll call when we've talked to him."

"That was Vickie," he told us after ending the call. "Colton got into Tavis Haldane's phone. He'd made two calls to Glendon Kerr's office last week, but none to Atlanta, which is where he was supposed to be headed."

"Who's Glendon Kerr?" Rake asked.

"A local realtor," Mom told him. "He handles most of the vacation rental properties in the area."

"Early last week," Mike continued, "there were three calls to London. With the computers down, Colt can't run Haldane's name, but Vickie's betting that being a nature photographer with family in Atlanta was a cover story. She wants us to swing by Glendon's place and ask him a few questions."

Mom was nodding. "That makes sense. If this mage Haldane was working with planned on being here awhile, he'd need a place to stay."

I had a thought. "He'd also need to know where the places of power were and where the ley lines ran. We keep that information to ourselves. Only certain locals know all of them."

Mom put the Defender in reverse to start a three-point turn to take us to Mr. Kerr's house. "We don't share that information with outsiders. Plus, the levels of each place fluctuate depending on the time of year or moon cycle. Even Widow's Peak. The mage would have to have had a local who was willing, or who could be coerced, into telling him."

"Does London mean anything to you?" I asked Rake.

"Nothing that gives me an answer to even one of our many questions, if that's what you mean."

"It is."

"Hopefully, Mr. Kerr will be more helpful."

Glendon Kerr was an older gentleman and practitioner who preferred to be called a wizard instead of mage or sorcerer. Sweetest old guy. He and his wife Nessa had run Weird Sisters' one real estate business for the past half century. Miss Nessa had passed on fifteen years ago, and Mr. Kerr had given no thought to remarrying. His red hair had gone to white while he'd been young. That, his good-natured personality, and a ruddy complexion had made him a natural to play Santa Claus every year for the local kids. The red velvet suit, beard, and bushy eyebrows hadn't fooled most of us—especially those of us who'd been budding seers. It didn't matter, we went along with the act. Besides, it made the grownups happy to think they'd pulled something over on us.

It was four miles to Mr. Kerr's, but it was a long four miles due to the road's curves and climb. I didn't even want to think what kind of driving Yasha would have done on these twisty mountain roads.

Rake had his human glamour firmly in place. We were keeping Rake's real identity on a need-to-know basis, and while we considered Glendon Kerr a close family friend, right now he didn't need to know.

The magetech generator had sealed us in Rake's hotel, and the next generation of that device had transported Rake's home in Regor to a vacant Manhattan lot. The more I thought about it, the less trouble I had believing the Wild Hunt had been brought to Weird Sisters from Scotland. If a softball-sized alien crystal could do intergalactic teleportation of a house, a portal path from Scotland to North Carolina would've been easy-peasy.

As Mom drove up the mountain, the sky continued to darken. I glanced at the clock on the Defender's dash. It was only 1:47 in the afternoon.

Early afternoon, darkening sky, but no clouds.

The mage warden was closing the door on our prison.

There was a massive tree down halfway up the gravel road that was Glendon Kerr's driveway. Not only was it massive, it appeared perfectly healthy. It'd had help getting horizontal.

None of us made any move to get out.

"Well, that looks new," Mike said.

Right now, new meant highly suspicious, which in turn meant dangerous. Everyone's paranoia was cranked to full volume.

"How much farther?" Rake asked.

"About a hundred yards," Mom replied.

Too far to go on foot out in the open with an ancient mage in the neighborhood. Or the Wild Hunt. Yes, it was daylight, but the sun had been dimmed by the dome. No one said any of the above, but we were all perfectly aware of our circumstances.

"I can move it," Rake said, "but it'll announce I'm here like sending up a flare."

"No choice," I said. "Can you do it from in here?"

He winced. "I'd rather not."

"Enough said."

"What does that mean?" Mike asked.

"When using magic to lift a tree that large, it would be… let's say, challenging for me not to move this vehicle as well."

Mom popped the locks on the back doors and tossed Rake a smile in the rearview mirror. "Hurry back."

Rake grinned. "That's the plan."

Even though Mom and Uncle Mike had heard Rake say he was going to "move" the tree using magic, they had no clue what they were about to witness.

Destroying the ward that the mage had put around Tavis Haldane's body had been impressive to me because I knew the power that had gone into making it. Rake had made it look easy. I'd seen him move big stuff before. The tree's diameter was about that of one of the Defender's snow tires. The base of the tree was just off the road, so I suspected Rake would go with breaking the rest of the roots and pushing it down the mountain on the other side.

I wished I could be standing outside looking through the windshield at Mom and Uncle Mike's faces.

Rake studied the roots, then crossed the road to take a look down the mountain. He was probably checking for obstructions to what he was about to do. He turned and gave us a quick thumbs-up.

"What is he…?"

Those three words were all Mike got out before Rake made a shoving motion with both arms and the massive tree obeyed, shooting across the road and over the edge.

Rake turned and jogged back to us, slid in, and shut the door. "We're good to go," he announced cheerily.

I reached over and squeezed his hand, biting the heck out of my bottom lip to keep from laughing.

Rake patted my thigh. *"I'll describe their expressions later."*

I coughed to cover a chortle. *"You'd better."*

The only sound was the crunch of our boots in the snow. At least the human boots were crunching. Rake was moving like a snow leopard.

Whatever had happened here was over. Just because we hadn't seen anyone, didn't mean we were going to let our guard down. Rake insisted on going up first to ensure there were no magical traps.

After what they'd seen Rake do with that tree, Mom and Mike let him.

Less than a minute later, he waved us up to the porch.

Mike knocked on the door and waited.

No answer.

He knocked again. "Glendon? It's Mike Bryant. I need to ask you a few questions."

Again, no answer.

Rake had gone around the side of the house. "It's open on this side."

When we walked around to where he stood, we clearly saw that when Rake had said "open," he wasn't referring to an unlocked door.

The entire side of the house was open. Open as in gone. I would've said peeled away, but that would indicate there were pieces and parts of it lying around.

There was nothing left.

What remained of Mr. Kerr's house was in good shape, all thing considered.

It reminded me of news coverage I'd seen after tornado touchdowns that'd left homes looking like dollhouses with removable walls, so you could play with your dolls inside. The furniture was still in place and clothes were still hanging in closets. It was almost as if when Mr. Kerr hadn't answered the door, the Big Bad Wolf had *really* wanted in. He'd huffed and puffed and vaporized the wall.

The Big Bad Wolf hadn't been playing around.

Shirts on hangers flapped in the breeze as if they were hanging outside on a clothesline, not in a second-floor closet.

There was a breeze blowing that was on the verge of

becoming a wind. That was probably why I hadn't smelled it at first.

Brimstone.

Black magic.

I glanced at Rake. He'd sensed it, too.

Mike didn't need a warrant, he just walked in, me and Mom right behind him. Rake stayed outside on guard.

The brimstone smell was inside as well.

The mage had been in Glendon Kerr's house.

Mr. Kerr's keys were on the kitchen counter, his car was in the garage, and his jacket, with his wallet inside, was hanging on the back of a kitchen chair.

The only thing not there was Mr. Kerr.

I wished it had been a tornado. He would've been able to see that coming and taken cover.

There'd been no cover for what had happened here.

We searched the house, calling his name but not shouting, so we couldn't be heard outside. There was no answer. Mr. Kerr wasn't here. On the upside, there were no signs of violence—or blood and bits. Hopefully, he was still alive. Somewhere.

Rake was studying multiple disturbances in the otherwise smooth snow.

"Hoofprints," he said. "Warhorse sized. I've walked all the way around the house. There were thirteen sets. They surrounded the house."

Mom tilted her head slightly, as if hearing something we could not, then walked slowly to the closest set of hoofprints. I started to follow, but Rake motioned for me to stay.

"His bootprints."

I didn't need to ask whose.

I wondered if we had Cernunnos to thank for the downed tree blocking the road.

"No," Rake responded in my head. *"That was the mage. He wanted to make sure Mr. Kerr couldn't escape."*

"He was here," Mom murmured, her eyes on the prints from where Cernunnos had dismounted and stood facing the wall.

She went to stand as close as she could and not be in them. "He's angry. Enraged. We're not the only ones looking for this mage, or I should say 'hunting.' That's what he's doing. Running him to ground. He wants him dead and ground to pulp beneath his horse's hooves."

I could get behind that sentiment—after we got some answers.

Mom's focus remained on the imprints of Cernunnos's boots. "This wasn't about Glendon. The mage was inside. Cernunnos wanted him, so he did this. I'm sure of it."

Judging from the lack of any patch of snow resembling a giant cherry Slushie, I'd say my dad didn't get what he wanted.

The wooden beams of where the side of the house had been connected to the sides, roof, and foundation were black and smooth with a glassy sheen, almost like amber, but you wouldn't catch anybody wanting to make a necklace out of this.

I took in the smooth lines of the remaining walls. I'd intended to take a sniff, but once within touching distance, I didn't need to. I'd smelled this before, on the road to Grandma's house.

Primitive magic, but with a strength not commanded by modern mages. This was a force of nature that could not be reproduced by mortal magic. This wasn't a magic you *had*. This was a magic you *were*. It was as much a part of its wielder as his blood and bones.

Cernunnos. The Master of the Wild Hunt.

My father.

He'd probably never considered knocking. He merely sheared off the wall to take what he wanted. It'd been entirely too easy. Our home was warded, but could Cernunnos do the same to get at me and my mom?

"There should be residual magic ricocheting all over the place," I said. "Could it have…I don't know…dispersed?"

"If there was any left, I would sense it," Rake said. "It's gone."

"Could it have happened long enough ago to—"

"No. It didn't blow away, evaporate, or in any way vanish. Cernunnos absorbed the force of this himself."

"That's not possible."

"Apparently, it is."

I was dumbfounded by what that implied. When a magic spell is worked, the power goes out from the practitioner. A big, violent spell is like a bomb. It's meant to destroy, or in this case, vaporize the side of a house. When a bomb goes off, the energy spreads outward until it contacts an obstacle, wreaking damage, then the energy continues radiating outward.

"Whoever did this reabsorbed all of the leftover energy," Rake said.

"Why would he do that?"

"To retain power. To never weaken. When a mage does

a working, it takes a lot out of them. Those at my level can keep going, but not indefinitely. It's like an MMA fighter. Matches have a time limit because mortals can only take so much before they need to rest and recharge. But what if you didn't need to rest? What if you could reabsorb the power of your punches to land another? Then another. Reabsorb and repeat. Ad infinitum. Unlimited power and stamina. Never weakening. Never dying.

"Eternal life and power. That could very well be what this mage wants. Why he lured your father here. What he plans to do with it if he gets it is anyone's guess."

It all clicked into place and made perfect sense.

"That's why he's trapped Cernunnos and the Wild Hunt here," I said. "And he's using me and Mom as bait to get him."

13

Mike waved from the kitchen to get our attention, held a finger to his lips for quiet, then crooked his fingers to get us inside.

What the heck?

We climbed up over the foundation and into the kitchen.

Mike kept his voice down. "I think I know where Glendon might be."

We followed him to the basement door.

"But we searched the basement," I reminded him.

Mike winked. "I don't think we got all of it."

"A safe room," Rake said.

Mike brushed the tip of his nose. "Point to the gentleman. I forgot about an 'amenity' down here Glendon told me about years ago."

"But wouldn't he have heard us calling him?" Mom asked.

"Not necessarily," Rake said. "It would depend on the thickness of the walls and where the air exhaust is located."

Mike put his hand on the doorknob. "Rake, you didn't search with us. Could you tell if Glendon is down there, and if so, locate the door to that room? I only know it's in the basement."

"Easily."

"I don't want to startle him. If he took cover in there against this mage or the Hunt, he could be a mite skittish. His magic doesn't have anywhere near the punch yours does, but I still wouldn't want to be on the receiving end."

"Understood."

We went down into the basement, Mike first, followed by Rake, Mom, and me. We stayed at the base of the stairs while Rake went to the middle of the room.

It was a finished basement, filled with the kind of things people typically stored. Exercise equipment bought in a moment of self-deception and good intentions, boxes of old documents kept "just in case," plastic storage boxes of miscellaneous stuff accumulated over a lifetime and no longer used, but too sentimental to be thrown out.

Glendon Kerr also had a sweet home-brewing setup.

Rake stood in silence for less than five seconds before jerking his thumb to the right. "Over there."

What looked like a wall with a pair of ladders leaning against it was in fact, a door. Apparently. I couldn't see the seams, but Rake pointed them out to us.

"So, who knows him best?" he asked.

"That would be me." Mom stepped up to one of the seams. "Glen! It's Maggie Fraser." She followed up her shout by pounding twice on the door/wall.

Nothing.

Then, muffled and barely audible, came two knocks. From the inside. Though considering how thick the door probably was, those were probably fist-pounds.

Rake's teeth flashed in a quick grin. "He's stuck. The locks are jammed."

I snorted. "You can read his mind, too?"

Rake tapped his ear twice. "I can hear him. He can't get out and he's tried everything."

Mike gestured at the door. "Can you…uh, lumberjack that, too?"

Rake chuckled. "I think so. Though I might need to buy Mr. Kerr a new lock system for Christmas."

"I'm sure he won't mind."

Rake closed his eyes. Seconds passed. His brow furrowed in concentration, them beads of sweat broke out on his forehead. He opened his eyes and blew out his breath. "Two of the mechanisms are bent. I think whatever Cernunnos did to vaporize the side of the house warped the locks. We're not getting in that way. Is it an actual concrete and steel safe room, or was it converted from a root cellar or something?"

"Don't know," Mike replied. "But I think it was here when he moved in. Can't we—"

A whirling sound came from inside the door, followed by a metallic grinding like nails on a chalkboard times a hundred. We all winced.

After a sharp click, the door began to slowly open, then stopped. "Help me, dammit!" shouted an irate voice from the other side.

Rake and I were closest. We grabbed the now-cracked door and pulled.

Never had Glendon Kerr looked more like Santa Claus. He was wearing a red sweater, which matched his face, now red from exertion. Those, along with his white hair and beard, gave him a definite St. Nick vibe. Though I'd never heard of Santa wearing Dockers and duck boots.

Or cussing a blue streak when Mike told him the entire side of his house was gone.

I introduced him to Rake.

Mr. Kerr's blue eyes twinkled as he slapped Rake on the shoulder with one big paw. "You loosened it for me, boy. My thanks." He stopped and took a closer look. Mr. Kerr wasn't a seer, but as a practitioner, he knew something about Rake was different.

"Yes, he's a Yankee," Mom said, saving the day. "But we're not holding it against him."

Mike steered us back to the business at hand. "Glendon, we need to ask you a few questions."

"We've rented seventeen properties for the holidays," Mr. Kerr was telling us.

Mike showed him a photo of Tavis Haldane. The one Aunt Nora had provided from her front desk security camera, not the dead one with his face set in a terrified rictus. "Have you seen this man?"

"I can't say that I have. Is he missing?"

"He was missing, now he's dead. The call history from his phone said he called your office twice last week. Do you think he might have rented a place? He worked for the mage who was here this morning."

"Did the mage kill him?"

"We have every reason to believe that he did."

"If he's been in the office, Dorothy would know him."

"Who's Dorothy?" Rake asked.

"My office manager. She has her license now, so she can sell and rent properties. If someone calls or comes into the office, and I'm out, she takes care of them."

"Is she in town for Christmas?" Mike asked.

"She is. I can have her meet us at the office."

"That'd be good, Glendon. We'd appreciate that."

Mr. Kerr took out his phone and typed a short text. Less than a minute later, he had a response.

"Dorothy can meet us there at 4:30. Does that work?"

"It does."

We moved up from the basement to Mr. Kerr's newly converted al fresco kitchen. As he viewed the damage, wide-eyed, he told us about his unexpected and extremely unwelcome visitors this morning.

"There's an old mining road that comes over the ridge behind the house," he was saying. "This mage of yours… mine…came that way. He had a driver. I couldn't see his face, but it was a man. He was wearing a long dark coat, gloves, and a fedora-type hat with the brim pulled down over half his face. Pale, no beard. That's all I got."

"Make and model?" Mike asked.

"Mercedes, G550. Black," Mr. Kerr replied.

"Must be a rental. No one in town has anything like that." He scowled. "If we had phone or Internet, I could find who rented it and from where. What time was all this?"

"Just before daybreak this morning," Mr. Kerr said. "When they drove up, it activated my flood lights. Damn bears keep setting them off, and I've been meaning to turn off the motion sensors. I won't be doing that now."

"Tell us what happened."

"When the floods came on, I looked out my bedroom window at the backyard, ready to yell at a bear. It was the man in the fedora, just standing there, looking up at me. Then the lights went out. They're supposed to stay on for three minutes. There's not a doubt in my mind that he did it. I never understood the meaning of 'my blood ran cold' until then. I've never feared any man, but I feared that one. I knew he wouldn't bother with knocking. He was going to come right in the house after me. I'm embarrassed to say that I hightailed it down the back stairs to the kitchen and down to the basement as fast as my feet could carry me and locked myself in."

Survivalist Santa.

"I'm glad I'm an early riser. If I hadn't been, this guy would've gotten the drop on me. He had the magical chops to take me by himself. From what I felt rolling off him, I wasn't about to take that chance. Didn't know, didn't want to find out. Way out of my league."

"There's no shame in running," I told him. "Only in being slaughtered."

"Damn right. I heard you went to work for SPI. I take it you learned that nugget of wisdom from experience."

"Unfortunately, yes. Running good, dying horribly bad."

"Smart girl."

"I try."

"So, you didn't see the Wild Hunt?" Mom asked.

Mr. Kerr kept looking at the open space that used to be his kitchen wall. "Did he do that, or the Hunt?"

"The Hunt," Mom replied. "They wanted the fedora-wearing man who wanted you."

"Did they get him?"

"We don't think so."

"Too damned bad."

"Agreed."

"Follow me," he told us. "I'll show you where that Mercedes was parked."

Rake went to stand on the left side of the Mercedes's tire tracks in the snow. The mage had walked the rest of the way to the house's back door. There was snow where they'd parked the car, so we had tire tracks and footprints, but Mr. Kerr said he'd cleared the walkway last night once the snow had stopped. On the right side of the tracks was another set from where the driver had gotten out and stood next to the SUV's door.

"What are you getting?" I asked him.

"It's our mage. Old, powerful. He came here for Mr. Kerr. The mage possibly needs more sacrifices to top off his tank. Your Mr. Kerr has enough power to be noticed. He's an earth mage, right?"

"Yeah. He's also our local ley line expert."

"That would have come in handy. How many locals know that he's a wizard or a ley line expert?"

"All of them who are clued in."

"How many is that?"

"Entirely too many."

Mike was hunkered down, studying the driver's prints. "From the size and tread, it's a man, size eleven work boot. Wolverine Journeyman."

"I take it that's a common boot around here?" Rake asked.

"Unfortunately, yes. They're fine boots. A lot of men in town own Wolverines."

All that the boots told us was that the mage's driver had good taste in footwear, bad taste in employers, and no problem with murder.

That narrowed it down somewhat, but not nearly enough.

One of our neighbors was helping this monster hunt us down.

14

"He did what?"

Grandma Fraser had seen and heard a lot of strangeness during her life in Weird Sisters, but Glendon Kerr telling her what'd happened to his house surprised even her.

I was a firm believer that a picture was worth a thousand words, so I showed Grandma the picture I'd taken with my phone of Mr. Kerr's newly aerated abode.

My father had vaporized the side of a two-story house to get at the juicy megamage inside.

At Mom's insistence, Mr. Kerr had packed a bag and followed us back home in his truck. He and Grandma were old friends. One more for Christmas was no inconvenience. A Southern woman could expand her household and meals to accommodate any who arrived on her doorstep anytime, but especially during the holidays.

We were all sitting at the kitchen table having a late lunch. Uncle Mike was out on the front porch talking to Vickie to get calls made and possibly officers out to check on the town's other earth mages. Rake didn't need to be told to have seconds, and I knew that thrilled Grandma to no end.

I knew why he was tanking up. As soon as the sun went down, things were going to get entirely too active around here. It was gonna be a long night.

Grandma knew that, too. So did Mom and Mr. Kerr. We all had healthy appetites.

Before he'd come to the table, Mr. Kerr had called Bill Crawford, the town's favorite contractor, and had explained his predicament. It being two days before Christmas, Bill was shorthanded, but he and two of his guys would get over there and close up the house as best they could. Bill promised to put Mr. Kerr first on his list for more substantial repairs two days after Christmas when more of his crew were back in town.

"Bill says even though it's just a temporary fix, it'll keep the bears out," he was telling us. "That's all any man can ask for. I appreciate you taking me in, Miss Agnes, but I don't want to bring my trouble to your doorstep."

"We know all about your trouble, Glendon," she assured him. "Be it mage or Wild Hunt, this house and those of us in it can take their trouble and shoot it right back at 'em."

I didn't know how Grandma planned to do that, but her confidence was contagious. Not to mention, it was still daylight. Once the sun went down, I had a feeling everyone's confidence would begin to erode, or at least turn into extreme caution.

We all thought the world of Glendon Kerr, but he did not need to know Cernunnos's relationship to me and my mom.

However, we told him what we believed his mage home intruder had wanted from him.

His soul.

Mr. Kerr put down his fork. "Miss Agnes, you know I love your sweet tea, but would you happen to have a wee dram for a man who's just had his life flash before his eyes?"

"You'll have nothing and keep your wits about you," Grandma retorted. "If this mage decides you're worth the trouble, he'll be back—and you'll be sober and grateful for it."

Mr. Kerr smiled. "You're a cruel woman, Miss Agnes."

Grandma huffed. "I've been called worse and will be again."

Mom's phone rang. She looked at the screen and got up to take it in the next room. Grandma didn't care if it was the Almighty himself on the other end, you did not talk on the phone at her table.

When the door swung open, Rake saw Uncle Mike on the front porch just finishing a call. He stood. "Excuse me, ladies, Mr. Kerr." He went out to talk to Uncle Mike.

The three of us sat unmoving, trading glances.

I was trying to decide if the pending conversation was going to be the good kind. I'd finished eating, so technically, there wasn't any need to stay. I put my napkin next to my empty plate and started to stand.

"Makenna."

Grandma's voice froze me where I half stood.

"Ma'am?"

"Don't you eavesdrop on those two. Their conversation is their own."

"I wouldn't dream of it, ma'am. I'm going to check on Mom."

"See to it that's all you do."

"Yes, ma'am."

I *was* going to check on Mom. I had no intention of eavesdropping on Rake and Uncle Mike.

I was gonna walk right out on the front porch and join them.

I paused on my way to the porch and raised an eyebrow to Mom.

"Vickie," she mouthed silently.

I nodded and proceeded to my destination, but out of courtesy for the conversation I was about to join, I paused, merely to determine at what point it wouldn't be rude to interrupt. Grandma couldn't find fault with that. I stood next to a window and peeked out the side.

"Jimmy got a drone up," Uncle Mike was saying. "The pocket dimension is approximately seven miles across. We've got five ley line intersections forming a pentagram—"

Rake held up a hand. "Margaret told me, but we needed confirmation."

Mike scowled. "He's using our natural power against us. Does him going after Glendon mean every magic user in town is in danger?"

"That depends," Rake told him.

"On what?"

"What the mage wants to do with the power boost. We know it involves Cernunnos and the Wild Hunt. A sacrifice doesn't need to be a practitioner. Instilling terror in a victim will work as well, if the mage gets desperate."

"How do you know all this? First up on Widow and now here." Uncle Mike's expression was flat. It was his cop face.

He didn't like what he was hearing, especially from a man his niece was in love with.

I could've stepped in at this point, but I knew I shouldn't. Rake needed to explain himself, and he was more than capable of doing so. This was best settled mano-a-mano. Uncle Mike wasn't sexist, but when it came to his family, he got protective in a primitive way. Aunt Vickie didn't mind, and neither did I.

"I have never taken a life to increase my power," Rake said point-blank. "Nor would I, but I know of those who have."

"How?"

"Makenna told me you served in the homicide department of the Atlanta police."

"I did."

"To catch a killer, you have had to think like a killer, to know their MO. By knowing how and why they chose their victims, you undoubtedly saved lives. It doesn't mean you gained that knowledge by committing those same acts yourself."

"I didn't mean to imply that you did," Mike said. "It's just that—"

"I'm not human, I have fangs, and goblins have well-deserved reputations in more than one area. I assure you, Mike, I love your niece more than my own life. Her safety and happiness are my only concerns. I do not blame you for questioning my sincerity or motives. Were I in your place, I would do the same." Rake smiled. "I may have even thrown in a barely veiled threat, so I admire your restraint."

Uncle Mike smiled back. "It's Christmas. I'm being generous until you give me reason not to be."

"Rest assured, I will never give you reason to doubt me in any way. When it comes to Makenna, I am what you see."

"And when it doesn't involve Makenna? Margaret told me you work with your people's intelligence service."

"Where I have had ample experience hunting and permanently stopping monsters like this mage, and those who enable them."

Mike's smile broadened into a grin as he extended his hand. Rake took it. "Then I'll look forward to working with and getting to know the other Rake Danescu."

"I see you're—" said Mom from right behind me.

I jumped and squeaked. "Jeez, don't sneak up—"

"I didn't sneak. You were too focused on your eavesdropping to—"

"It's tactical listening. Gathering intelligence for—"

"Call it what you like, dear." She gave me a little smile. "Well…?"

"Well, what?"

"What did they say?"

"They seemed to have worked it out. Mutual respect. I think Mike likes him. Maybe. Probably."

"I'd take it if I were you."

"I will. What did Aunt Vickie have to say?"

"Not good." She reached for the front doorknob. "They need to hear this, too."

Grandma joined us. "Glendon went upstairs to shower." She looked from me to Mom and back again. "So, who said what? Catch me up."

15

"I sent out a town-wide red alert," Mom told us, after she had Rake and Mike come back inside. Daytime or not, now was not the time to stand out in clear view of anything waiting in the woods. "That's a message sent via e-mail as well as phones, both voice and text," she explained for Rake's benefit. "We use it for weather and…certain situations when it's best to shelter in place."

"Like last year, when the Cameron boy was having adjustment issues during full moons," Grandma added.

"Local werewolf family," I told Rake.

His lips twitched at the corners. "I thought that might be the case."

"At that time, it was safer for everyone to stay where they were," Mom continued. "I asked Vickie to put out the alert this morning after we found Tavis Haldane. We asked everyone to check in and tell us if they'd seen any strangers. Several people didn't respond, which isn't unusual considering it's the holidays. Calls and texts that went to people outside the seven-mile perimeter simply bounced back. Of those inside who didn't respond, Vickie contacted their nearest neighbor and asked them to go make sure everything was all right. Eight of them reported that the individual or family was out of town, and some had asked them to keep an eye on their places and get the mail." Mom paused. "We have five people missing. Violently missing. Their homes had been broken into, a struggle had obviously taken place, and they are no longer there."

Mike swore. "Who?"

"Fletcher Parks, Elaine Abbot, Abigail Sellers, Douglas Ross, and Minnie McVane."

"Old-timers, like me," Grandma said.

"Practitioners?" Rake asked her.

She gave a tight nod. "Earth magic. Those are five of the sweetest souls God ever made."

"We'll get them back, Miss Agnes," Mike promised.

"Damn right, we will."

"Mr. Kerr is luckier than he knows," I said. "He's an earth mage and knows where all the power points are."

Mom nodded. "The mage must have recruited ghouls as kidnappers. There were multiple sightings near those houses. Vickie's been busy following up on calls."

Horrified silence met that news.

"Was any blood found in those houses?" I asked.

"Thankfully, none."

I knew only too well that ghouls were extremely proficient kidnappers. A team of ghouls had taken my friend Oliver Barrington-Smythe on one of my first big cases at SPI. And an immortal supervillain, known only as Janus, had abducted my SPI partner with the help of ghouls. Both had been rescued. Barely.

I suddenly couldn't breathe. We'd saved Ian, but Janus had escaped, vowing to return.

"Rake…"

"Janus is only about four thousand years old. What I felt on Widow's Peak was much older, and quite frankly, stronger."

"Who's Janus?" Mom demanded.

I gave everyone the *Reader's Digest* condensed version of one of SPI's scariest adversaries.

"How can you be sure it's not him?" Mike asked.

Rake answered him. "Janus *might* be strong enough to face the Master of the Wild Hunt—not defeat, merely face him. But he's not nearly old enough to account for what I felt."

I remembered Bannerman Island and all of our agents and allies from this world and others who had battled with everything we had to defeat him and the Fomorians. We'd nearly lost. This time, it was just us, a tiny police department, and townspeople who were depending on us to protect them.

The being who had cut us off from the outside world made even Janus look like a lightweight in comparison.

"If he's worse than this Janus, what do we do?" Grandma asked.

"Pray," I told her.

It was time to call a town meeting.

Last night, Cernunnos had appointed himself and his Wild Hunt as Rake's and my official welcoming committee. While terrifying, it hadn't necessitated warning the entire town. Mom knew why Cernunnos had come.

Until this morning, the mage had only killed his own accomplice. Again, while horrifying, it didn't involve the safety of the entire town. Now that Cernunnos had vaporized the side of Glendon Kerr's house to get at the mage who had come to add Mr. Kerr's soul to his arsenal, and now that one of our own neighbors could be pointing out those of us with earth magic…that made it personal, and the entire town needed to know.

Mom called Vickie and had her turn the red alert into a be-in-town-by-sundown to circle-the-wagons broadcast. Mom estimated that there were only eighty-four townspeople inside the pocket dimension, including the five that had been kidnapped. Christmas Eve was tomorrow, so Mom told everyone to bring their family gifts and any food they had prepared, and we'd share it among everyone. Between the three restaurants in town, there'd be enough fridge space.

Main Street in Weird Sisters wasn't long and running under it was a cavern about half the size of a football field. It came complete with its own fresh-water spring.

With the situation we found ourselves in, defending it might not be so easy, but it was what we had, and more than once during Weird Sisters' history, it had been enough and our people had been grateful for it.

I was in my bedroom, getting my lethal accessories out of my luggage and on me where they belonged. "So, it's a lockdown, but a party."

Mom had already packed a bag and was standing by the door watching me arm myself with increasing concern.

I shrugged into my shoulder harness with a pistol under each arm. Only one was loaded with bullets. The other had paintballs. "If this bothers you, don't watch," I told her. "I'm not stepping foot outside this house without every gun and knife I brought with me. Don't worry, I've been trained how to use them. If I wasn't good *and* safe, I wouldn't be carrying."

"I'm not worried—okay, maybe a little. I'm proud, but at the same time, I hope you don't need to use any of those."

Heck, I just hoped any of them would work. From what we'd sensed from this mage so far, I might as well be packing a pair of water guns for all the good it'd do us.

My phone buzzed with an incoming text. "It's Aunt Vickie,' I told Mom. "Dr. Crombie's finished her initial autopsy of Tavis Haldane. She wants to know if Rake and I can meet her at Dr. Greenleaf's office in half an hour."

I typed my response.

We'll be there.

There were so many questions we wanted to ask the late Tavis Haldane.

Unfortunately, his soul was gone, so even with a proficient necromancer, talking to him wasn't possible.

Dr. Jean Crombie was one of our regional medical examiners. Dr. Mark Greenleaf was our town doctor. Dr. Crombie's office and lab were in Asheville, but she lived in Weird Sisters. Lucky for us—though she probably felt otherwise—her home was inside the dome.

When you worked in a town where many of the citizens either weren't human all the time, or looked human but had never been human, it helped to have a medical examiner who had a flexible mind.

Jean had a lot in common with one of Manhattan's top medical examiners, Dr. Anika Van Daal. Both had the skill to hold a glamour on a dead body. When dealing with a body that only looked human when they were alive, time was not your friend. Not too long after death, any magic they'd used to glamour themselves as human quickly faded, leaving them as they really were.

That could be a very unpleasant surprise for the uninitiated.

"How did he die?" Vickie was asking Dr. Crombie.

"Unknown. There's no sign of injury, illness, or violence—the appearance of the face notwithstanding. The internal organs are perfectly healthy for a human of his age."

I looked down at him. Dr. Crombie had sewn up the Y incision. I refused to let my eyes go above that incision to his face. I'd gotten a good look at it this morning, and that was more than enough. When I got a chance to sleep again, I was sure I'd be seeing it in my nightmares. I swallowed against a wave of nausea.

"I don't have access to a lab, so the toxicology report is out of the question for now," Dr. Crombie was saying. "No drugs or alcohol that I could tell. No needle tracks or liver damage."

"Time of death?" I asked.

"Best I can tell just under twenty-four hours."

"Late afternoon yesterday."

"Or thereabouts."

Right when Rake and I had been ambushed by the Wild Hunt.

"How was the soul taken?" Rake asked. He was wearing his human glamour. "Excised or left on its own?"

Dr. Crombie glanced at Vickie, who nodded. "It's okay, Jean. He needs to know. We all do."

"Muscles can do strange things, post-mortem," she said. "However, it's my belief the contortions on the face were caused by very real fear and pain, agony even. That being said, I didn't detect any sign of restraint or physical assault."

All of which went entirely too well with Rake's assessment of a spell holding Tavis Haldane still while the mage did whatever horrific things he had done.

"He did not pass peacefully," she continued. "There's no official cause of death. He simply stopped."

"How about unofficial?" Vickie pressed.

"His soul was taken, slowly, and with extreme care and precision." Dr. Jean Crombie had been our medical examiner for as long as I could remember. If she hadn't seen it all, she had at least seen a lot. She looked as if she were about to be sick. "The closest comparison would be surgery, except without anesthesia." Her eyes met Rake's. "Chief Fraser tells me you have had experience with mages able and willing to do this."

"I wish I had not, but to stop such monsters, someone has to. To my great regret, this only confirms my theory. The mage who killed this man needs souls. He's using them as an external power source, a battery if you will, and he needs them to be…intact. There are devices that can be used to store the soul until it is needed."

"Dear God," Vickie breathed.

Rake's gaze went to Tavis Haldane's tortured face,

and he did not look away. I knew why. Rake was not only acknowledging what had been done to him, he was making a pledge that he would find the mage who had done it and make him pay and pay dearly.

"The soul would have fought him," Rake continued. "Which is what the mage would have needed and wanted. For his evil purposes, this man's soul would have needed to have been taken at full strength, fighting for his life." Rake paused and swallowed on what I knew was a dry mouth. "An individual capable of such an act would have enjoyed every moment of it. Power over others, domination, subjugation. We're looking not only for an obscenely strong mage, but a sadist."

Dr. Crombie reached for Tavis Haldane's right hand. "I found something I wanted to show you. It might be helpful." She turned the hand palm up and pried open the slightly curled fingers.

There was a tattoo on his palm.

A scarab.

I'd seen the exact same tattoo in one of my first cases at SPI. It had been on the palm of Dr. Adam Falke, a Danish historian and archeologist who had assisted Vivienne Sagadraco's sister Tiamat in obtaining artifacts critical to controlling a pair of grendels. Grendels that Tiamat intended to turn loose in Times Square at midnight on New Year's Eve.

It was the mark of the cabal.

The cabal had killed my three predecessors. They wanted me dead. Now one of them was here, had trapped us, and was preying on our townspeople.

This was all my fault. Mine.

The smells in the room suddenly overwhelmed me. I took the smallest breath I needed to get the next couple of words out. "Can we continue this outside?"

I didn't wait for an answer. I fled. When we'd come in, I'd seen where the restroom was, and I ran for it.

Rake must have waited a few minutes before he followed. I'd just flushed the toilet after I'd thrown up and had moved over to the sink. There was a Dixie cup dispenser next to it with a big pump bottle of mouthwash.

I made use of both.

While working at SPI, I'd learned that the scents of death assaulted more than the nose. Your taste buds could take a hit, too.

I was pumping a second dose of mouthwash into a cup when Rake quietly knocked on the door and then opened it just enough to look inside.

"You okay?" he asked softly.

I was swishing and concentrating really hard on not throwing up again from the wintergreen taste of the mouthwash. God, I hated wintergreen. Rake would wait.

I spat it in the sink, and hung my head over it, my hands braced on either side, the cool porcelain doing a little to make me feel human again.

"It's a cabal mage," I managed. "Or someone they hired." I stared down at the drain. "He used me and Mom to lure my father and the Wild Hunt here. Somehow, someway, he found out Cernunnos was my father. I don't know how, and right now, I don't care. What I care about is that he's torn people who I've known all my life from their homes. Grandma's right. They're some of the kindest, sweetest people there are."

A sob rose in my throat and I shoved it down and kept going. "He's going to do to them what he did to that poor man on Dr. Crombie's slab. This is all my fault."

Rake didn't respond. He didn't need to. Once again, I was doing a fine job of pointing out the obvious.

"It's not your fault," he said. "He's using you as a tool, the same way—"

"The hell it isn't," I spat. I ran the water long enough to rinse out the sink. "If I could, I would leave right now and draw him away, but he's fixed it so I can't even do that."

"Makenna, don't take this the wrong way, but this isn't all about you."

I turned on him. "What is *that* supposed to mean?"

Rake came into the small bathroom and closed the door. "And you took it the wrong way. I didn't express myself properly. I mean that you're not his main goal. Your involvement is a piece of some twisted puzzle, but there's a much bigger picture in play here."

"Like what?"

"This is about power. Obtaining enough of it to reach his goal, whatever that is. Right now, you need to clear your head." Rake put his hands on my shoulders and gently turned me to face him. He enfolded me in his arms and kissed the top of my head.

"I'm here," he murmured against my hair. "Your formidable family is here. We can do this. They have greatly underestimated who they're dealing with."

They.

We knew we weren't just dealing with one mage.

We were up against the cabal.

16

I splashed water on my face and dried off with a paper towel. I hadn't bothered with makeup this morning, and I was glad I hadn't. The mascara alone would've made me look like a raccoon by now.

I took a deep breath, nodded to Rake, and together, we left the restroom.

Aunt Vickie was waiting for us in the hall, arms crossed, leaning against the wall.

"Sorry about that," I told her. "It won't happen again."

She pushed away from the wall, standing straight. "It's not a problem if it does. Happens to the best of us."

With that, she wasn't treating me as her niece. I was one of her officers. I clenched my teeth to stop any misties.

"I take it you know who's doing this?" she asked me.

"A member of the cabal who we've never gone up against before or someone they hired. A serious heavy hitter. They use that exact scarab tattoo. I've seen it before."

"It sounds like there's a lot more we need to unpack here. Everyone needs to hear it, and I don't want you to have to repeat yourself." She glanced at her watch. "We're closing the town in just under two hours. The town council will be meeting thirty minutes before that. We need a full report, everything you can tell us about them."

"You'll have it."

It was two blocks to Aunt Nora's inn, the Three Sisters. I'd called earlier and asked if she could show us the room Tavis Haldane had stayed in. There was a chance, albeit slim, that we could find or sense something that had been missed in Vickie and Mike's investigation.

Aunt Vickie left us to get there on our own. She had straggling townies to gather. I welcomed the chance to have some time with Rake.

He put his arm around my waist and pulled me close. "Vickie said they're closing the town. Exactly what does that mean?"

"They test the system a couple times a year, usually in the middle of the night and when we don't have tourists wandering around. Thanks to the cabal's hired gun, Weird Sisters is a tourist-free zone right now. He killed the one tourist we had, and stuck us in a pocket dimension so more can't get in."

"And this system of yours is…"

"Ward stones. Seventy-seven of them. When activated,

they put the entire downtown in a protective lattice. It's like a ginormous bug zapper. Or in our case, ghoul zapper. We haven't had the chance to test against someone this powerful. Hopefully tonight won't be a first—or last."

The Three Sisters Inn was a turreted two-story Victorian centrally located on the corner of Laurel Street and Azalea Avenue, one block off the town square.

The house was pink.

Fortunately for the homes and shops around it, the pink was pale and actually tasteful. Aunt Nora was many things, and most of them were over the top, but tacky had never been one of them.

The house's trim paint was a soft eggshell white and the landscaping was what I liked to call Victorian immaculate chaos. My aunt loved wildflowers, which were notoriously hard to control. They were called wild for a reason.

Eleanor Fraser controlled those flowers like she managed everything about her life and business—with a steel hand covered in a lace glove. Don't get me wrong, Aunt Nora was one of the kindest and most generous people I'd ever known. She simply didn't tolerate disorder.

She was standing on the inn's wraparound porch waiting for us. Vickie hadn't called her to let her know we were on our way. She didn't need to. Aside from being the most talented medium I'd ever known, Nora had an uncanny knack for knowing where the people she loved were at all times. When asked how she did it, she'd merely smile and say she had the help of some dear friends. It didn't take much to figure out those dear friends were of the dearly departed kind.

That was why I wanted to drop in on Aunt Nora.

Well, that and I needed one of her world-famous hugs. Maybe two.

Nora took one look at me and said: "You need a cup of tea."

I laughed. I couldn't help it. Surprisingly, it felt good and not crazy. "Make it a whole pot—with some of your shortbread cookies." I paused. "You have baked shortbread, haven't you?"

Nora just looked at me.

"Sorry, of course you have."

"Tea and cookies in a minute." She opened her arms. "First, I want a hug."

Once Aunt Nora had deemed me and Rake to have been adequately hugged, she welcomed us inside, and the house did essentially the same thing. Next to the word "cozy" in the dictionary should have been a picture of Nora's inn. The pink Victorian did a thriving business. People only had to stay there once, and they were guaranteed to come back—and tell all their friends that they'd never had a more relaxing vacation.

As she took us up to Tavis Haldane's room, we told her who we thought her guest had apprenticed with.

"How disappointing. He seemed like such a nice young man. I sensed a tension in him, but that's not unusual with those who find their way here. I'm normally such a good judge of character."

"He might have been nice," I told her. "He just had seriously bad taste in mentors."

"It certainly wouldn't be the first time something like *that* happened." Nora stopped in front of the closed door. "Margaret said you might be able to sense something in his room. I haven't touched it since he was last in it two days ago. I was supposed to have a full house last night, but this pocket dimension is playing havoc with all our Christmas plans."

That was Aunt Nora. Regardless of how far the world had swirled down the universe's toilet, it was nothing more than a minor inconvenience. This too shall pass, was her response to any situation, be it minor snafu or major catastrophe.

Tavis Haldane had stayed in the Blue Ridge Room. Just because Nora had a raging passion for the color pink didn't mean she subjected her guests to it. The Blue Ridge Room was, as the name suggested, mainly blue, with accents of soothing green and masculine browns. No clawfoot tub, this room had a shower only, but it was a shower that could easily accommodate two. Practical, with the possibility of romance, if that's what you wanted.

Tavis Haldane hadn't been here for romance. He'd been a clueless murder victim in waiting. I wondered what the mage had told him to lure him here. I also wondered why he hadn't stayed wherever the mage was hiding himself. There were probably too many clues lying around giving away the mage's real reason for being here. Can't have your sacrifice learning they're on the murder menu. The mage would've wanted that realization to happen on Widow's Peak. When it came to terror, the more, the merrier.

Hysterical laughter bubbled up and I pushed it back down. Yep, Rake was right. When you spent enough time around psychotic killers, you started knowing how they thought. While good for figuring out their next moves, it was rough on your continued emotional stability.

Be the rock, Mac.

And ignore the hammers that keep hitting it.

Vickie and Mike had done a thorough job of searching—and sensing—Tavis Haldane's room. She had told me what they'd gotten from it. Neither Rake nor I picked up anything they hadn't already found.

"Have you sensed him?" I asked Nora.

"No," she said sadly. "And I've tried, multiple times."

Rake told her what he thought had happened to Tavis Haldane's soul.

"No one deserves that fate." Nora's blue eyes flashed with a rare anger. "And now this mage has taken five of our own."

"Yes."

"Do you believe they're still alive?" she asked Rake.

"I do."

"We were hoping you could confirm that," I said.

She carefully closed the door to Tavis Haldane's room and locked it.

"Then let's go downstairs and see if we can find them."

Aunt Nora had tea parties in her frilly Victorian parlor.

She also held séances.

Nora didn't *summon* anyone. She always asked politely. If they wanted to drop in for a visit, that was their choice. And right now. Weird Sisters had enough unwelcome guests, and Nora wasn't about to add to it.

She invited me and Rake to take a seat at the table with her. "Business first, then tea and cookies."

"Who are you calling?" I asked.

"Whoever might have the answers we need."

Nora pulled down the room-darkening blinds and lit the candles around the room, ending with the ones on the table. In the center of the table was my great-grandmother's silver tea stand. Nora went to the china cabinet and removed a silver tea caddy, and a tea towel I recognized as one that had also belonged to great-grandmother. Nora opened the caddy and carefully went through the contents, selecting several items inside and placing them close together in the center of the towel.

A thimble, a small ladies' pen on a chain, a coin, a pipe stem, a worry stone worn smooth, a brooch, a small gold cross pendant, an amethyst crystal, and a few others I couldn't identify.

If all of the people responded who had owned those objects during their lives, it was about to get crowded in here.

I knew who the pipe stem had belonged to.

Stephen McRae had built this house in 1882—and had never left.

The house had been turned into an inn during the early 1970s. The previous owners had suspected it was haunted, but Stephen had never made himself known to the couple. When they were ready to retire, they'd put the inn on the market. Glendon Kerr had the listing, and when he'd shown Nora the property, she'd found Stephen standing by the parlor fireplace smoking a pipe.

Nora had asked Mr. Kerr to give her some time alone to "get a feel for the place." He left, and Nora began negotiating with the true owner of the house. They reached an agreement, Nora moved in, and Stephen McRae remained as a permanent guest—who eventually became much more to her.

Aunt Nora gently folded the four corners of the tea towel over the objects and placed her hands over it. She then bowed her head and closed her eyes.

No one spoke. I tried to breathe as quietly as possible and not fidget. Even the flames on the candles had ceased to flicker.

Then that changed.

Brief puffs of cold air darted past me, making the flames dance on their wicks. The temperature dropped as I sensed more and more presences in the parlor. The air was thick with them. Even though I knew the ghosts didn't take up any physical space, I was starting to feel claustrophobic.

It was worse for Rake.

Aunt Nora's lips curled in a small smile, but she never opened her eyes. "They are curious to meet the man Margaret's little girl has brought home. Relax, Rake. They approve."

That's easy for her to say. Rake sat upright and frozen. Only his eyes moved, flicking from one side to the other, then up and down as the ghosts swirled all around him.

Over the next few minutes, the stifling sense of a packed room faded, and the temperature returned to normal.

Nora opened her eyes and sat back in her chair, a little pale from the experience. I felt a presence still in the room. I couldn't see Stephen, but I sensed him standing right behind Aunt Nora. He must have laid a comforting hand on her shoulder because she reached up to pat it. "The five who have been taken are alive," she said. "They're being held together in a place that's unknown to them and have not been harmed."

Yet.

Nora didn't say it, because we all knew it.

≈ **17**

After Aunt Nora had deemed us adequately fortified with tea and shortbread, she fixed us to-go cups and sent us on our way down Main Street to Glendon Kerr's office.

Beginning the weekend after Thanksgiving, downtown looked like something out of a Hallmark movie. The buildings were an eclectic blend of country, alpine, and Victorian, and were decked out in twinkling lights with evergreen wreaths and swags everywhere. Elves were a particularly popular decorative element among the locals. Several shops had decorated Christmas or Yule trees in their windows. Some had the nine-candle menorahs of Hanukkah or the seven-candle kinara of Kwanzaa.

The citizens of Weird Sisters were a mix of races and species covering the full range of magic talent and encompassing the entire spectrum of religious beliefs. We embraced our diversity and respected each other's opinions and beliefs.

In short, we all got along.

And yes, it's possible.

Rake was looking at the smiling locals greeting and chatting with each other. He was clearly confused. "Your mom told them about the ghouls?"

"Yep."

"And they're…happy?"

"What can I say? We love the holidays." I popped the last bite of shortbread in my mouth. "Plus, it takes a lot to rattle our locals." Though I had caught a couple of words of concerned conversations regarding Santa Claus. Some of the children were worried that Santa wouldn't be able to find them because they'd be in town rather than in their homes.

I was scanning the crowd for a pale man in a fedora. I didn't think he'd be out in public, but stranger things had happened.

I wasn't the only one on villain watch.

Clarissa St. James was standing just outside Weird Sisters' coffee shop, the Witch's Brew. She smiled at me and Rake, raising her cup in salute, then went back to casually surveying the people as they came into town.

Vickie and Mike would rather find, apprehend, and interrogate our Benedict Arnold quietly and with minimum fuss. When they did get him or her in a room with two chairs and a small table, I knew who'd be sitting across from them. Clarissa wasn't an official member of the Weird Sisters police department but was on a retainer as a consultant. Any locals who had been naughty in the eyes of the law simply confessed to whatever misdemeanor they'd committed when confronted with Clarissa.

She was a human lie detector. She also had a knack for identifying the outlier in a crowd. Right now she'd be scanning for anyone feeling particularly pleased with themselves, who considered themselves a wolf successfully concealed in a herd of sheep. They might look like a sheep to everyone else, but Clarissa would recognize them for the traitorous scum they were.

The search for our traitor was in the very best hands.

Rake was getting a lot of looks, not because he was a goblin or he had some strange aura of otherness about him. Rake was wearing his human glamour and had the lid locked down tight on his dark magic.

Rake was hot. He was almost as hot a human as he was a goblin.

"What is everyone staring at?" he asked from behind his cup.

I grinned and linked my arm through his. "That would be you."

"Why?"

"One, they've never seen me with a man before, let alone snuggled up. Two, you look like a hot human, but they're wondering, 'What is he, really?'"

Rake gave me a quick, wicked grin. "I could drop my glamour and answer their question."

"Darlin', that'd be like dropping your jeans. I wouldn't mind, but I'm pretty sure it'd be a bit much for everyone else right now."

I was being recognized. A few spoke in passing. All were intensely curious, but no one asked. I pushed my lips together against a grin. That is, no one would ask until we'd passed, and by the time we'd strolled to the end of the street, we'd probably be able to hear the buzz of fresh gossip if we listened closely enough. If I stopped and introduced Rake to one or two people, everyone else would take that as an open invitation to a mob scene. We needed to get to Mr. Kerr's office. After we got safely sealed in for the night, then I'd introduce Rake around.

Jimmy had confirmed that we were completely cut off by what was essentially a pocket dimension that extended like a dome over the town and surrounding area. His drone had hit the top at about two hundred feet. Once it reached that altitude, it was like a fly trapped in a jar. After bumping into the pocket dimension's "lid" a few times, Jimmy brought it back down.

The last time we'd been in a pocket dimension, it'd only covered Rake's hotel, but the magetech generator that powered it had unpowered Rake's magic, much to his frustration and embarrassment. Yes, he'd moved that tree this morning, and had tried to force open Glendon Kerr's safe room, but those had been several hours ago.

I nudged Rake. "How's your magic holding up?"

He smiled slowly, eyes glittering. "I can assure you with complete confidence that I am fully functional in every way."

I gave him a quick grin. "That's what I like to hear."

Grandma Fraser was waiting for us outside Glendon Kerr's office, a big mug of spiced apple cider in one hand, her iPhone in the other. "Took a walk down Main Street, did you?"

"And Rake made quite the impression."

"So I heard. My phone hasn't stopped buzzing." She opened the door to Mr. Kerr's storefront office. "We've got something to show you."

Dorothy McGuire was seated at her desk. Glendon, Vickie, Mike, and Mom were gathered around. Everyone's attention was on her computer screen—and no one looked happy.

Mom gestured me over and gave me her spot directly behind Dorothy. "Tell us what you see."

I looked, I saw, and the bottom fell out of my stomach.

It was a short video, running in a loop, taken from the office security camera, showing Tavis Haldane getting out of a black Mercedes G550 and entering the office. There was a man in the passenger seat. The camera was good quality, not top-of-the-line equipment, but good enough to pick the passenger out of a lineup.

I spat the mother superior of all cuss words, and Grandma didn't threaten to wash my mouth out with soap.

It was a pale man in a dark fedora.

It was Janus.

Rake knew my realization as soon as I had it. Then the two of us just stood there staring in disbelief at the screen.

Aunt Vickie cleared her throat. "Care to share with the rest of us?"

I turned to Glendon Kerr. "Is that the man who was at your house this morning?"

"I didn't get a clear look at his face other than it being pale, but that's the hat, and from what I can see of his coat—"

"But his face looks odd," Mom said. "Almost as if—"

"Yeah, he has more than one," I finished for her. "That's Janus. If you see him in person, and I hope you don't, it'll be clearer than it is here. Seers will get faint impressions of multiple faces, each different from the one before, layered one on the other, stretching back into the distance like looking into a wall of fun-house mirrors." I paused. "All those faces have been real enough at one point in time or another. Janus can shapeshift. In my experience with him, a ghoul has been a favorite disguise, though he's powerful enough to assume any form he wants."

"What's his last name?" Mike asked. "Or is it an alias?"

"Just Janus. This guy only needs one name. He's four thousand years old and so are his grudges. Raging psychopath. Turn-ons include plotting world domination and battles on the beach. The last time we fought him, he had an army of Irish sea monsters. Lucky for us, we're in the mountains, so he's back to having to make do with ghouls."

Aunt Vickie just stood there. "You're completely serious."

"And I wish I weren't."

Grandma moved around the desk to get a better look at the screen. "But you said it couldn't be him. He's not strong enough."

"I can't explain it," I told her. "Rake and I know Janus's magic signature. What we've sensed wasn't him. He can change his appearance, but not what his power feels like or his age. Magical power is like fingerprints. No two are alike. But..." I waved a hand helplessly at the screen. "There he is. It's him." I turned to Rake. "You got anything?"

Rake was staring at the screen, utterly still, his face an intimidating mask. Janus had tricked him; he'd tricked us both. But I wasn't a mage. Rake was. This went beyond personal for him. I could read his thoughts as they seared their way through his mind. Precious time had been lost while Janus had kept him in the dark. One man was dead and five more taken. I had nearly been carried away by Cernunnos. If he could've recognized Janus on that road when we'd been ambushed by the Hunt, he could've acted and prevented our earth mages from being kidnapped, kept us from being cut off from help, kept the town from having to huddle behind wards.

Rake blamed himself for all of it.

I'd never seen him as angry as he was right now. I was right there with him. Janus was playing with us, and he'd picked my hometown as his playground, and the people I loved as toys.

Rake silently swore by his power that Janus would pay with his life for all he had done, was doing, and planned to do.

Everyone was completely silent. They didn't have a psychic bond with Rake, but they didn't need one to recognize his rage.

Rake quietly took a breath and slowly exhaled, once again in complete control. "Somehow Janus has acquired power that neither he nor anyone else should have. If he's been collecting the souls of mages for years and absorbing that power, it would only explain a small part of the strength I've sensed. Nothing explains the age."

"Someone besides Glendon has to have seen him," Mom said. "We're not paranoid about strangers, but we definitely make note of them. We've had mages come through here before, but nothing like this." She glanced out the window onto the street. There was a car parked where the Mercedes had been on the security footage. Mom's gaze went beyond it to the small park on the edge of town.

"Other than knowing that an immortal psychopath is kidnapping our earth mages and holding the rest of us hostage, we've got nothing," she continued. "We need more, and I'm going to get it. Rake, Vickie, Mike, I want you to come with me, but stay back. I don't want to antagonize him—more than necessary."

I drew in a sharp breath. "Mom? What are you doing?"

"What I should have done last night. I'm going to have a talk with your father."

18

Considering who my father was, I should have been afraid for my mom.

I wasn't.

To tell you the truth, I had questions for my father—a lot of questions. Rake literally had our backs, as well as Vickie and Mike. I didn't know what bullets would do to Cernunnos, but lead and steel couldn't feel good. If he came with the intent to harm or kill either me or my mother, then he damned well deserved anything he got. As to carrying me or Mom off to Wild Hunt Never-never Land, that wasn't possible, at least as long as we were trapped in the dome.

Mom briskly crossed the street and entered the park. A woman on a mission.

I had to jog to catch up to her.

Mom didn't need to look to know I was coming up behind her. "Makenna Anne, I said stay back."

Technically, she hadn't, but I didn't think now was the time to smart off and point it out.

"I'm going with you, Mom. No arguments."

"I'm not going to give you one. If this goes well, I *want* you to meet your father, but first give me a few minutes alone with him."

A father who could do a lot in a few seconds, let alone minutes.

I didn't want to do it, but Mom had more of a stake in this than I did. I owed her that much.

"Okay, but we're gonna be right there." I indicated where Rake, Vickie, and Mike waited by a picnic table.

She gave me a tight smile and quick hug. "Now, go."

I went.

Mom turned her back to us and walked a few steps farther to the edge of the park. She stood facing the deep forest beyond, which had already slipped into late afternoon shadow. While it wouldn't be full dark for another hour, it was dark enough for the Wild Hunt.

I inhaled confidence and exhaled fear. When my father appeared, I couldn't show any weakness. He was a hunter. He was *the* hunter. I was his child, and I wouldn't be seen as prey.

As the minutes passed, I tried not to fidget. If Mom could stand perfectly still, so could I.

One moment it was just the edge of a forest; the next, thirteen riders with hounds appeared between the trees.

Cernunnos, Master of the Wild Hunt, Celtic god of

fertility and death, my father, the lover of my mother, was now directly in front of her.

Still, she did not move.

The sun had set behind the mountains, casting the horses, the riders, and the trees around them into shadow. I could barely tell where the horses ended and their riders began. The evening cold was setting in and I was frozen in place: not with cold, nor fear, but with anticipation.

Last night, everything had happened so fast, I hadn't had time to really look at my father.

I had time now.

Cernunnos and his horse were both armored in matte black—both metal and leather. The stallion was similar to a Friesian. Black, sleek, and graceful, yet with the size and musculature to carry an armored knight. A horse of war.

Cernunnos made no move to draw a weapon. One hand loosely held his mount's reins; the other rested negligently on a leather-sheathed thigh. Then he threw one leg over his horse's muscled neck and slid smoothly from his saddle. I swear I felt the earth tremble when his boots hit the ground.

He was tall, but not inhumanly so. His hair was blond, his face pale, and his features sharp. His eyes were green, like mine, only mine didn't glow. I couldn't see them from where I waited, but I'd gotten an all-too-close look at them the day before. Every other Fraser had blue or hazel eyes. I'd been the green-eyed oddball.

No more.

Cernunnos held up his hand, silently commanding his Hunt to stay where they were. He left his horse to come meet my mother alone. He stopped at least five feet from her. It wasn't for his own sake. I doubted anything scared my father. This was for her benefit, so she would feel less threatened. It was a distinctly non-villainous thing to do.

Then he inclined his regal, antlered head in a bow.

"Well done," Rake murmured.

There were gasps from behind us.

I turned my head to look.

Oh jeez, half the town was watching.

Cernunnos wasn't doing anything to disguise himself, so the locals were getting the full impact of his appearance.

Mom had to know this would happen. She was tired of hiding.

She could've gone farther into the forest. She'd chosen the park on purpose. She wanted the people of Weird Sisters to witness this.

I'd never been more proud of her.

Rake's eyes were on my mother. "Very well done."

I couldn't hear what she was saying, but her body language was loud and clear. Mom was giving the Celtic god of sex and death a complete and thorough piece of her mind.

"So that's where you get it," Rake murmured.

I glanced at him. He was smiling.

They were standing in profile, Cernunnos taller than my mother by at least a foot, even more with the antlers.

I could catch a word or two here and there. I saw him not as my father, but as my mother had when she'd encountered him in that stone circle. He probably looked exactly the same now, thirty years later. He was achingly beautiful. In the prime of his life, but as ageless and implacable as the death he brought—one you'd eagerly embrace. His voice was a dark baritone, rich with the depth of the forest primeval from whence he'd come.

I totally and completely understood why Mom had thrown caution and clothes to the wind that night in a Scottish stone circle.

It was also clear that Cernunnos found her just as beautiful and desirable as he had the night I'd been conceived.

As one, they closed the distance between them and Cernunnos bent and kissed my mother. She rose on her tiptoes as he gathered her to him. After a few seconds, she gently pushed away. A few more words were exchanged, and her hands went to either side of his antlered head. I saw her lips form the words "Be careful."

She turned and gestured me to join them.

Oh boy.

"Stay here," I told Rake.

"I will. He is no danger to you."

I went to join my parents.

Yep, I remembered correctly.

His eyes were green with flecks of glittering gold. They didn't burn me as I had expected they would, but they held me where I stood, though I had no intention of running.

As my mother took a step back, Cernunnos placed his hands on my shoulders, bent and kissed my forehead in greeting or blessing or both.

A second collective gasp came from the townspeople, as they realized my mother—their mayor—had just introduced me to my father. I looked like a smaller female version of him. There was no mistaking that we were related.

This was every kind of cool.

"So, you're not here to carry me off?" I asked before I could stop myself.

He slowly turned his regal head, taking in his Hunt. "Do you see any horse without a rider?"

"No."

"Then there is no place for you."

Okay, that hurt a little.

"I am here to meet and protect my daughter, not to take her."

"But the—"

"Legends? Do you truly believe I follow rules? That I am subject to laws laid out in a mere story?" He smiled, taking my chin in his bare hand, his fingers warm against my chilled face. "The laws of nature cannot contain me. I appear when I choose. It is merely easier at certain times and places. You are my child, and I would never harm you." His eyes narrowed ominously. "Or allow any other being to do so. If the laws of nature cannot hold me, then how could the will of one sorcerer, albeit one of great power, command me?"

"You told him what we know about Janus?" I asked Mom.

"I did. They've crossed paths before."

"It was he who attacked your strange conveyance last night. I pulled you from it to keep you from more harm."

And then Rake walloped the entire Wild Hunt with one of the biggest spells in his arsenal. Oops.

Cernunnos's eyes flickered over my face, drinking me in. "I see her in you—and myself."

When I had time to think, I could see myself reevaluating who I was. It made me doubt who I'd always believed myself to be. Now, I was more, and more was scary.

"Why does it frighten you to doubt?" he asked. "There is no growth in certainty. Only arrogance. You are part of me. All that I am, you are."

Cernunnos. Father, god, philosopher, and life coach.

"It's not arrogant to not like surprises," I told him.

He laughed. "Is that what I am? A surprise?"

"Just the biggest one ever."

Unlike the rest of the Hunt, Cernunnos didn't wear a helmet. Antlers rose, proud and majestic, directly from his head. The mountain girl in me did a quick count.

Twelve points.

Wow.

Cernunnos leaned toward me, his teeth bright white against the shadows.

"I have no intention of allowing myself to be brought down, either."

I raised my hands. "I was simply admiring the headgear. Impressive."

He inclined said headgear in acknowledgment of my compliment.

"Why did Janus lure you here?" I asked.

"Some time ago, he offered me a partnership. I refused. I do not partner. I hunt."

"Considering what he did to his apprentice, good call."

Cernunnos scowled. "The one whose soul he sacrificed to bring me hence. This might account for the strange compulsion I felt, a pull from Janus to me that should not be possible. I opened a portal to confront him. Once I was here, he closed the portal behind us and told me he had found my mate and child."

"I'm not your mate," Mom told him.

"Did we not mate that night? The evidence stands here between us."

"Once, maybe twice," she said as an aside to me.

Cernunnos threw back his head and laughed, his voice booming as it carried across the park. "Nay, it was thrice and more, and still you desired me."

Go Mom.

Applause and wolf whistles came from the townies.

His green eyes glittered. "Your inner fire called to me, as mine called to you. We passed the hours of dark together. I have not encountered your like before or since. You are my mate. You are mine and I am yours."

"We'll discuss your possessiveness issues later."

Cernunnos's good humor vanished. "Janus told me he had once had my child's throat in his hands. If I denied him, he would again. This time he would end your life."

"He can try."

"Small, yet fierce."

"He's trapped all of us here. We're bait. You're the quarry, whether you like it or not. We believe he wants your power."

"He has taken five of our people," Mom told him. "Their magic comes from the earth. He has them but has yet to kill them."

Cernunnos's gaze grew distant. "Five sacrifices," he mused.

"Not if we have anything to say about it," I told him.

"There are five points of power on the edges of this prison he has conjured."

Mom nodded. "There must be a connection, but we

don't know what it is. This partnership, did Janus say why he wanted it?"

"He did not. No doubt I would find it distasteful." Cernunnos drew himself up to his full height, his eyes burning. "Last night he vanished into the fog like the coward he is. In the early hours of this day, he escaped me. Tonight will be thrice—and he will be done."

19

The secret the women in my family had kept for thirty years and nine months was now the talk of the town.

Once we knew Cernunnos wasn't here to carry either me or Mom away, there was no reason not to admit who he was in relation to us. Which was exactly what Mom had done. Honestly, matter-of-factly, and publicly, like it was no biggie that she'd had sex with the Celtic god of fertility and given birth to his daughter. Plus, Cernunnos had made it obvious he still found my mother eminently desirable.

Now that the town had gotten a good look at said fertility god, her standing had increased even more. Heck, they'd probably want to elect her mayor for life.

Yep, my mom had just leveled up in the townspeople's estimation.

But that was all they were going to know. As far as anyone outside the family was concerned, Cernunnos had come to town to meet his daughter, and while he was here, hunt down the mage and ghouls threatening to ruin everyone's holidays, and assist our local law enforcement in the rescue of our five kidnapped townspeople.

None of that was a lie. Tonight, Cernunnos and his Wild Hunt would be hunting Janus, and he'd promised to leave evidence of his success on the park's picnic table. Just what every woman wanted for Christmas, a freshly severed head. Though I'd have no problem waking up tomorrow morning to find Janus's head turned into a holiday centerpiece. It'd be the best present ever. I knew Ian would love it. If it happened, I'd have to take a picture and text it to him in Bora Bora with "Merry Christmas, Partner!"

Hoo boy, would *that* get me a phone call.

Once everyone who was trapped by the dome arrived in town, Mom and the six other members of the town council activated the ward stones, sealing downtown Weird Sisters and hopefully protecting us from attack.

Normally, the town council met in the conference room next to Mom's office in the small town hall a block off Main Street. Instead, they adjourned with us back to Glendon Kerr's office.

We still had Janus's rental lair to locate.

We knew which house Tavis Haldane had signed up for, but whether Janus was actually there was a point being debated.

The town council was made up of Mom, Aunt Nora, Glendon, pub owner Cynthia Browne, diner owner Delia Lees, volunteer fire chief Clark Findlay, and town doctor

Mark Greenleaf. Rake, Aunt Vickie, Grandma Fraser, Dorothy McGuire, and I rounded out our meeting.

The real estate office was almost as crowded as the conference room would've been, but Mr. Kerr had an old, pulldown map of Weird Sisters that showed the five power points, as well as detailed interior photos of every house available. When you sold and rented homes to supernaturals, or psychically or magically gifted humans, you needed to know where all the local power points were. I wouldn't call it allergies, but some people couldn't handle being that close to crossed ley lines. The types of adverse reactions varied.

Fortunately, all the properties that were presently rented were outside the dome, including the Newsome house Tavis Haldane had rented for Janus.

"Could he have rented one place, but be staying in another?" Delia asked. "This time of year, no one would notice if there was a squatter."

"The Newsome house is rather small," Dorothy agreed. She lowered her voice. "This doesn't leave this room, but it's our worst property. Mr. Newsome could get more money more often if he'd just put in a little work."

"Or had any taste whatsoever," Rake said in my mind.

Looking at the photos, I had to agree. "Yeah, I can't see Janus setting foot in that place, let alone staying there. All it's missing is one of those Big Mouth Billy Bass singing fish things mounted over the fireplace."

Dorothy giggled. "It's in the bathroom, dear. Motion activated."

I snorted. "Janus is *so* not staying there. Did you try to talk Tavis Haldane out of renting it?"

"Oh yes. But Mr. Haldane insisted on the Newsome house."

"It's just outside the dome at the southwestern power point," Rake noted. "Is there any significance to that?"

"The annual solstice surge begins at the southwest point," Mom told him.

"Could Janus be going in and out of the dome, since he's the one who constructed it?" Mom asked.

"I have every reason to believe he can," Rake said.

I was there when Rake had discovered that unpleasant bit of information. Isidor Silvanus had a back door, so to speak, in the Hell dimension he'd trapped us in. If Isidor could do it, it'd be a no-brainer for Janus.

"If there's a way out, could one of our people go out that way for help?"

Rake shook his head. "My theory is that he's used the power latent in the five points to build and maintain the dome. Any door in it would be keyed to Janus. Only he could open and close it."

Mom shrugged. "I had to ask."

"It was a very good question; I just wish I could've given a different answer."

Grandma squinted at the map. "Isn't that tacky Newsome house near the Bishop place?"

"It is," Glendon said. "About a quarter mile west."

"Looks like it's just inside the dome."

"It's more than that. It's built almost on top of the southwest power point."

"Is it still in one piece?"

Glendon shrugged. "More or less. The family lives in

Savannah, and I've been trying to sell it for them for nearly two years, but there's been no takers. The size isn't the problem. I've sold larger houses. But combine the size with the amount of work it needs…"

"Sounds like Janus's kind of place," Rake said.

"It was built after the Civil War by Hadley Bishop," Grandma told him. "He was a Confederate captain and plantation owner who got run out of Georgia by his own people. Killed his brother in an argument over their inheritance. He escaped with his life and a strongbox of gold."

"And Janus's kind of people," Rake added. "I take it you have photos of the house?"

"We do." Dorothy scrolled through the listings on her laptop, clicked on one, and the Bishop house appeared on the big wall-mounted flatscreen.

No house was more out of place in the North Carolina mountains. It looked like the house from *Psycho.*

"That was taken two years ago when it went on the market," Glendon said. "Part of the roof collapsed last month. The owner doesn't want to pay to make the repairs. I can't say that I blame him. The rest of the roof isn't stable enough to stand on. If Janus is in there, he's getting snowed on."

"You're missing the entire side of your house," Grandma said. "You could still live there. Janus is even older than we are. I'm sure he's dealt with discomfort."

"Janus is perfectly capable of making the house comfortable for himself while maintaining the illusion that it's falling apart," Rake told them both.

Dr. Mark Greenleaf spoke. "What do we know of where he's holding our people?"

Aunt Nora half raised her hand. "I can speak to that. A few hours ago, I contacted some of our departed to ask if they knew of their whereabouts and condition. All five are alive and they are being held in one place—at least they were at that time. They did not appear to be under duress or unduly frightened. As to Janus's intentions, unfortunately, our departed were unable to communicate with them aside from determining their general condition."

Heads were nodding around the room as people voiced concern and impatience that we were unable to do more to find and rescue them right now. No one questioned what Aunt Nora had seen or disputed its accuracy. Try that in any other town council meeting.

Mom stepped up beside the flatscreen showing the Bishop place. "As we discussed earlier, we don't know what Janus intends to do with those he's taken, but Makenna and Rake tell me SPI's past encounters with Janus have involved power accumulation. Our hemisphere's winter solstice was yesterday. Our local solstice is Christmas Eve. At midnight on Christmas Eve the ley lines running under our five points reach their greatest power. We believe Janus intends to use our five earth mages to channel that power to him. How he will do this and what it will do to our people is unknown, but we should assume their lives are in the greatest danger."

Aunt Vickie spoke. "As soon as the sun's up in the morning, Mike and all our officers as well as some others we have deputized will go to the Bishop house and the southwestern power point, and the other four if necessary. We *will* find and rescue our people. However, there is something we need to do tonight. One of our locals is helping Janus."

"I'm surprised Janus came into town," I said. "Even if he didn't get out of the car. He doesn't do his own legwork. One of our people told him who our earth mages were and where they lived."

Glendon Kerr then hit the highlights of Janus and our mystery local paying him a visit early this morning. He said that Cernunnos and his Wild Hunt showing up and running Janus off had probably saved his life.

Delia scowled. "We have a traitor."

Vickie nodded. "We're all but positive. And we believe that person is inside the ward with us tonight, with the intent to discover our plans and relay them to Janus. Mike and I aren't about to leave a wolf in here with our people. We will find him or her tonight. Clarissa St. James has been walking around since late afternoon. She'll be reporting to me when we leave here. If this person knows how our ward stones work, they could be planning sabotage."

Cynthia looked horrified. "That's possible?"

"We don't know of any way it can be done, but this mage easily trapped us inside a seven-mile-wide pocket dimension. Any action is on the table. He could have given his spy a device of some kind or told them what they'd need to do to bring down our ward. We also don't know how many ghouls are out there, but we don't want even one in here with our children."

I wasn't about to say it, but I wondered what Janus had offered those ghouls as payment to come here. They had little use for money, but they could eat their weight in human flesh twice a day. They'd take a couple of bites out of one and move on to the next. They preferred live food, but they'd take dead. For them, the fun was in the pursuit and torture of their victims. Sadistic bastards.

Rake's expression was set in stone. He knew what ghouls could do, and he knew how to handle enemy spies who were indirectly responsible for bringing them down on us. That was his job. It was a good thing my family already liked him. When it came to getting needed information, Rake had no qualms about violence. Or so I'd been told. I'd never witnessed it firsthand, and I really didn't think violence would be necessary tonight. Janus's informant would be in here with us. Alone. Janus wasn't coming to help him, and Rake would make that abundantly clear. Traitors were almost always cowards. With no one to back them up, their bluster collapsed like a house of cards.

Mom looked into each and every face. "Are there any questions? That we have answers for," she added. "Okay, if not, then I think we're done. Delia?"

"With the holidays, I'm short-staffed at the diner, so I've recruited kitchen help. We'll be serving dinner in the Hall in about forty minutes. It won't be fancy, but it'll be hot and good. Glendon, if you'll come with me, we'll get you fed so you can get changed for the kids."

Glendon stood and took a garment bag off the coat rack behind his desk. I knew what was in there.

His Santa suit.

He tossed the garment bag over his shoulder like Santa's bag of toys. "We only have fourteen children in town, but Santa will drop in after dinner to assure them that he knows exactly where they are and has presents for each and every one of them."

Now that I knew Janus was behind all this, all I wanted for Christmas was his severed head from my dad.

20

Some things you kept in the family.

The town council meeting was to be followed by a Fraser family meeting.

Mom asked Cynthia if she could get us a quiet corner table and a round of her steak sandwiches and fries.

Weird Sisters had two pubs, both owned and run by Cynthia Browne and her husband Barry. The Cauldron was for the tourists and locals who understood they had to either be human or be able to look that way.

In the Cauldron, it was all *Macbeth* all the time.

The town was named after the three witches in *Macbeth,* and our little theater performed the play every summer in an amphitheater just outside of town that was partially constructed, but mostly natural tiers of stone seating surrounding a large flat area of rock that served as the stage. The production and psychic festival were Weird Sisters' two main summer events.

The Cauldron was decorated with photos, props, and costumes from the local theater. Instead of columns to separate the areas, there were illuminated glass display cases with mannequins dressed in costumes from various productions. Cynthia and Barry were particularly proud of two costumes they'd acquired from the Globe Theatre in London. The bar as well as the tables, chairs and booths were dark wood with a distinctly Elizabethan vibe.

The second pub, the Cellar, located downstairs from the Cauldron, was for supernatural and clued-in human locals only, and was accessed from the small parking lot running behind the Main Street shops. There were two doors—one marked "Deliveries" and a second unmarked with a pull handle. There was a small buzzer next to the unmarked door. Everyone knew the drill. You pressed the buzzer and a camera hidden inside what looked like a broken light fixture over the door showed whoever was tending bar the new arrival. Once you were identified and approved, there'd be a click, the door would unlock, and you were in.

The Cauldron was great, but the Cellar rocked.

The Cellar was a place where people could go and let their hair down, so to speak. Glamours were optional, which was a welcome relief for a lot of our locals. Civilized behavior was not optional. It was expected and enforced. Cynthia's husband and head barkeep, Barry, was a quarter troll and had no problem whatsoever in keeping the peace by tossing the offender into the parking lot or the street if he was working the bar upstairs.

Mom and Aunt Vickie had a few things to take care of, then they and Uncle Mike would be joining us. Grandma, Rake, and I went down to the Cellar.

Based on our earlier conversation, Rake decided not to drop his glamour. Most folks in town had only heard of goblins and had never seen one. I'd caused enough of a stir by bringing a man home. I just wanted an hour of peace and relative quiet at a dark corner table. I also wanted one of Cynthia's homebrewed ales, but since Janus was out there somewhere with who knew how many ghoul minions, I'd have sweet tea instead.

Like the Cauldron, the Cellar's interior was all dark wood and dim lighting. There was a stone fireplace that shared a chimney with an identical fireplace upstairs. One thing the Cauldron didn't have that the Cellar did was one of two steel doors that led into the Great Hall.

Barry got us set up at a corner table, and we ordered sweet teas. Once this was all over, I'd introduce Rake to the malty ambrosia that was Cynthia's ale.

Rake took off his coat and hung it over the back of his chair and put his gloves in the pockets. I took off my gloves but kept my coat on, at least until I'd warmed up.

I dropped into my chair and sagged. "Have we been here a week yet?"

Rake glanced at his watch. "In another twelve minutes, it'll be twenty-four hours."

"Longest twenty-four hours ever."

"What's this 'hall' Delia mentioned?" Rake asked.

"The Great Hall," Grandma told him. "A cavern that runs about half the length of Main Street. We use it for town gatherings and shelter for emergencies. The walls are cave stone, just the way we found it. It has its own water source, two entrances with steel doors lockable from the inside, and a ward stone at each corner."

Rake nodded in approval. "Nice thing to have."

While we were greeted with waves and friendly smiles, no one came by to talk to us. I was wiped out, so I was relieved not to have to make introductions and small talk, but at the same time, I was hurt that the people I'd known all my life were hesitant to get anywhere near me.

I knew why.

Cernunnos. My dad.

Yes, it was Mom who'd had sex with Cernunnos, but I was the result of said sex.

And yes, my dad was the Celtic god of fertility, but he was best known for being the god of death and hunting, or more to the point, hunting resulting in death. Gory, violent death. In the eyes of the people of Weird Sisters, that made me an unknown factor even though they'd known me all my life. Some of them had even been hunting with me, and they knew perfectly well I hadn't wacked out and gone on a killing spree. Other than being able to see portals and ride a horse without falling off, I didn't know of anything else I'd genetically inherited from Cernunnos, other than green eyes and blond hair. Though, as far as the locals were concerned, I could be a Cernunnos mini-me. Plus, I'd gone off to New York, joined SPI, and helped save the supernatural world a few times. Most of them didn't know that, but some did.

They didn't know what to think about me anymore.

Truth be told, I didn't know what to think about me, either.

Barry brought our sweet teas over himself. Whenever I'd come home before, I'd gotten myself a big ol' Barry hug. They were the best. All things considered, I thought I'd let him make the first—

Barry put down the tray, gave me a big smile, and spread his arms. "Do I get my hug? Or now that you're a big city girl, are you—"

I grinned and launched myself at him. Barry lifted me off the floor into one of his patented rib-crushing hugs.

"You're still Makenna Fraser," he rumbled in my ear. "Don't let anyone tell you any different."

"Thank you." I kissed him on the cheek, and he set me back on my feet.

The social ice now resoundingly broken, others started coming up to say hello and be introduced to Rake.

I was still just as tired but felt so much better. *This* was the homecoming I'd hoped for.

Mom, Vickie, and Mike showed up a few minutes later, then Barry took their drink orders and served all of us our sandwiches and fries.

I dug in, suddenly ravenous. "So, who's in charge of protecting the town right now?" I asked Vickie and Mike between bites.

Mike grinned. "That's what deputies are for."

When you worked in law enforcement, you ate first and talked later—if there was any time left. When a waiter had cleared our plates and left us a pitcher of tea, we got down to business.

Aunt Vickie was sitting across from Rake. She leaned forward, forearms on the table. "Any chance of getting this dome down?"

"I've never seen or heard of anything this big. I'm a battlemage. Ley lines are way out of my skillset—and Janus has had thousands of years of practice with them. They're one of his specialties. That being said, I want to get a look at that southwestern power point as early as possible tomorrow. Janus has never supplemented his magic with technology, at least not that I know of, but other members of the cabal are known for it."

He proceeded to tell them about the magetech generator that Phaeon Silvanus had invented and his brother Isidor had used against SPI in Rake's New York hotel.

"Is Janus a member of this cabal?" Mike asked.

"He knows them, but I believe he uses them rather than works with them. He's a loner, and I believe he's alone now. I've only sensed one mage, and now we know that mage is Janus. He often uses ghouls as muscle."

"And if there is one of these generators at the southwestern point?" Vickie asked.

"I know how to disable it. You wouldn't happen to have a gem mage in town, would you?"

"We do," Mike replied. "But she's visiting her daughter and grandbabies up in Richmond."

Mom refilled her glass and topped off mine. "How could a gem mage help?"

"Magetech generators are powered by a rare crystal," I said. "I can't see Janus having any trouble getting his hands on either one. If he was using a generator and it wasn't at the southwest point, a gem mage could bird-dog it. If it's there and Rake disables it, most of our problems would be taken care of when that dome comes down. There have to be at least two SPI commando units waiting just on the other side. Our New York people. Ms. Sagadraco has probably called in the two Atlanta teams as well, or at least has them on standby." I chuckled. "That doesn't even include Rake's royally pissed-off chief of security, Gethen Nazar, and every goblin battlemage I'm sure he's brought with him."

Rake groaned.

I nudged him with my shoulder. "Honey, Gethen's not gonna let us go anywhere alone ever again. But on the upside, it'll be open season on Janus the instant that dome comes down." I sighed. "It'll be a beautiful thing and I want a front-row seat—with my phone so I can record it for Ian."

Our people at SPI lived for things like this. I just didn't want any people in town to die for it.

"Two of Janus's other specialties are portals and pocket dimensions," I continued. "It looks like he's doing the triple-threat thing here: portals, pocket dimensions, and ley lines." I told them how Janus had hidden Ian from us on a six-acre island in upstate New York. "We knew Ian was there, his girlfriend sensed him, we searched every square inch. Turned out Janus had a prison cell-sized pocket dimension. Ian was right under our noses the entire time, but we couldn't get to him." I described the alien starfield we saw in the escape portal that Janus had instantly snapped open that night.

Mom exhaled heavily. "So, our people could be beyond our reach."

"Until the last minute. Janus seems to be replaying his greatest hits. It's not what we want, but at least we have an idea of what he's doing."

Rake took my hand. "But he failed. We won. If it hadn't

been for you slicing through his shield *and* his chest, he would have won, and his Fomorian army would have been loosed on this world."

Mike blinked. "Squirt did what?"

Rake grinned. "Let me tell you about your niece."

He proceeded to tell my family about what I'd been up to since becoming a SPI agent. Though "regaled" might be a better term. Rake was quite the storyteller, though all of it was true. After a few minutes, I felt a blush coming on.

"You're no longer the child they raised or the niece they knew." Rake told me in my mind as he continued his stories to my family. Nifty trick. I was nowhere near that psychically coordinated. *"They need to know what you've done, so they realize what you're capable of. Tomorrow and tomorrow night, we won't have time to tell them that you know what you're doing and to stay out of your way when this starts to go down."*

"You think I know what I'm doing?"

Rake paused mid-sentence to give me a wink. *"You're still alive, aren't you?"*

"Hope those won't be famous last words."

"I didn't say them out loud, so they don't count."

"Your lips to God's ears."

He told them about the time I'd attacked a grendel in Times Square, went verbally toe-to-toe with the most powerful vampire godfather on the East Coast, read an ancient dragon/Russian oligarch's mind to know how to save all the supernaturals in the tri-state area while struggling against a harpy to keep from being turned to stone by a gorgon, fought a buka (aka a goblin-world Sasquatch) to save Rake, and attacked Janus to save my partner and quite possibly the world (or at least its coastal regions) from being overrun with Fomorian sea monsters.

I chimed in about how Rake saved me from going to literal Hell by jumping in a draining pit of molten brimstone and climbing out of the pit with me on his back without either one of us bursting into flames, how he flew the battle dragon that carried us to the island when Janus was about to sacrifice my partner, and that he was the one who learned an ancient curse in an instant and used it to banish the Fomorian army back to where they'd been imprisoned for millennia. And then there was the time when he'd—

Grandma Fraser raised her hand. "Enough already. We get it. You're qualified for whatever this Janus has up his sleeve."

No one could pull the wool over my grandma's eyes.

This time, I winked at Rake.

Rake wasn't looking at me, and his eyes were glittering dangerously. "Janus's little traitor just made his move."

21

I hadn't seen anything, but Rake had a link to his personal items that was a pickpocket's worst nightmare. He didn't just do it for fun. Personal possessions, like my brush and Mom's sweater, could be used against him.

Rake reached around behind his chair to his coat. "He took one of my gloves. Vickie, is anyone heading for the kitchen? Waitstaff?"

To anyone watching, it looked as though Aunt Vickie merely glanced around the pub. "Male, five foot eleven, blue knit hat. His back's to me, can't see his face. Took a left at the kitchen into the Hall." Amazingly, she barely moved her lips while relaying all of this.

"Glove?" Mike asked.

Rake stood. "Janus can use it like Margaret's sweater and Makenna's brush."

Bingo.

"Or worse," I added, standing with him. "Like a voodoo doll."

Barry came around from behind the bar. He knew something was wrong.

"Blue knit cap?" Mike said, headed for the Hall. "You know him?"

"Minnie McVane's grandson, visiting from up north."

Grandma actually growled. "Little bastard betrayed his own grandmother."

"The Hall's getting full. Can you point him out in that crowd?" Mike asked Barry grimly.

"He the traitor Cyndi told me about?"

"We believe so."

Barry's eyes glittered as he tossed his bar towel over his shoulder. "Glad to help."

"One piece, Barry," Grandma said. "We need him in one piece. At first."

We followed our quarry into the Hall, and Barry pointed out Jason McVane, who had changed from a blue cap to a red one, thinking that was gonna fool anyone. Way to go, Jason.

That done, Barry posted himself at the door between the Cellar and the Hall, arms crossed over his massive chest, expression set on "Just try it."

Vickie caught Jimmy Kennedy's attention with a glance, and with another glance directed him to cover the second and only other way out of the Hall.

A werewolf officer and a part-troll barkeep acting as

bouncers. Though in Jason McVane's case, he wouldn't be thrown out, but back in.

I got the slightest whiff of ability from him, nothing big. "What's he capable of?" I asked Grandma.

She snorted. "Nearly nothing. And to hear Minnie talk, he's resented it his entire life."

Janus had offered him power over a town whose citizens had what he didn't.

"And he gave his own grandmother to Janus?" I could not get past that part.

"Minnie has money. Filthy little vermin always wanted it."

Rake heard what Grandma said, then grimly turned and spoke quickly to Vickie, Mike, and Mom. Aunt Vickie gave Rake the "be our guest" gesture, and Rake went to stand in the middle of the Hall.

Oh boy.

For the most part, folks had finished eating, but were still sitting at tables, chatting and socializing. The kids had gathered around the decorated tree that'd been set up in the Hall's far corner to wait for Santa. A few people noticed Vickie, Mike, and Jimmy, and two other officers who had just come in the door Jimmy was guarding. They knew something was up, but no one said or did anything, getting the sense that Vickie and Mike wanted it kept quiet.

Mom came up next to me. "Rake thinks Jason isn't acting alone. If they're in this room, Rake wants to see if he can make them run for it."

"Run? What is he going—"

"Jason McVane." Rake's voice boomed in the small cavern. "You've taken something of mine. I want it back."

The entire room went silent, even the kids.

Jason turned, saw Rake, and smirked. He'd probably already handed the glove off to his accomplice, and figured that if it wasn't found on him, Rake wouldn't do anything. Was he in for a shock.

Rake smiled, slow and confident. He was enjoying himself. "Janus didn't tell you about me, did he?"

Here we go.

"I don't know what or who you're talking about."

"Let me see if I can enlighten you."

Rake dropped the glamour on his power.

Those people in the room who were sensitives instantly recognized Rake as a mage of a level they had never seen before. Those who weren't sensitives saw a seriously pissed-off man who was more than capable of making Jason McVane exceedingly sorry.

Jason immediately started having second thoughts. "I had to take it."

"No, you didn't," Rake told him. "And you didn't have to betray your grandmother and those other four good people to Janus and his ghouls, but you did. Was it money, Jason? Or was it the power you have never had." Rake slowly stalked closer to where Jason was, townspeople parting like the Red Sea on either side of him. "Return my property and tell me where Janus is."

"I can't."

"You will."

Rake powered up, and the lights dimmed as he glowed red.

He wasn't bragging. It ain't bragging if you got it. It

was more like a friendly warning to Jason, and anyone else so inclined, to stop being stupid. If you thought about it like that, Rake flexing his magical muscles was more like a public service.

Jason spent the next two seconds comparing what Janus had threatened to do to him with what Rake was able—and all too willing—to deliver right now in a room full of witnesses.

He did not choose wisely.

Rake was a firm believer in the more public an object lesson, the less likely he would need to repeat it. Public object lessons spread even faster than the juiciest gossip.

Rake took one more step forward. "This grows tiresome."

I knew he wasn't going to get violent. Jason McVane was a small fish, tiny even. Small fish were easily frightened when confronted by a shark. Rake's magic marked him as not merely a shark, but a megalodon.

Rake raised his hand toward the ceiling—and Jason rose right along with it.

The hand gesture wasn't necessary, but Rake believed theatrics helped convert any witnesses who were also unbelievers. Word would spread, and any future inquiries would be met with swift cooperation.

Not everyone's eyes were on the dangling thief. My family and others, including Clarissa St. James, were watching Rake's audience for any sign that one or two people *really* wanted to be somewhere else.

Rake flipped Jason McVane upside down and objects started falling out of his pockets. Among them were jewelry and cash—but no glove.

"That's Miss Minnie's brooch!" someone shouted.

"And diamond bracelet!"

More cash began fluttering down. Ben Franklins. No one moved. The room went silent.

"Miss Minnie kept cash in her mattress." It was Simon Carlson, president of the local bank. "I told her it'd be safer in the bank."

Jason McVane might not agree, but he was safer being tacked to the ceiling. Rake wasn't violent, but the people of Weird Sisters were about to be.

There was a scuffle from the far corner, and Clarissa St. James's voice rang out. "Brad Hodges, stop!"

I'd never considered Santa Claus as the militant type, but dangerous times called for dangerous Santas.

Glendon Kerr was a Santa on a mission—bring happiness *and* protection to the children of Weird Sisters. Santa swung his sack of toys and slammed the escaping Brad Hodges into the nearest wall.

The children froze as they gazed up at him, eyes wide in wonder.

Glendon/Santa dropped the sack next to the Christmas tree. "Bradley has been a very naughty boy."

～ 22

The children had gathered around Rake, eyes wide and mouths agape. Two of the braver ones wanted Rake to toss them in the air, too.

Weird Sisters kids had a different idea of fun.

"What am I?" Glendon/Santa muttered. "Chopped liver?" He cleared his throat loudly. "Ho, ho, ho?"

Thus redirected, the kids clamored around Santa, all of them telling him at once they'd been extra good this year, not naughty at all.

Chatter around the room restarted. Rake was on the receiving end of more than a few nods and friendly smiles— and discreet admiring glances. I couldn't begrudge them that. My Rake was blistering hot. And if by chance anyone had been filming, all they would've gotten was a blur—of everyone and everything. When Rake's magic had dimmed the lights, most electronic or battery powered devices would have taken a momentary leave of their senses. I was relieved to see that everyone was still upright, meaning no one in the room had a pacemaker.

That Makenna Fraser had brought home a man who had that much power under the hood had to be some of the juiciest town gossip in years. When the dome was down and the Internet up, googling "Rake Danescu" would tell them even more. If only they knew about the goblin, colonial governor, and royal duke parts. That'd probably bump it up to the juiciest since the town's founding, closely rivaled by the news about my father.

Rake went to where Brad Hodges was starting to come around, searched him, and found his glove. Mike hauled the traitor and thief to his feet.

I knew Brad Hodges. Everyone in Weird Sisters knew him, and none of us liked what we knew.

Like Jason McVane, he was only marginally gifted in either magic or good judgment. Brad could sense power in others, and that, combined with a sense of entitlement, made him resentful of pretty much most of the town. He had a decent veil, and he could pick up obvious thoughts from others, which in Brad's case let him know who in town thought he was creepy, which was pretty much anyone who knew him. He had a small business as a hunting guide, but even that earned disdain from the locals. Hunting is considered a sport and a skill, but it's neither sporting nor skillful when your idea of hunting is veiling yourself to cover all five senses and walking right up to a deer to kill it.

Santa had swung that toy bag with purpose, not giving Brad a chance to veil. Although even if he had, I could see through veils, so that wouldn't have worked for him. My trigger finger had been itching for my paintball gun.

Grandma was smiling, and I saw the girl who had made plenty of trouble in her younger days. "I'll say this for your young man, he knows how to make an impression."

There were still a few people in the Cellar. Barry helpfully shooed them into the Hall so the pub could be used for interrogations. Vickie took Jason to a corner table. Mike took Brad to the kitchen. Their officers split the guard duties. Clarissa St. James went from Jason's questioning to Brad's. This was a situation custom-made for a human lie detector. After an initial questioning of both men, Rake left them to Vickie and Mike, and came over to where Mom and I stood near the pub's back entrance.

"He doesn't know anything," he told us. "When I asked him to tell me where Janus was, he said, 'I can't.' He really can't. Janus put a geas on him. Not that I believe Janus would trust anyone, let alone a human he considers a tool to be used and disposed of. The other one may know more, but I'm not counting on it. Janus didn't even want Tavis Haldane anywhere near his true lair. Janus considers himself a god. To him, humans aren't worthy of consideration, let alone trust."

"They're probably lucky they never made it out of here with your glove," I said. "Janus would've taken it and killed them."

"Ghouls don't work for free," Rake agreed.

I put a hand over my stomach. "Gee, thanks. I just wolfed back a steak sandwich."

Mom looked a little pale. "Janus would've given them to his ghouls as payment?"

Rake nodded once. "Tools to be used and disposed of. Or in this case, be useful one last time as food. Don't feel sorry for them. Jason wanted his grandmother's money, and Brad Hodges knew it. Brad also knew all the earth mages in town and was the one who actually dealt with Janus—and who directed the ghouls to their homes."

"Then ghoul chow would've been a fitting end," I said.

"Even Stephen can't help?"

We all recognized the voice as Grandma's, and she must have been standing on this side of the Hall door.

And asking about Stephen meant she had to be talking to Aunt Nora.

Oy.

Mom rolled her eyes. "Mother won't take no for an answer even from dead people."

"Who's Stephen?" Rake asked. "And who's she talking to?"

"Nora," Mom told him. "Stephen is Nora's…" She searched for the right word to describe Stephen. "Special spectral friend."

Rake raised his eyebrows. "Are you saying—"

"Also known as her ghost with the most," I chimed in with a smile.

"Makenna," Mom admonished.

I raised my hands. "Aunt Nora is a *very* happy woman. Just saying."

"That is…interesting," Rake managed.

"We may tease her," Mom told him, "but we think it's

wonderful. As Makenna said, he makes her happy; and after Nora passes, he'll be waiting for her."

"Mother, he's standing right here," we heard Nora say to Grandma. "Have some tact. He says that he can hear them, but they can't hear him. There's nothing he can do about that. They're alive and unharmed. Minnie told them about her grandson betraying her, so now they're also angry."

Silence from Grandma and Nora. And still more silence.

"Mother, are you okay?" Nora asked.

Silence.

Nora squeaked. "Oops, sorry. I'll leave you alone."

I had no earthly idea what was going on.

Nora came out into the pub, saw us, and scurried over.

Mom raised a brow. Nora gave a quick nod. Rake and I were utterly clueless.

So, we all stood there in awkward silence.

While we waited, I wondered if Stephen had skedaddled with Nora and was here with us. I also wondered if it was rude not to greet someone you couldn't see. The awkward just kept coming.

"Girls?" Grandma called.

"Yes, ma'am?" all three said—even the one in the middle of interrogating a suspect.

"It's time to see Edwina."

That announcement caused a flurry of activity.

The four Fraser women were now having a heated discussion in the middle of the pub. Mike and two of the officers had taken the suspects into custody—and over to the police station's small jail. Rake and I were back at our pub table, watching, and trying to make sense of things.

We weren't having much luck.

"She's an elderly lady who lives up the mountain from us," I was telling Rake. "Folks think of her as kind of an oracle. I've never actually met her."

Rake was incredulous. "And no one brought her into town?"

"I would have thought so, but judging from the back-and-forth over there in the huddle, I'm getting the sense that she's not here, and…no one seems to be concerned. At all. Which in itself is cause for concern."

"Curiouser and curiouser."

"You said it."

"Makenna," Grandma gestured for me to join them.

I did as told.

Rake was not summoned. He stayed put. A wise man, Rake.

"She wants to see you," Grandma told me.

"Miss Edwina?"

"Yes."

"Why?"

"Your father."

"What's Miss Edwina know about my father?"

"Apparently things we don't know but need to," Mom said.

"She's not in the Hall with everyone else?"

Grandma snorted. "Of course not. She's perfectly safe where she is and wouldn't have left her cave regardless."

I blinked. "Cave?"

Mom came to my rescue, bless her. "Mother, I think it's time Makenna was told about Edwina."

My mouth just fell open. "There's something *else* you haven't told me?"

"Edwina's location is need-to-know," Grandma told me. "She likes it that way, so that's the way it is."

"Who knows?"

The four Fraser women raised their hands, Nora sheepishly.

I knew about my dad and was about to learn about Edwina. I guess that made me the fifth Fraser woman. As little as I'd liked being excluded all this time, it was nice to finally be included in the club.

"Edwina has been here as long as the town has," Grandma said. "Each generation, one of us is chosen to be her channel to the town. Right now, that's me. She contacted me and said she needs to see the hunter's child. That would be you."

"She's an actual, honest-to-God oracle and you haven't asked her about all this?" I threw my arms wide in disbelief. "This is the biggest catastrophe to happen in the history of Weird Sisters, and a woman who's been here since the beginning has nothing to say about it?"

"She does now," my grandmother said matter-of-factly. "She knew last night when you and Rake were attacked. She contacted me and said it was Cernunnos. I got back home as fast as I could. I reached out to her late last night and again this morning. She was there, but she had nothing to say. Edwina talks when she is ready." Grandma paused. "She's ready."

"Fine. How do we get there?"

"We need to go home."

〜 23

Agnes Millicent Fraser, matriarch of both the Fraser family and the town of Weird Sisters, had decided what she was going to do, and no one with a lick of sense was about to try to change her mind.

Edwina would only see two of us—her channel and the hunter's child—and Grandma said she wasn't about to go to Edwina's cave leading a parade.

Needless to say, this caused a bit of a scene.

Rake put his foot down. I wasn't going anywhere without him. Especially not at night with the entire area crawling with ghouls. Janus was out there and who knew what else. Mom was incensed that she was being left out, even though we'd be coming back and telling her everything that was said. Like Rake, she was having a fit at the thought of us going alone.

And don't even get me started on Vickie and Mike. Nora, having determined that she didn't have a dog in this fight, was standing quietly off to the side—probably with Stephen—enjoying watching the family throw everything they had at Grandma Fraser without putting so much as a dint in her argument.

Grandma just stood there, letting everyone voice their objections, anger, frustration, and anything else they needed to vent. Then and only then did she speak.

"I may be old, but I'm not crazy. Do you think I'd risk my granddaughter by driving home through ghoul-invested woods without a proper escort? Makenna and I will be the only ones going into Edwina's cave. To get there and back in one piece, I'll be taking adequate precautions. Victoria, I want the Hummer. Jimmy can drive." When Mike drew breath to protest, Grandma snapped her index finger in the air. "I'll thank the lot of you to be quiet until I'm finished. I've known Jimmy since I was a little girl, and it's close enough to the full moon for him to turn if necessary. Rake, you're going—but only as far as the cave," she added when he started to smile. "Edwina doesn't like men in her home. That's all," she told us. "No arguments."

"But you—" Mom started.

"No arguments, Margaret." She turned to Rake. "I understand from Makenna that you can keep anyone from hearing, seeing, or even smelling the Hummer and anyone inside."

"Yes, ma'am."

"But that the fewer people you have to hide, the easier it is on you. Correct?"

"Yes, ma'am."

"Then a few is all we're taking. Me and Makenna to talk to Edwina. Jimmy to drive and turn if necessary, and Rake to cloak us and unleash magical hell if needed. The rest of you have a town to protect." She regarded each of us in turn, smiled, and clapped her hands together. "I think that covers everything. Don't just stand there. Let's move."

Rake was biting his bottom lip hard against a grin. *"I love that little woman."*

"If anyone could know what Janus wants with your father, it will be Edwina," Mom was telling me. "As well as what he intends to do with our earth mages, the power points, and ley lines tomorrow at midnight."

"Yes, Mom. I'll ask her everything, and I've got a great memory, so I'll remember everything."

Mom pressed her lips together, sniffed twice, nodded once, and hugged me. Hard.

Aww jeez, Mom.

It was a good thing she didn't live anywhere near New York. If she did, every time I went out on a mission, I'd be doing it with bruised ribs from her goodbye hugs.

Don't get me wrong. I loved her hugs, but I could do without the bruises. And the borderline waterworks. Okay, okay, from both of us.

Jimmy was the only one who hadn't been in the room when Grandma had volunteered him to join us on our little road trip. His fist pump after learning he'd be our driver and ghoul shredder pretty much said it all. I'd always wondered if the bat-out-of-hell driving style and penchant for turning monsters into hood ornaments was a Yasha thing or a werewolf thing. Looked like we were about to find out.

Grandma was now telling Mom that another reason she had to stay in town was in case Cernunnos brought her the gift of Janus's head sometime during the night. She said it'd be downright rude for her not to be here to accept it, and that she didn't raise no ill-mannered children.

Less than an hour later, Mike brought the Hummer around to the end of Main Street. The town council would deactivate the three ward stones at the end of the street just long enough for us to drive through.

Grandma had told everyone that we'd probably stay at home for the night and not to expect us back before morning.

Jimmy got into the driver's seat. Grandma was riding shotgun. Literally. Rake and I were in the back seat. Rake was weaving and speaking the spell into place that would keep anyone or anything from seeing, hearing, or smelling us. Though if Grandma opened fire, we would definitely be heard.

Me? My job was to point out any veiled ghouls or warded beasties that made the poor choice to try to keep us from getting home.

Janus needed to take Rake off the game board. His plan was in danger with Rake around. His solution? Get his human minions to steal something belonging to Rake. The glove wasn't the best option, but it certainly would've worked with a mage of Janus's power. Skin cells, sweat, perhaps a hair or two—Janus could've used any of it to diminish Rake's power, or disable it altogether. I batted my mind away from the ultimate use: kill Rake outright.

What did he have planned for Cernunnos? Janus wanted power. He wanted my father's help and possibly his power. Janus had asked nicely. Now he'd imprisoned all of us inside this dome. For what purpose? Janus would make his move tomorrow night, Christmas Eve. We needed to know his plan. Now. We hadn't been able to deduce much on our own. We needed help. Hopefully, Edwina would be the source of that much-needed enlightenment.

The town council opened the way out of town, and Jimmy drove through. I waved through the back window, but didn't look back. I'd prepared myself to go to work, and I couldn't allow emotion to get in the way. It was yet another valuable teaching from Ian. I had my game face on.

Time to go to work.

Dead ghouls were everywhere.

Though a more accurate description would be ghoul pieces and parts.

The road back home was dotted with the end results of skirmishes between the Wild Hunt and Janus's ghouls. Though I didn't think you could rightfully call it a skirmish when only one side ended up on the receiving end.

I'd seen what swords and axes could do in the hands of experts, and Dad and his boys certainly qualified. They were doing a fine job decreasing the ghoul minion population. Some of the pieces were still twitching, which meant the kills were relatively fresh.

"Ain't nothing getting up from that," Grandma said in admiration.

Just how many ghouls had Janus brought with him?

"He plans to gift them the entire town," Rake said in my mind.

I knew this, but wasn't about to say it out loud, or even allow the thought in my head for long. I imagine Grandma and Jimmy were perfectly aware of what Janus intended for the people of Weird Sisters, but Dad and his Hunt had seen to it that the dozens of ghouls they'd encountered tonight wouldn't be eating anyone ever again.

I smiled grimly as I gazed out the window at yet another scene of carnage. The night was still young, and my father was still hunting.

Jimmy was scowling at the sight. Grandma reached over and patted his arm. "I'm sure there'll be some ghouls left for you to play with."

Yasha and Jimmy were definitely werewolf brothers from another mother.

Our family home was lit and welcoming, inside and out.

"I use timers," Grandma said for Rake's benefit.

"There doesn't appear to be signs of forced entry," he noted.

"That's because there aren't any. No one's getting inside that house who doesn't belong."

"Ward stones around the house and property?"

Grandma beamed with pride. "Mostly a house that hates trespassers—with a vengeance."

Jimmy backed the Hummer into the space between the house and garage in front of the short, enclosed breezeway.

It was a perfect fit, with just enough room to open the doors and get out.

After Grandma slid down from the Hummer, she closed the door and patted it. "The house will protect it like it was its own." She went through the front door without hesitating, Jimmy at her heels. Rake and I hesitated. I knew I could cross, but Rake had been using his magic to hide us and the Hummer. I didn't know if the house would sense his dark magic and take offense.

Grandma was headed for the kitchen and didn't look back. "The house won't bite you, Rake. Get in here and quit dawdling."

We did as told.

The fireplace wasn't lit, but that was the only difference from when Rake and I had crossed the threshold last night. The same lights were on, and the same sense of peace and warmth welcomed us.

Grandma led us through the kitchen and down into the basement. We had barns and storage sheds for most of the things that filled most basements. Ours was lined with shelves filled with neatly labeled and meticulously organized preserves. That was another proclivity of folks in Weird Sisters. We made survivalists look like amateurs.

A low hum came from a freestanding walk-in refrigerator and freezer. Inside were meats and cheeses kept cool and dry. Grandma hadn't put away all this on her own. The locals had a network set up where one family would raise or grow one food animal or crop and share it with their neighbors. As a result, everyone had plenty of the basics without needing to rely on the outside world.

We were mountain people. We took care of our own.

Grandma went to what looked like just another shelf of preserves and pulled out a jar of apple butter from the far end.

The shelf smoothly slid to the left, revealing an iron door.

I'd never seen this before. Why? Yet another "Fraser woman" secret I hadn't been privy to growing up? I had a twinge of hurt feelings that I pushed aside.

Grandma was watching me and nodded in approval. "Well, you know now." She opened the door to a whole lot of pitch dark. "There is a reason our home was built here."

She reached inside to the other side of the wall and I heard the click of a switch.

Wow.

Below and beyond stretched a cavern that was lit by bulbs strung on wire and attached to whatever surface was available. Stalagmites and stalactites populated the space that extended into the darkness beyond.

"Wow." I said it out loud this time. "It's probably a good thing I didn't know about this. If I had, you'd never have gotten me out."

"Exactly," Grandma said. "Edwina doesn't like uninvited visitors. Rake, Jimmy, you can go with us a ways. I'll let you know when you need to stop."

Grandma could've told Rake and Jimmy to wait in the house and they'd never have known where the entrance was or that all of this was down here. She'd known Jimmy all her life, so I could see her letting him in on the family secret. But she'd only met Rake in person last night. Either she'd accepted Rake, or our situation was so far down the crapper that she'd discarded her usual borderline paranoia of outsiders.

Grandma started down the stairs into the cavern. "Let's go talk to an old friend and get some answers."

≈ 24

Everyone in Weird Sisters had grown up in and around area caves. Plenty of local businesses and careers had sprung up as a result. Some of our people went on to explore cave systems around the world. Some became cave rescue specialists and cave divers. The grownups knew we'd be going in regardless of whether we had permission or not, because they'd done the same thing when they were kids. People had learned soon after settling here that telling the kids they couldn't or shouldn't do something just made them want it all the more. As a result, every generation was taken into the cave system and taught to explore safely. Every citizen of Weird Sisters grew up taking numerous camping trips and expeditions. For many, having adults take you into the caves and teach you how not to be an idiot and get yourself killed sucked the fun right out of it. If it wasn't forbidden, they didn't want to do it. But where it really helped was with those kids who didn't really want to go in, but would have given in to peer pressure to keep from being called a scaredy-cat, chicken-shit, and all the other names some kids came up with to make themselves feel braver by verbally punching down on kids who had more sense than they did.

As a result of the unofficial cave education program, more kids born in Weird Sisters actually survived to adulthood.

But the caves we'd explored were nothing like this. If they had been, like I'd just told Grandma, the grownups would've never gotten us to leave.

I would've loved to have lived down here—as long as I could go up once a day and see the sky.

The temperature was perfect. There must have been a hot spring really close by. We passed below openings where snow was falling through. I had expected it to be depressing, and was all set to feel sorry for Edwina, but it was enchanting.

The wattage of the lights gradually decreased, and the temperature increased further, along with the humidity.

Just as I was about to ask, the reason showed itself.

Glow worms.

How they made the twinkling blue strands was gross, but the starry-night illusion it created was anything but.

It was absolutely magical.

"Jimmy, you and Rake need to wait here," Grandma said. "There's some flat rocks over there by the wall that Edwina uses for visitors. They're not in the drip zone so you won't be sitting in worm goo. Makenna and I will go ahead a ways while you boys sit here and enjoy the light show."

Rake was gazing around in wonder at the sparkling strands, his pupils wide to accommodate the near absence of light. Goblins were mainly nocturnal. Living among humans, Rake had had to adjust to daytime hours.

My sweetie was in his element.

And as a werewolf, Jimmy would be comfy here, too.

Grandma continued and I followed, but stopped when I saw the wall. Grandma just kept going.

I sucked in air to warn her—

"Makenna Anne, do you think I'd walk into a wall?"

The wall suddenly became an opening. I couldn't detect any veil, and I hadn't known it was there. No wonder Grandma had told us Edwina was perfectly safe down here.

Grandma stepped through. "Hurry up. We don't want to keep Edwina waiting."

I went in and the veil closed silently and completely behind us.

Vivienne Sagadraco was a dragon, and dragons loved their sparklies. My boss would've loved Edwina's subterranean home.

Edwina's cave, or at least the entry space, was a massive geode. A lit, and somehow smokeless, brazier stood in the middle of the room, its light flickering and reflecting in every crystal, setting the space ablaze with firelight.

It was dazzling—and more than a little dizzying.

I sensed Grandma patiently waiting on the far side. "Pretty, isn't it?"

My mouth was hanging open in amazement, so all I managed was an "uh-huh."

Grandma walked through what looked like yet another solid wall and into Edwina's main living space.

It was warm and earthy, and dare I say cozy.

There was a small hearth complete with a fire for cooking. It also seemed to be producing heat, but no smoke. I took a sniff. Nope, no smoke.

Plants and roots were hanging to dry, and here and there, natural indentions in the rock formed shelves that were filled with glass and earthenware jars. The chairs were made of intricately twisted branches and vines with patchwork or needlework cushions. A squat stalagmite with a flat top functioned as a table. A wide alcove with a low rock shelf formed the seat of a sofa, spread with a brightly colored quilt and more pillows.

For the first time since Rake and I had arrived, I relaxed. I was safe. I didn't blame Edwina one bit; I wouldn't have left this to come into town, either.

"Thank you for accepting my invitation."

I jumped and squeaked. The voice had come from behind me.

I slowly turned.

Edwina was sitting in one of the highbacked, twisted branch and vine chairs. I'd looked right at her and hadn't seen her. The browns of her smooth skin and eyes completely blended in with the warm wood; and her hair, with its dark brown mixed with gray, was the exact color of the bark. What I had thought was a quilt was her dress. If she had been standing, Edwina might have been five foot tall, but barely.

When she greeted me, then and only then did I feel the thrum of the ley lines running directly beneath us. She had even kept those hidden from us. We had to be at the exact center of the five points of the star. It felt like we were on a tiny island with huge waves crashing on it from all directions. In her chair, Edwina was sitting at the center of the ley lines, the apex of their power. Positioned as she was, she could probably feel the barest touch at the farthest strand.

Edwina was a force of nature personified.

She smiled at me. "Welcome, Daughter of the Hunter."

I instinctively bowed.

Growing up, I was taught not to judge by appearances. This became even more important when I went to work for SPI. Vivienne Sagadraco wasn't much taller than Edwina, but her true form was that of a three-story-tall, fire-breathing dragon. Edwina was a few inches shorter than Ms. Sagadraco, but she radiated even more power. Janus had lived thousands of years and had worn many faces and forms. I instinctively knew Edwina had always looked just as I was seeing her now. No deceptions, no disguises. As she was, she had always been. She was even older than Janus. Much, much older. Grandma said she'd come to Weird Sisters two hundred or so years ago. For Edwina, that had been very recently.

"I came because I was needed and would be needed," she said in response to my thoughts. "The world above is in chaos."

She could say that again.

"The one who brought the chaos, who you call Janus, has long been an adversary."

She gestured that Grandma and I sit in two of the other chairs.

"I have called you here not because of the being you know as Janus, but the other, even more ancient than he."

I was confused. "Cernunnos?"

"Not in his present incarnation, the man who is your father. I sense the first and most powerful Master of the Wild Hunt. An ancient hunter long dead, whose power continues on in the hunters who have come after him. The power your father possesses by wearing the mantle of the Master is great, but it pales in comparison to that of the First Master. It is this power that I sense. It should not be, yet it is."

Sounded like Rake and I weren't the only ones who'd been confused by what we thought was Janus's power.

"This First Master is here?" Grandma asked.

"That is what the great rivers tell me. Their strength extends far beneath these mountains and beyond and across this world. The knowledge they carry to me has never been false. I began to sense him one moon cycle ago. It grew stronger with each day. The First Master has not been of this world since the time when the great dragons ruled." Her eyes grew sad. "In his arrogance and lust for blood, the First Master brought most of them down and took their souls to increase his power."

That sounded entirely too familiar.

"With his death and the continued passing of his mantle to subsequent Masters, the Wild Hunt pursued mortal game, yet the Master retained the knowledge and understanding of the sky's greatest predators."

Those eyes turned to me. "You hear the thoughts of dragons."

She didn't ask it as a question, but clearly wanted a response.

My heart fluttered in my chest as I remembered reading

Vivienne Sagadraco's thoughts, and much less pleasantly, Viktor Kain's and Tiamat's. "Yes, ma'am."

"Like your father, and the Master before him, and all the ones before him."

I felt a little sick. "I'm going to be a Master of the Wild Hunt?"

"Nay, child, but you have inherited part of what he is and what he can do. You see veils and portals."

I swallowed. "Yes, ma'am. But not the veil that hid your home."

Edwina smiled. "That is not surprising. I use a magic long since gone from this world. Older than even the First Master."

Grandma spoke. "But this First Master, this ancient and dead First Master, is *here* inside Janus's dome with us?"

"He is, in some form, and he should not be. When he roamed the earth, the world was young then and still being formed, the sky was filled with fire, the land with wild waters, steam, and molten rock. The First Master reveled in the chaos. The chaos has come again, and if it is unleashed, this world will not survive."

25

How much trouble could one dead guy cause?

In a normal world? None.

But in a world where it was entirely possible that said ancient dead guy was in cahoots with a less ancient alive guy?

There would be no limit to the trouble they could cause.

Like Edwina said, chaos that the world would not survive.

Grandma asked my next question before I could. "Define dead."

"Death is not the end, but a transition to a new beginning."

Oh, that definitely wasn't good.

"Miss Edwina?" I asked.

"Yes?"

"How does one incarnation of Cernunnos choose his successor?"

"The Cernunnos of that time seeks out a worthy replacement. One who is willing and able to protect all nature. One who reveres all life, and respects its natural conclusion, death. When that man is found, he is marked as the chosen. The man must either ride with the Wild Hunt or become their prey. He is chosen, but he still has a choice."

"Ride or die isn't much of a choice."

"It is still a choice. However, some men volunteer, or even seek out Cernunnos."

"Why would they do that?"

Edwina shrugged. "To possess the power to protect their people, their loved ones. To carry the crown of Cernunnos is to carry the power of the earth, all of nature."

"A force of nature," Grandma murmured.

"Indeed."

"Being Cernunnos makes you immortal?" I asked.

"No being is truly immortal. Even myself—and Janus. He seeks to cheat death in all its forms. He makes a mockery of life and death. Such disdain and disrespect will not go unpunished." Her dark eyes sparkled. "Death is patient, but relentless."

Cernunnos was a god of death, and as we spoke, was doing his darnedest to collect Janus. But I'd seen Janus in action, and that was before he'd somehow become new and improved. I didn't like the thought of my dad, powerful though he was, being out there in the dark with him.

"Cernunnos and his Wild Hunt are cursed to endlessly ride and hunt," I said. "Why would Janus want that? My father said he can come and go as he pleases, but it is easier at certain times and places. Janus is a master of portals and he jumps through dimensions like that." I snapped my fingers. "Master of the Wild Hunt would be a demotion for him." I hesitated. "How does Cernunnos transfer his power to his successor?"

"The chosen, the student, must face the Master in single combat and kill him."

"And if the Master wins?"

"The search for a worthy replacement continues."

I felt sick. "So, to free himself from the curse, Cernunnos has to die?"

"You are concerned for your father."

"Very."

I felt a light, warm pressure around my shoulders like I'd just been given a hug.

Edwina was still in her chair.

"Worry not about your father. Not all incarnations of Cernunnos are the same. Your father is one of the cleverest there has ever been."

I managed a tight smile. My father might be a clever, all-powerful god of nature, but he was out there with Janus and this First Master.

"And I should remind you Cernunnos is also a god of death." Her brown eyes gleamed with humor.

"In other words," Grandma chimed in, "who better to cheat death than the god of death?"

Okay, that made me feel a little better.

This would normally be when the dots started to connect to form at least an outline of an SPI villain du jour's evil master plan. There were still way too many question marks and not nearly enough dots.

One thing I did know, without any doubt, was why Janus was doing whatever it was he was doing.

Power, with a big side order of revenge.

Janus had held a grudge against the bloodline of Lugh Lámhfhada for millennia. He'd hunted my partner Ian, the last of his family line, for years, then came entirely too close to sacrificing him on Bannerman Island in order to free his people, the Fomorians (aka sea monsters), from a millennia-long curse. If Janus held grudges for that long, there was room in his black heart for one or two more.

Power and revenge. The supervillain double-header.

Though something was missing. Janus had offered Cernunnos some kind of partnership. My father had refused. So, Janus used my hairbrush and Mom's sweater as bait to lure him here and trap us all. Then he'd kidnapped the town's five best earth mages. I knew from experience that Janus didn't kidnap people to let them live.

Cernunnos had mentioned feeling a strange compulsion, a pull from Janus that should not be possible. Had Janus used the First Master of the Wild Hunt's presence to compel my father to obey? Then what would he be able to do when the power of the ley lines was the strongest, and with the souls of the five earth mages as a power boost?

Become the reincarnation of the First Master? Bring the First Master back to life? Transfer the soul of the First Master into my father's body? The possibilities were endless and horrifying, and horrifyingly endless.

Cernunnos was the Master of the Wild Hunt, an ageless force of nature, wielder of the power of the earth itself.

I connected the dots and did not like what I saw. "You said that the First Master was the embodiment of chaos, correct?"

"That is true."

"Are you familiar with Tiamat, the Babylonian goddess of chaos?"

"I am. She is one of the few remaining great dragons."

"She and Viktor Kain, another great dragon, operate a cabal of what we call megamages. They're like regular mages, but with way more power than anyone who's not a Bond supervillain needs."

Edwina's brow furrowed in confusion. Must have been the Bond reference. I'd explain later when we had time.

"Janus has been known to work alongside this cabal when his goals intersect with theirs," I continued.

Grandma saw where I was going. "And now Janus is cozying up to this First Master, who just so happens to be the ultimate dragonslayer."

"Who's dead, whatever that means."

"That doesn't seem to bother Janus none."

"No, it doesn't, and that bothers *me*."

Ley lines surging tomorrow night, five kidnapped earth mages, an ancient supervillain, and the First Master of the Wild Hunt. My father, the current incarnation of Cernunnos, was out there somewhere with his Wild Hunt, slaughtering Janus's ghoul minions and presumably getting closer to the man himself.

Which might be precisely what Janus was counting on.

26

Edwina stood. "I am going with you."

Grandma choked on her own breath. "You're what? But… you don't leave your cave."

"You will have great need of me. Just because you have never seen me outside of this cave does not mean I have not left it. I do, and quite often. I travel this world, going where I am needed, then returning here." She gazed around her small sitting room, formed from nature and adapted for her comfort. "I am fond of all this. It suits me. This is the longest I have made my home in one place." She stood. "There are things I must attend to here, and then I will follow you."

"I'll leave the door in the basement unbarred."

Edwina smiled. "That will not be necessary. Until this situation is resolved, you must take every precaution. Now go. I will be with you soon."

Grandma and I passed through the geode and the veil and into the chamber where Rake and Jimmy waited.

We told them what Edwina had said and that she would be joining us up in the house soon. Jimmy's reaction to Edwina leaving her cave was much like Grandma's had been. Apparently having Janus and the First Master in the neighborhood caused all sorts of unheard-of things to happen.

The walk back up to the house felt a lot shorter, though that was probably due to scary scenarios of everything that could possibly go wrong in the next twenty-four hours running in high definition through my overactive imagination. I wasn't being pessimistic, just preparing myself for all possibilities as a good SPI agent should. It was just that given recent events, I didn't see things taking a turn for the better anytime soon.

The last time SPI had taken on Janus, we'd had two teams of SPI commandos, every battle-ready agent we could field, a squadron of battledragons from Rake's home world, werewolf allies, a team of vampire mercenaries, and a special guest appearance by a host of the Tuatha Dé Danann.

What did we have now? Me, Rake, five family members, a couple of police officers, and eighty-four, not-battle-ready citizens of Weird Sisters (fourteen of whom were kids). The special guest appearance would be my father, Cernunnos, and his twelve riders of the Wild Hunt.

And Edwina. I didn't know what she was capable of, but it had to be major-league power. She and Cernunnos might turn out to be our MVPs.

We came home to a house that was quiet and secure, and Rake proclaimed it to be ghoul-free before we all went inside. Just what anyone would want to hear when coming home after visiting a neighbor during the holidays.

Grandma gave a derisive snort at Rake's ghoul-free comment. "This house would never permit a ghoul inside." Then she stopped in her tracks, listening.

Seconds later, the set of heavy chimes hanging from the eaves of the front porch began to ring. The wind was picking up.

Then I remembered. A storm front was supposed to come through tonight from the southwest, probably bringing freezing rain, definitely sleet, and maybe some snow for the sprinkles on top. Typical North Carolina winter weather— plenty of ick and no fun.

I glanced over at the grandfather clock. It was nearly ten thirty. Only about an hour and a half and it would be Christmas Eve day. We were running out of time.

Grandma went to the front door, opened it without hesitation, and stepped out onto the front porch. We followed. She was staring up at the sky just visible through where the trees had been cleared for the house a little over two hundred years ago. Her eyes narrowed as she squinted up at the clouds racing overhead in the moonlight.

"Those look normal to you?" she asked me, knowing danged well they didn't.

I looked and I studied. "They're moving fast, south to north, but there's some swirl in there that's not normal."

"No, it's not," she said, never taking her eyes from the oddly roiling clouds. "And it ain't good."

Grandma could feel storms in a way few could. She didn't bother to chalk it up to arthritis or a bad leg, or even over-sensitive sinuses. She didn't need to see the sky or even be outside to know when bad weather was coming. When I was growing up, whenever Grandma told us to grab an umbrella, coat, or put the tire chains on the truck for tomorrow, we didn't question her. We just did it.

Grandma continued to stand silently for nearly a minute, her eyes going from the storm clouds to the forest gloom and back again.

There was a loud pop as if an entire box of fuses had blown at the same time. The floodlights went out, as did every light in the house.

"Something's coming," she said calmly. "Get in the house."

We did as told, and she locked and bolted the door after us. Rake and I posted ourselves to the side of one of the front windows and peered out.

A little over a minute later, there they were, complete with winter camo.

"Ghouls," I muttered. "Why does it have to be ghouls?"

It'd been four months, two weeks, and five days since I'd last seen a ghoul—and it hadn't been nearly long enough.

Ghouls looked more or less like humans, but the resemblance ended there. Their eyes were solid black, but would roll over white like a shark when they fed. Their jaws were longer and their mouths wider to make room for jagged teeth. Their skin was a pasty whitish gray. But a more applicable problem in our case: they were next to impossible to kill.

Ghouls ate human flesh, preferably while it was still alive; but in a pinch, corpses would do. And while they would eat alone, they preferred to dine with friends, and right now there were entirely too many friends out there. I wondered again how many ghouls Janus had recruited. We'd seen the pieces and parts of what had to be dozens of them courtesy of the Wild Hunt. Yet, there seemed to be just as many gathering around our house.

Sharp zaps and crackles came from the wraparound porch and behind the house as the ghouls threw themselves repeatedly at the wards. It'd always reminded me of a supernatural-strength bug zapper. Unfortunately, what was trying to get in wasn't mosquitos.

"The wards will hold," Grandma reassured us as she quickly unlocked her gun cabinet.

"They're impressive," Rake said. He'd dispensed with his human glamour. He could hold his glamour and fight at the same time, but it was easier if he didn't have to.

"Should be. We've got a big-ass crystal buried under the foundation."

"A ward crystal?"

Grandma snorted. "Not any of that New Age frou-frou crap. This one's got kick. It was a house-warming gift from Edwina to the Fraser who built this house."

The wards provided two additional benefits that helped those of us without goblin night vision. They glowed like supercharged floodlights, giving us at least a half-decent look at what all was outside. Rake had conjured a few light orbs and deployed them around the room. They were bright enough to help us not break our necks on a coffee table but dim enough to not be helpful to the ghouls outside.

I peered out the window again. The ghouls that'd gotten themselves fried were being replaced by fresh troops, though fresh wasn't the best word to describe a ghoul. These were staying outside the wards and were not happy at what had happened to their more eager buddies.

"This next batch isn't gonna be nearly as friendly," I noted.

"Neither am I." Grandma worked the pump on her favorite twelve-gauge, definitely-not-legal, sawed-off shotgun that she used for intruders and varmints. Ghouls qualified as both.

She threw open a window and let two of the closest ghouls have it with both barrels.

That was the second ward benefit. You could shoot out, but bullets or arrows or whatever shot from outside couldn't get in.

What was left of those ghouls did not get up. They were still twitching a little, but they were now what I'd heard one of SPI's commando team leaders refer to as "combat ineffective."

I knew what was in those shells. Iron shot through with silver. No need to waste pure silver against ghouls. A smidgen of silver in with the iron would do the trick, or in this case, do the ghoul. Grandma loaded her own shells, the casings color-coded for the contents: Iron/silver, just iron, just silver, rock salt, and rock salt with iron. A practical woman, my grandma. She never wasted ammo. Know your target and the most efficient way to kill it and load your firearm accordingly.

Jimmy had his own gun and was trying to raise one of the side windows. "This one's stuck, Miss Agnes."

"Break it. Glass is replaceable. We're not."

Jimmy broke it, opened fire, and decreased the ghoul population by a few more.

There was a clap of thunder and the entire house shook.

Somebody had just broken out the big guns, and it wasn't us.

It was magic, and it was strong.

"Good evening, Agent Fraser and Lord Danescu," boomed a deep and cultured voice that'd starred in many of my nightmares. "Is this any way to greet a visitor during the holidays?"

Janus.

27

It was Janus. At least it looked like Janus conferring with two ghouls in our front yard. He had his usual array of multiple faces, but something was off. Way off.

He felt even more ancient, if that was possible. But there was no sign of anything that looked like a First Master.

That didn't even take into account his new mode of transportation.

I loved horses. What he was sitting on was shaped like a horse, but the eyes were glowing red; and instead of hooves, I could swear this thing had claws. The two ghouls just behind him were mounted on the same demon horses; and judging from the red glowing eyes on the edges of the forest, there were more staying just out of the ward's light.

"What is wrong with this picture?" I whispered to Rake.

"Entirely too much."

"Is that Janus?"

"Yes…and no."

"Big help."

"You asked."

This odd Janus also didn't have any personal shields around himself.

"Is it me being exhausted or does he not have any shields?"

"You may be exhausted, but you are also correct. No shields."

Grandma peered out at Janus from her position by the window on the other side of the door. "Does he bleed?" she asked, keeping her voice down.

"I once sliced open his chest with a spearhead," I said. "His skin smoked, if that counts."

"It does." Grandma glanced at Rake. "You think we can start ourselves a bonfire?"

"I'd love nothing more, but—"

Janus's voice boomed through the walls. "Agent Fraser, if you will come out to me, I will allow everyone else in the house—including Lord Danescu—to live. If you refuse, I will be forced to do something unpleasant."

While Janus made his demands, Grandma coolly switched to gray-jacketed shells. Gray meant pure silver cooled in holy water. If that didn't punch a hole in Janus, it'd at least hurt like hell.

She paused and glanced at Rake.

He nodded.

In one smooth move my grandma pumped and fired both barrels out the open window. She hadn't taken time to aim.

She didn't need to. She was that good. When it came to her shotgun, the Force was strong with my grandma.

As soon as her finger had tightened on the trigger, my eyes had looked back at Janus. Her aim was dead on.

A nanosecond before impact, a light in the center of his chest pulsed green, and Grandma's shot came straight back at her.

I'd never reach her in time.

Rake dove across the space separating them, taking my grandmother to the floor, shielding her body with his just as the silver shot shattered the window, the panes, and obliterated the frame around it.

The ward should have stopped it.

It failed.

How?

Rake dragged her away from the window with my grandma hissing and spitting like an enraged bobcat. Her fury wasn't aimed at Rake, at least not yet, though he had an arm locked around her waist and wasn't about to let go. She wanted Janus. Badly. Janus had used magic and that magic had cheated her of a sure kill. In her mind, he should be ghoul chow.

Janus wasn't ghoul chow. He was pissed off.

Well, you play, you pay.

"Agent Fraser, I only need you marginally alive." He turned toward the forest. "Burn them out!"

"It's my fault," Grandma said. "I'm so—"

"Don't be sorry," I told her. "He was gonna do this anyway."

"At what cost?"

Rake got to his feet, bringing Grandma with him. "No cost to us. I need the three of you to go back to—"

My attention was drawn back out the window. "What are *those*?" I breathed.

The riders came out of the forest. They were ghouls, and they were ablaze—but not burning.

Rake came to the window and looked out. "Fire ghouls."

"*Fire* ghouls?"

"It's another kind of ghoul."

"There's more than one?"

"They're rare, and they don't work cheap. As I was saying, I need the three of you to go back to the caves."

"This house won't burn," Grandma told him.

"The house might not burn, but smoke kills before fire does. I can take out those fire ghouls, but I can only shield myself while I do it."

The first fireball was aimed at the hole where the window had been. The ward was back and deflected most of it; but wards, like shields, let air in, or in this case, smoke.

More fireballs were launched, slamming against the wards on the roof, sides, and back of the house. Smoke began filling the rooms.

The house that had been built and warded for the ages was now on fire.

"Caves!" Rake shouted over the fiery roar of one launch after another. "Go, now!"

Edwina swept past us all in a flurry of a patchwork cape and went directly to the front wall and did what I could only describe as a laying on of hands. She bowed her head and breathed in and out. I could swear I saw the walls flexing, as if the house was breathing with her, expelling the smoke and cooling the air. When the air was clear enough to breathe, and before anyone could stop her, Edwina stepped through the empty space where the window had been and out onto the front porch.

"These people and this town are under my protection." Edwina was tiny, but her voice was not. It rang with a volume and authority you questioned at your peril.

I risked a glance out the window and was stunned.

Janus was rattled. Edwina had said he had long been her adversary, and that adversary was afraid of her. In a blink the fear was gone, replaced with steely determination as the center of Janus's chest began to glow bright green. If it'd been blue, it would've looked like Iron Man's Arc Reactor. It wasn't that, but whatever it was, we knew it could ricochet bullets, and no doubt, much more.

Edwina saw it and her anger increased. "You have stolen a power that does not belong to you or to this age."

"It is mine now. It has accepted me, and even you cannot take it away."

The wind picked up and the clouds overhead swirled faster. The storm may have started naturally, but Janus was focusing its fury squarely on us. I could feel a charge building in the air as lightning began striking around the edge of the forest. The house had lightning rods along the roofline, but they could only take so much, and then the house would be toast and us along with it.

A bolt hit the roof with explosive force, knocking pictures from the walls and sending dishes in the kitchen cabinets crashing to the floor.

The next bolt flashed the night sky white.

It didn't strike the house.

It was caught before it could.

By Cernunnos. My father had arrived and his Wild Hunt along with him.

28

His arms were raised to the sky, calling the lightning down on himself. When it struck, he dropped his arms and spread his fingers, sending white-hot charges into the chests of every ghoul within his sight. My mind flashed to the final scene of *Raiders of the Lost Ark* when the lightning from inside the Ark took out all the Nazis.

It was painfully bright, and I had to cover my eyes. When I opened them again, there were puffs of smoke where the ghouls had been and a whole lot of stink, but no pieces or parts. They'd been vaporized.

That had to be one of the most badass acts of magic ever.

Janus and his surviving ghouls fled into the forest with Cernunnos and his Hunt on their heels, hounds baying in the excitement of the chase. There were a few more flashes of lightning, each fainter, the storm fading now that Janus was no longer here to feed it with his magic.

Edwina came in from the porch with not a single hair out of place.

Rake's eyes widened in what I could only call shock and awe, but he instantly recovered. Apparently, Janus wasn't the only one who recognized Edwina. He stepped forward, stopped at a respectful distance, knelt, and bowed deeply.

My honey had the best manners.

Edwina's tiny smile in response had "What a nice young man" written all over it.

Grandma stalked into her kitchen and let out an enraged scream when she got there. I could only imagine what it looked like. Then she closed the door behind her in complete silence, and soon we heard sweeping and scraping as she began cleaning up what Janus's lightning strikes had done.

Rake stared after her, unmoving. "That is one angry woman."

I stomped off toward the kitchen. "Only when she doesn't get to finish what she started. That runs in the family, too."

Grandma had gone into what most people would consider a typical kitchen. For Agnes Fraser, it doubled as her personal armory. It was a room full of knives and other cast-iron and stainless-steel implements. Rake respected her and her ability to inflict damage. Janus had come to her town and had declared war on her family.

I think what pissed Grandma off the most was she now knew she couldn't kill Janus on her own, and like most of the older mountain folk, she did not like things she couldn't do for herself. Folks around here took their feuding seriously. Whether he realized it or not, that was exactly what Janus had started. He'd come to her town, kidnapped her friends, shot at her using her own ammo, threatened her granddaughter, then tried to burn down her family home. In mountain-people parlance, Janus had just started the ultimate feud. Agnes Millicent Fraser, matriarch of our little clan, wanted to finish it and him more than anything.

Could she do anything about it now? No. All she could do was sweep up her broken dishes. She was overflowing with bottled-up rage with nowhere for it to go.

I totally understood.

I slowly opened the door and poked my head around the corner. Dang, it looked like a bomb had gone off in here. Dishes, cans, jars, glasses, pots and pans. If it'd been in a cabinet, most of it was now on the floor and much of it broken. "Is there anything I can do to help?"

Grandma looked around, realized the futility of using a broom instead of a bulldozer, and dropped into a kitchen chair. "Makenna, I'm too old for this shit."

I pulled up a chair, and after checking it for broken bits, plopped down beside her, and rested my head on her small shoulder. "You can't say that. I was gonna say that."

I felt her chuckle. "Then that makes me doubly too old for this shit."

"I don't think Janus would agree. If he hadn't had that flashy thingie, you'd have blown him away." I lifted my head and gave her a nudge with my shoulder. "Good job. I've only gotten a piece of him. It's satisfying and at the same time infuriating because we weren't able to finish the job. I do hate to tell you this, but us wanting to kill Janus puts us at the end of a very long line."

Her blue eyes glittered. "They're not here. We are."

"Actually, Rake's in line, too." I shrugged. "You're family, so I'd give you my place in line, but I can't speak for Rake."

"It does not matter who does it," Edwina said from the open door. "It simply needs to be done. Agnes, yet more needs to be done this night, and we must act quickly."

"I know your grandmother is tough," Rake was saying as we waited for her to "get a few things." "That's obvious to everyone. She's confident that she can not only take on but take out anyone she goes up against."

I nodded. "Terrier syndrome. I've got it myself."

"Yes, you do."

I paused and blew out a shaky breath. "Thank you for saving her. I couldn't have reached her in time."

"It was my fault. I should never have encouraged her to shoot. This is Janus. Him standing there with no shields should've been a red flag, not green."

"You understood how important it was that she be able to defend me and her own home."

Rake gave me a wistful smile. "My own grandmother was much the same. She passed years ago, but I wanted to give Agnes what I would've given her."

I stood on tiptoe and kissed him very gently. "Yet another reason why I love you." I paused. "Do you think Janus wanted me to come out for revenge for what I did on Bannerman Island, or as bait for my dad?"

"Yes."

"That's what I thought."

"I'm ready," Grandma announced from the great room.

Rake and I both sighed. We knew she wasn't just ready to go; she was ready, willing, and all too eager to take the fight to anything stupid enough to get in her way.

Jimmy stood in front of the wreckage staring in complete disbelief. "They killed the Hummer."

It'd been struck by lightning. A lot. What wasn't melted slag had been burned to a crisp.

"We asked too much of the house," Grandma said solemnly. "It could protect us and itself, or risk both to protect the Hummer, too. The house chose to sacrifice the Hummer for the greater good." She patted one of the house's massive logs. "We know you did all you could."

Jimmy had transferred his disbelief to Grandma. "Uh, Miss Agnes, making the house feel better about itself is all fine and good, but how are we gonna get where we need to go?"

I remembered something. Something wonderful. "Did Bobby Ray finish the work?"

Grandma's expression brightened. "Yes, he did. Why didn't I think of that? Will we all fit?"

I waved a negligent hand as I headed for the barn. "Oh, sure."

I was cautious opening the doors. Just because it looked like all the ghouls were gone didn't mean they were. Rake deemed the barn ghoul-free, so I swung open the doors and grinned at the shape under the tarp.

I pulled it off and beamed. "Get in, everybody. We're going huntin'."

I'd missed my Jeep Wrangler so much. Rake had arranged to have the one we'd used in Las Vegas sent back to New York, and I loved it, but it wasn't the same. This was *my* Jeep, bought with my own hard-earned money, and we'd been through a lot together. When I'd moved to New York, I'd had to leave the Jeep behind. Forget homesickness, I pined for my Jeep. Once I knew I'd be coming home for Christmas, I'd asked Mom to have local mechanic Bobby Ray Benton give her a tune-up, a new set of all-terrain tires, and a reinforced grill for Christmas. My girl was ready to rock the snow and any ghouls that got in our way. Yasha would have approved.

According to Cernunnos, Janus had flipped our rental Jeep. Vehicle death number one. Now he'd taken out the Hummer. Number two.

Janus better not even think about killing my Jeep.

I was driving and Rake was riding shotgun—though right now, he *was* the shotgun.

If we were attacked by any of Janus's henchghouls, Rake was eminently qualified to make them regret that decision. My job would be to keep the Jeep from going off the side of the mountain.

Fortunately, Grandma and Edwina were petite, so Jimmy fit between them. He didn't fit particularly well, but it worked.

Grandma had put her first-aid kit in the small cargo space in the back. It looked like what you'd find at an aid station on the front lines of a war. Until I'd left home, I thought everybody's grandmother put in stitches like others put on a Band-Aid.

The Jeep was carrying all she could, but it wasn't like we were going all that far.

We were going to the old Bishop place.

At night.

I didn't like it, but Rake and I agreed with Edwina.

She had recognized the thick, glowing medallion Janus was wearing as having come from the First Master. It had been a vessel of sorts for much of his power, which came from all the souls he had harvested during his time as the First Master of the Wild Hunt. The souls—literally eons' worth of them—were imprisoned inside. From the description Edwina had given us, the shape and size of it sounded like a petri dish. Rake and I now knew why we hadn't recognized Janus's magical signature. He had the medallion, but Edwina said she sensed the essence of the First Master himself, and that sense was coming from the Bishop place. For us to stand any chance of ending this, and to finish what Janus had started, there was only one course of action. Suicidal or not.

Go to that house and take or destroy what was there.

She said Janus and Cernunnos would keep each other occupied for the rest of the night. Now that he had used the First Master's medallion, Edwina could track where he was. Right now, Janus was miles away on the other side of the dome from us, and to take on the Wild Hunt, he'd need all the help he could get. We knew he wouldn't have left the Bishop place unguarded, but we had to do what we had to do.

Rake was hiding the Jeep and us from sight, sound, and smell. If any ghouls on guard duty at the Bishop place thought something was there, Rake's spell would make them think the Jeep was a really big bear. Ghouls were adventuresome diners, but they preferred humans, and had a healthy respect for all large-clawed predators like lions, tigers, and bears. Big cats didn't live around here, but big bears did. Any ghouls would either ignore us or give us a wide berth.

I wasn't getting the sense that we were driving into a trap, but I knew we weren't taking an evening drive through the woods.

We were less than a mile from our destination when Jimmy took a couple of big whiffs from the backseat.

"I smell ghouls," he said. We had the windows partially open so the werewolf officer could put his preternatural sense of smell to good use. "They're not here now, but their stench has some serious hang time."

I'd always thought the forests around Weird Sisters looked like they could be in a fairy tale. The trees were old growth, their canopies arching far overhead, shutting out most of the light and sound. During the summer when the trees had a full canopy of leaves, if a plane flew overhead, you'd be hard-pressed to hear it. What sound the trees didn't block out, the moss-covered forest floor muffled. Tonight, the snow did that job.

I'd always loved it, just not now.

What was the saying about outer space? That no one can hear you scream?

Normally, there were sounds coming from the forest itself, even on a winter night. The silence was unnatural. Either the animals had fled, or they were remaining motionless as they would in the presence of a predator.

That predator sure as heck wasn't me, because I was feeling the same threat, my primitive survival instincts telling me to run or hide and hope I wasn't found.

I brought the Jeep to a stop as soon as I spotted it, or at least the block of blackness down in the hollow.

The Bishop place.

We all sat in silence while Rake did a scan of the house and grounds that wouldn't set off any wards Janus had installed.

"No guards, no wards," Rake said, his voice a bare whisper. "It's wide open. It's like he wants us to see what's in there."

This wasn't just a red flag. It was a siren with flashing red lights.

We didn't trust it, not one bit, but we had no choice but to go in.

29

Hadley Bishop had been an acquitted murderer and rumored evil sorcerer. The evil part was known fact, the sorcerer part rumored. Thanks to a slick lawyer, Bishop had been acquitted of his brother's killing. He'd come here, built a house here, and had died here, struck by the lightning that'd gone through the roof, through the house, and down into the basement, where it was highly suspected but never proven that Bishop had been conjuring that which should be left unconjured.

It was a beautiful house, but it looked totally out of place in a mountain hollow.

Second Empire. The architecture style most often associated with haunted houses.

The house an ancient sorcerer had now illegally appropriated as his hideout, probably surrounded by ghoul guards.

The house we had to go into.

Thankfully we weren't going in the front door.

This haunted house had a basement entrance—because of course it did.

According to Glendon Kerr, it was also the safest way to get into the house. The wood floors upstairs were less than trustworthy, and the less weight on them, the better. Besides, the basement was the closest to the ley lines and was the likeliest place to find what Janus had brought with him on holiday.

We got out of the Jeep. Rake adjusted the shield so it would keep our getaway Jeep safe and sound. I wished I had the same confidence about us. Yes, Rake would continue to shield us, but we were about to walk into a haunted house to find this primeval "essence" Edwina had sensed, whatever that turned out to be. I so wanted to be sitting in front of a warm fireplace in a house that hadn't nearly been burned to the ground by fire ghouls, drinking Grandma's spiced cider and eating her iced gingerbread cookies.

We were all armed to the teeth for our excursion.

Jimmy was sniffing this way and that, working his werewolf nose for all it was worth. I trusted a werewolf's sense of smell to detect unfriendlies nearly as much as Rake's scans.

"Definitely no ghouls," Jimmy announced. "They were here, but not now."

"I want to go in first," Rake said. "If you stay right here, the shield will continue to conceal you."

"I will go with you," Edwina told him.

Grandma adjusted her shotgun's sling over her shoulder. "We will *all* go with you."

Rake had expected this, but it didn't mean he liked it. He didn't. "If it's a trap, I can get out faster than any of you—except possibly for Jimmy, if he were turned."

Silence met his logic.

"It is important that the hunter's daughter see what is inside," Edwina said. "The blood of Cernunnos flows through her veins. He is here because of Janus. We must know his intentions, and I believe Makenna will know what those intentions are. Listen to your blood," she told me. "It always speaks the truth."

Rake held out his hand to me. "I'm not letting go of you."

I put my hand in his and gave it a squeeze. "That's good because I'm not gonna let you let go of me."

"Jimmy, how fast can you change?" Rake asked.

"If I don't care about ripping my clothes to shreds, about twenty seconds."

Impressive. That was Yasha's speed.

"Forget the clothes," Grandma said. "It's not like the whole town hasn't seen you naked before."

Rake tightened his grip on my hand. "Let's go."

Rake and Jimmy had natural night vision. Edwina lived in a cave. Grandma and I followed in Rake and Jimmy's footsteps. Grandma and I stumbled a time or two, so those shields more than earned their keep.

The closer we got to the house, the more I felt the ley line convergence that ran beneath it.

"Rake, this feels like North Brother Island." I didn't say it out loud because I didn't want to make any noise, and I didn't

want anyone else to know the reality of just how deep the black-magic mess waiting for us in that house could be. Rake knew exactly what I meant.

The Dragon Eggs.

The Dragon Eggs were cursed diamonds stolen to "cure" supernaturals or humans infected by supernaturals, bringing them back to their human state. This included reversing vampirism, gorgonism, and those bitten by werewolves. It would also negate glamours used to make supernaturals such as elves, goblins, trolls, ogres, dryads, etc., look like humans, instantly outing them to their human neighbors. The curing part sounded like a good thing, except when you realized that vampires and werewolves would instantly return to mortal humans, but keep all of the years, decades, or centuries that their mortal bodies would have aged—turning them instantly into extreme old age, bones, or dust.

If the Dragon Eggs had been activated that night over the convergence of ley lines, the force of that magical blast, for want of a better word, would've extended to every supernatural in the tri-state area.

Janus had been at the Metropolitan Museum gala the night that the diamonds had been stolen. He'd wanted those diamonds, but a gorgon had beaten him to it.

In short, a convergence of ley lines plus the activation of an object of power on top of them equaled very bad things.

"Any idea what's in the house?" Rake asked.

"You'll know as soon as I do."

We were cautious as we made our way around to the back of the house. To be anything else would be crazy. No, not crazy, suicidal. I had no idea what was inside that house, but it was beginning to give me a serious come-hither. I had finely honed survival instincts, but those seemed to have been deactivated.

Against every sane thought, I wanted to go inside.

The ley lines throbbed like a heartbeat, a warm, comforting heartbeat, welcoming me home, to where I belonged, had always belonged. I didn't just want to get closer, I *had* to.

Rake squeezed my hand.

He knew what was happening. With our psychic connection, he felt what I did, especially when it was strong.

"I'll never let you go."

Rake determined that there were no traps of any kind. This did not fill me with the warm and fuzzies. I would almost rather we'd been met with a gauntlet of traps we'd need to disable. I kind of felt like Indiana Jones just before the giant boulder made its appearance.

A flight of stone stairs against the house's foundation led down to a basement-level door. It was unlocked. Rake determined nothing was waiting to ambush us on the other side. He went first, one hand glowing red with defensive magic, the other with a firm grip on me.

There was light in the basement. Janus wanted us to get a good look at his latest project.

He'd been a busy psycho. There was a pit in the middle of the earthen floor. The light was coming from inside the pit. Glendon Kerr definitely didn't have a photo of this in his sales listing.

Jimmy stopped and sniffed. "Our five people aren't here. Only one person is here, and it's dead. It's been long dead... except it's not."

Edwina slowly went to the edge of the pit and looked down. Her head remained bowed.

Morbid curiosity and something else much stronger, beckoned me forward. Rake slid his arm tight around my waist and went with me to the edge of the pit.

Janus had a history of tomb robbing.

It wasn't the first time Janus had stolen remains. Regardless of what he'd been originally, Janus was really a ghoul at heart. If he even had one.

It was a man—or at least it had been.

His armor, which resembled dragon scales, was dull, his cloak hung in rags, but my eyes kept going back to his face. The skin was leathery and taut over the skull, but I could tell that he'd been very handsome, beautiful even. He had been the very first Master of the Wild Hunt in the time when the earth was young.

I glanced at Edwina. Her cheeks were wet with tears.

"The First Master?" I quietly asked.

She didn't take her eyes from the corpse. "Yes."

My grandmother came up next to her. "You knew him?"

Edwina swallowed. "He was my son. He wanted too much power. Regardless of how much he had, it was never enough. The power took him, changed him, and then it killed him." Her jaw clenched in anger. "Janus brought him here. I did not know his body had survived."

Words could not describe the obscenity of what Janus had done.

"Why hasn't he crumbled into dust?" I whispered.

"Latent power," Edwina replied.

His body hovered about fifteen feet below the pit's edge,

encased in what looked like clear crystal. The crystal was lit from within—

No, the body itself was faintly glowing, in time with the thrum of the ley lines running below. It was horrifying and mesmerizing at the same time.

Living beings inhaled air. The First Master inhaled power and was still inhaling it. He was suspended over one of the five points of power and was absorbing energy from it, like charging a battery.

"What will happen when he's...charged?"

"Other than a monstrous obscenity, I know not. Janus does."

A hole had been drilled into the crystal. The piece had been removed, then replaced.

As one, Rake and I leaned forward and looked more closely at the First Master's—Edwina's son's—armor. There was something missing. It'd been taken from the center of his chestplate. Circular. A little larger than my palm. We'd seen it a couple of hours ago in the center of Janus's chest.

There was power centered there—or it had been. The vessel for eons of harvested souls.

"Yes," Edwina replied inside my head.

I was glad she could hear my thoughts. I wouldn't need to tell her with words how I was feeling now. Tears welled up in my own eyes and I hugged her. She was a grieving mother who should never have to see this, to be put through—

I wiped my eyes with the back of my hand. "You were right," I told her. "We have work to do this night. Janus must pay for this. Rake, I need you to let me go."

"No."

"We need to know how strong the pull is, what happens when I give in to it. It will be stronger for my dad. We can't help him"—I looked down at Edwina's son—"or him, if we don't know how it will affect Cernunnos."

"I'll be right here," Rake promised.

I looked in his eyes. "I'm counting on it."

Rake released me and took a step back, tamping down his own magic so all I felt was that which emanated from the ancestor of my father's power.

Your power.

I froze. Those two words had not come from me. Or Rake, or Edwina.

The light from his crystal cocoon blinded me to all that was not the First Master. I realized that's what it was. A chrysalis, protecting what was inside until it could grow into what it would become.

Then it would emerge.

I am the First. You are the Last. A vessel waiting to be filled. I can return through you.

Then he showed me the power that could soon be mine.

Images flashed before my dazed eyes. The world was blood-red and filled with prey, both winged and ground-bound. They were mine for the taking. Their terror filled my senses, their blood was mine to shed. All would fall before me. The world was mine to take. This world, not then, but now.

I teetered on the edge of the pit, drunk with the promise of power. Tomorrow—no, tonight, it was after midnight now—it could all be mine.

To have, to hold, to wield.

To reign.

I stumbled back and Rake caught me, his magic surrounding me, severing the spell the First Master was weaving. Yes, weaving like a spider trapping its prey before it fed.

I took breath after shuddering breath, trying to push the narcotic fog of the First Master's thoughts out of my head.

Rake held me close. "Makenna?"

I nodded, swallowing on a dry mouth. I turned my head toward Edwina, a wave of nausea accompanying the movement. "I see what you mean by your son being a power junkie. He still is. He wants to come back, but he needs a body. Apparently, mine will do, but my dad's would be best. I thought Janus wanted me for bait. Not bait. A backup body if he can't get Cernunnos. Your son's power will possess my father, pushing all that is him aside, taking over. He wants to work with Janus. Or so he says. He needs a body, one that can contain all the power he had before and then some. Though if the First Master comes back, Janus had better watch *his* back." I didn't dare risk a glance back into the pit. "Your son has no intention of sharing power with anyone."

Then I remembered. The last words Janus had spoken before he'd opened that portal and escaped Bannerman Island and the curse of the Tuatha Dé Danann.

"Those greater than I await their chance," Janus had said. *"They have begun to awaken. They will find you. I will be there to guide them, and this time, you will not escape."*

I told everyone what he'd said.

"Janus is playing with fire," Rake said. "He's been planning this for a long time. This is his contingency plan if Bannerman Island failed."

"What worries me is the plural," I said. "Janus said 'they,' not 'he.' More than one is awakening."

"Let's deal with one catastrophe at a time. We'll worry about the rest later."

Edwina's face had been devoid of expression while we'd spoken. "Janus and the Fomorians were exiled from this world. On this Bannerman Island, he failed to break the curse. I believe he wants to use my son's strength to anchor himself here. The curse of the Tuatha Dé Danann would be no match for my son's full power. The medallion has given Janus but a small taste of it. He needs more, all of it. If he awakens my son…" Her eyes were dry as she looked down into the pit at what had been her child. "My son. Loosed on the world again. That will not happen. He cannot happen."

"What do we do to stop him?" Grandma asked.

"I could destroy him now," Edwina said. "But my working would destroy all who are trapped inside this dome, this prison of Janus's making."

"That would be bad," Jimmy murmured.

"So, we go after Janus," I said. "Find him, exterminate him. Once he's dead, the dome will fall. Problem solved." I glanced at the light coming from the pit. It was stronger now. "Maybe."

30

Janus wanted to bring back the First Master and break the curse of the Tuatha Dé Danann, but he needed Cernunnos's body as a vessel for that power. We couldn't let any of that happen.

We had to get back to town. Now.

Mom could call Cernunnos back to town with his Wild Hunt. They'd be safer there while we figured out a way to bring down the dome. They probably had a few ideas of their own. The more the merrier.

Our luck ran out half a mile from the Bishop place.

Rake had been shielding us and the Jeep from sight, sound, and smell. It was working great—until it wasn't.

I saw two ghouls rise up on either side of the road, snap assault rifles to their shoulders and with gleefully vindictive smiles, open fire.

It always annoyed me to hear anyone over the age of ten whine about something being unfair. That's a word kids use when they don't get to stay up late or have to eat their broccoli before they can have dessert.

I didn't say it out loud, because I was too busy surviving, but that Janus's ghouls were about to mow us down in a hail of ridiculously high-powered bullets?

It was unfair.

My three predecessors in New York had been killed by the cabal, which had made it look like accidents. I'd been walking around with a bullseye on my back, and head, and chest since the day I'd started at SPI. There'd been multiple attempts to turn me into vulture chow—or in my case, baby demon chow. All efforts had failed.

Now I was about to be blown away by the hunter's version of a machine gun.

It just wasn't fair.

That didn't mean I was just gonna sit here and let us get filled with holes like empty beer cans on the back of an old washing machine.

I ducked and more or less kept driving, taking occasional peeks over the dash, as other ghouls in snowmobiles and ATVs joined in the chase.

My Jeep was a soft top, which some called a rag top.

That had never been more accurate than it was less than a minute later. The top had been reduced to rags. If the fireball from a fire ghoul hadn't torched it and nearly us, Rake would have had to have ripped it off himself. Once again, Edwina kept us from going up in flames.

Rake's shields were no longer fooling the ghouls, but his battle magic was getting the job done.

Rake was standing up in the back, facing our ghoul pursuers, his feet braced under the back seat, one hand on the rollbar, the other glowing like a blood-red sun. I hadn't turned to look. I'd witnessed Rake unleashing magical whoop-ass enough to recognize the angry red glow in my rearview mirror.

Jimmy had switched with Rake and he was now in the front passenger seat. He'd been in the army and had more experience shooting out of a moving vehicle. Grandma acknowledged his superior skill and did her part by keeping his guns loaded.

Entirely too soon, Jimmy clicked on an empty chamber. No more ammo.

"Well, shit."

Jimmy spoke for all of us.

At least the road ahead was clear.

And then it wasn't.

Normally when something appeared in the middle of the road, you slammed on the brakes. It was a ghoul, so I downshifted for more power and accelerated. The ghoul made a solid thump as it slammed into the Jeep's new and improved grill and went under her new tires.

If Rake had been human, me punching the gas would've turned him into a hood ornament at best, another speed bump for the Jeep at worst.

Then came a sharp curve. I turned into it.

It did not go well.

Crap.

But Rake wasn't human, so he stayed right where he'd been before my sudden maneuver turned the Jeep from a four-wheeled vehicle into a Tilt-A-Whirl fair ride. I'd hated those things as a kid and having my Jeep acting like one did nothing to change my opinion. Not to mention, it was embarrassing for me as a Jeep owner. I was shaming my people.

My hands had a death grip on the steering wheel as I turned into the direction of the spin, sending up a rooster tail of powdery snow. My girl did good, taking that curve like a champion slalom skier.

Rake leaned with the skid. His back was to me, but I sensed his flash of fangs. "You *are* good!"

I grinned. "I try." I also tried not to breathe as I geared down to get out of the snowbank and gently nudged the gas, getting out of the drift and back up to speed. I still had the shakes, but I was keeping them under control. For now. Near-death experiences of the messy kind did that to me. Just because we hadn't been run off the road by ghouls and gone over the side of the mountain or been filled with bullets, didn't mean my imagination wasn't going to pick up where our most recent brush with death had left off. I was sure I'd have a front-row seat to what could have happened the next time my head hit the pillow. Thankfully, it was looking like that wasn't going to be anytime soon.

Edwina broke her silence. "Makenna, there's a turn-off ahead. Pull in and stop."

I shot a horrified look at her in the rearview mirror. "Stop?"

"Stop. Trust me."

"I do, but—"

"You do or you do not."

I pulled in.

"Turn off the engine."

I hesitated, but I did it.

Edwina began to sing softly. A song without words, or at

least words that I could understand. Words weaving a spell of quiet, of forests dark and deep, of us belonging to nature, being at one with it, part of it.

A two-ghoul snowmobile drove past, then another. The drivers kept their eyes ahead, but the ghouls armed with assault rifles in the second seats scanned the road on either side. They looked right at us.

And didn't see us.

Edwina's song continued uninterrupted.

I sensed the animals coming out of hiding, an owl launching itself to glide silently overhead. Snow began softly falling. It was so beautiful, so peaceful.

Edwina had only begun.

In the road we'd turned off of, an exact duplicate of not only my Jeep, but each one of us appeared and solidified from swirling snow. Then a second exact replica appeared. And a third and fourth.

With an impish grin, Edwina waved her hands with a delicate flourish, and two of the Jeeps continued in the direction we'd been going, following the ghouls. Then one of them split off and took Lead Mine Road. The other two Jeeps went back the way we'd come, with one turning off onto Troll Den Ridge Road.

Going north, south, east, and west.

All four Jeeps made plenty of noise. The four Jimmys in the replicas had more ammo than he knew what to do with. The Jeeps may have been illusions, but somehow the ammo wasn't.

The ghouls in their snowmobiles and ATVs split up and took off in pursuit, each convinced they were chasing the real us.

"I am finished," Edwina announced. "Makenna, take us to town."

A few ghouls weren't fooled by the faux Jeeps and found us again. Either that, or they got lucky. We picked up a tail, four of them. The road had straightened out and they were gaining on us.

I nudged the gas. "Grandma, call Mom and have them get that ward down. We're coming in."

Grandma made the call, having to shout over the engine and wind. "Get the ward open on the south side of town… *South side.* We just passed the gas station and Makenna's bringing us in at full speed. Close it quick after us. We got pissed-off ghouls on our tail and we're out of ammo."

I hoped Mom moved fast because I wasn't stopping, and running into that ward would be a messy end to our escape.

I could see the south side ward ahead. It was still up.

"Mom," I said through gritted teeth. "Hurry, Mom."

The ward lattice vanished just as my grill got there. I drove through, hit a patch of ice, and slid sideways to a stop in the diner parking lot.

The sounds of my panting filled my ears. Then I grinned like a maniac. "Who's up for pancakes?"

Uncle Mike was standing in the parking lot, fists on hips, his hard eyes on Jimmy and what he was not driving.

"Where's the Hummer?"

Jimmy jumped out of the Jeep, slipped on the ice, but recovered nicely. "Sir, that's quite the story."

Mike's arms were now crossed over his chest. "I got nothing going on right now, why don't you tell me?"

We all headed inside. I gave my Jeep two pats on the flank. "You're such a good girl. Best Jeep ever."

The Hummer was a smoking ruin in our front yard, but my Jeep had survived. I'd even briefly turned a ghoul trying to kill us into a hood ornament. Yasha would be so proud. I'd have to tell him all about it. I didn't know how, but we *would* get out of here.

～

Unlike most small towns, Weird Sisters didn't roll up the sidewalks when the sun went down. The towns that did were populated by humans.

Those with kids were probably bedded down in the Great Hall. The Cellar and the Cauldron catered to the alcohol-lovers, and Delia's Diner offered the comfort of hot coffee, sweet iced tea, and Southern home cooking 24/7—for everyone. Humans got one menu. Delia kept a special menu under the counter for the local supernaturals. Home-cooked goodness for all.

She served breakfast day and night. It was well after midnight, which made it morning—Christmas Eve morning, to be exact—and morning at Delia's meant pancakes. I preferred mine loaded with blueberries with a huge glass of milk. I suggested to my chocoholic boyfriend that he try the chocolate chip pancakes.

Just as the kitchen was the heart of a house, Delia's was the heart of Weird Sisters. If it happened in town, Delia knew about it. She served some of the best food I'd ever had—with a side of local gossip.

Rake had just been soundly replaced as the town's latest hot gossip by the woman seated next to me.

Edwina.

When she'd walked in with us, you could've heard a toothpick drop. Our townies sensed who she was even if they'd never seen her. There were plenty of whispers while Edwina enjoyed a bowl of fresh fruit in amused silence.

If the people of Weird Sisters didn't know we were experiencing a capital "E" Event before, they did now.

Delia had set us up with the big corner booth, where we told Mom, Vickie, and Mike everything. We started when we'd left town, and when we reached what had happened at home, Rake regaled everyone with how Grandma was the only one of us to get a shot off on Janus.

"It didn't bring him down, so it doesn't count," she said, but she smiled ever so slightly when Rake saluted her with his coffee cup.

Mom paled when we got to the part about the Bishop place, finding the First Master, my link with him, and Janus's evil master plan, but kept her thoughts to herself.

"Your father needs to know," she said when we'd finished. "I'll go back to the edge of the ward at the park and wait."

I blinked. "Go *back*? You've been there all night?"

"He promised to be back just before dawn. You were due back after daybreak." She shrugged. "So, I waited. We saw the lightning strikes and fire, so we thought the gunfire coming into town from the other side was Cernunnos being shot at since y'all were supposed to spend the night at the house."

I gave her a little smile. "Sorry to disappoint you."

She reached across the table for my hand. "No, don't ever say that." She managed a smile, squeezed my hand, and sat back. "You're here and safe. Now I only have your father to worry about."

As Rake continued with his assessment of the Bishop place and the newly exposed ley lines, Mom gazed down into her coffee, and I could almost see the wheels turning. "The dome is powered by ley lines at normal strength," she began slowly. "At midnight tonight, there'll be a surge. Janus has dug a pit above where the lines cross at the Bishop house. The

First Master…" She paused, glancing at Edwina, her eyes sad, one mother to another. "Janus is using the power to reanimate him. I'm so sorry, Edwina."

Edwina inclined her head in acknowledgment of her sympathy and gestured that Mom continue working out her thoughts.

Mom reached for her napkin. "Does anyone have a pen?"

Delia was passing and pulled a pen out of her apron pocket. "Right here, Mayor. You got an idea?"

The edge of a smile appeared. "I just might."

"Then let me freshen up that coffee." She leaned over and topped it off. "And I'll brew a fresh pot for the table."

"Thank you, Delia." Mom clicked the pen and started to draw. "This may be crazy, but—"

"Those are the best ideas," Grandma told her.

"The surge takes the route of a five-point star. It comes up under the Bishop house and goes up to the north point, then down to the southeast, back up and across to the northwest, straight across to the northeast, then back across and down to its starting point."

Mom had drawn a five-pointed star, just like everyone had drawn as kids. It formed a star, but the center of the star made a pentagon.

"The surge passes twice through the town square here." She drew a small "x" at the bottom of the pentagon. "From here the surge returns to the Bishop house, completing the circuit. Our town square is another point where the ley lines have eroded the ground between them and the surface, such that we had to take down the gazebo and fence off the area to keep people away from it."

She turned to Edwina, whose lips were creased with a tiny smile as Mom worked out her theory.

"Is there a way to redirect the flow, to keep it from making that last run to the Bishop house? If the dome is powered by ley lines at normal strength, could the surge be redirected straight up to shatter it? Like I said, this is crazy talk, but—"

Rake was with her. "The surge gathers speed and strength as it makes the circuit. The concentrated power of the surge meets the weaker dome. It'd be like a hammer coming up to shatter glass. I like it."

"Is that even possible?" Mom asked Edwina. "And would it work?"

Grandma leaned forward. "If we opened the ground over the ley line like what Janus did at the Bishop place, could you redirect the surge to destroy the dome?"

"Or would it kill all of us?" Jimmy asked.

"No, it won't." Edwina's tiny smile grew. "Yes, it would work. And yes, I believe I can do it, but I will need help."

Mom's napkin wasn't enough.

Delia brought over a stack of the paper placemats she gave kids for coloring, along with another pen and some brand-new crayons. Coffee was consumed, plans discussed, and decisions made.

Grandma talked Mom into coming back to Nora's to get a couple hours of sleep. She'd been waiting for Cernunnos for the past few hours and was worn out. Grandma said she'd ask Glendon to keep watch at the park. He'd call the inn when Cernunnos came back.

No one was gonna say "if."

I'd eaten, I hadn't had any coffee, I was warm, and no

one was trying to kill me. My body exchanged adrenaline for exhaustion, and I didn't fight it. I'd save my fight for tomorrow. I actually let Rake drive the Jeep to Nora's inn, then carry me upstairs to the room Nora had set aside for us.

I was asleep before Rake put me on the bed.

 **32**

I woke up snuggled under blankets in a canopy bed. Sunlight was streaming through the lace curtains.

Nice.

Rake was on the bed beside me. Fully clothed.

Too bad.

He raised an eyebrow. "You look disappointed to see me."

"I'm disappointed to see you with clothes on."

"I can fix that."

I sniffed. "Coffee?"

"And scones. Nora brought up a tray."

"Coffee first, fun later."

Rake rolled off the bed. "As my lady desires. Nora thought you might like to have something before you came downstairs. There's a bigger breakfast laid out in the dining room."

I blinked at the bright sunshine. "What time is—" Then I remembered and bolted upright in bed. "Did my dad—"

"No, but it doesn't mean that—"

"It doesn't mean anything good. Mom. Oh God. Mom."

"She's fine," Rake said. "She's found something she can do to help and she's busy doing it. She's calling it her *de*construction project."

I fell back on the pillows, staring up at the canopy, my mind racing. "Why didn't you wake me up?"

"You needed the sleep and there's nothing you can do right now. It's going to be a long day and an even longer night." He got back on the bed and pulled me close. "Makenna, your father has hunted two-legged prey for hundreds of years. He's good at it. The best."

"Janus isn't just any prey."

"You father is his equal. He's more than proved that. He's Cernunnos, the Master of the Wild Hunt. No one is in his league. Actually, your father is a one-man league."

That made me proud, but I was still worried sick.

About a man I'd known about for only a day. My father. I'd accepted that he was my biological father as soon as Mom had told me. After she'd formally introduced me to him, I'd started thinking of him as "my dad," but the surge of fear and worry was raw—and new. I had a dad only to possibly lose him, and it would be Janus's doing. Fear turned to anger.

Rake was reading my thoughts as I had them, and I was glad. I didn't want to say any of it out loud and risk getting emotional. I didn't need that now, and it didn't do anyone any good.

"You need to eat." He kissed me, got up again, brought

the tray over, and set it up across my lap, a mischievous glint in his dark eyes. "I know something you don't know."

I knew he was trying to distract me, and I needed it, so I let him.

"You know a lot of things I don't know."

"This one's about Edwina. Or to be more exact, who Edwina is."

"Uh, she's a lady who lives in a really cool cave?"

"Think about it. She's the *mother* of the first god of *nature*."

It clicked. Loudly. Distraction achieved.

"Mother Nature? *The* Mother Nature?"

"I don't believe there's more than one on this world."

"That's why you bowed to her."

"Aside from my unwholesomely good looks, I have impeccable instincts and faultless manners. I give obeisance when and where it is due. That's another reason I'm confident about your mother's plan. If Edwina says she can destroy the dome with that ley line surge, I believe her."

"Janus must know who she is, too. Last night at the house, he was unnerved." I grinned. "It must be true what they say, 'You don't mess with Mother Nature.'"

I took a big bite of Aunt Nora's famous cinnamon scones and a good-sized sip of her notoriously strong coffee. Sugar and caffeine thus entering my system, I switched the topic back to my mother.

"Where's Mom?"

"She was up bright and early, and has already met with the town council to tell them the plan."

"And?"

Rake chuckled. "These are sane people, Makenna. Naturally, they would have concerns. However, they also live in Weird Sisters and acknowledge that unusual circumstances must be overcome with unique solutions."

"So, they're cool with digging a pit in the town square for a ley line surge that might destroy much of downtown?"

"They're cool with the offer I asked Margaret to relay to the council. Should such destruction occur, I've offered to pay to have the entire town rebuilt."

"Wow. Merry Christmas to them."

"Indeed. Your mother told me more than a few of them seemed to be perfectly fine now with whatever may occur."

"I imagine you'd already planned to make a substantial donation to the town anyway."

"I do feel somewhat responsible for Janus targeting them."

"None of it's your fault. If anything, it's mine. I'm Cernunnos's daughter. But since you're the billionaire philanthropist and I'm not, you have my blessing to throw as much cash around as you'd like. They're good people here. They deserve some nice things."

"Then nice things they shall have." He gave me a slow, wickedly sexy smile. "You deserve nice things, too. Is there anything I can do for *you*?"

After a shower that was steamy in all the best ways, Rake and I started down the stairs to breakfast.

"Are you sure?" Grandma asked from the foyer.

"Mother, of course I'm sure." It was Nora. "Stephen wouldn't have said it unless he'd heard it." She heard us and came to the foot of the stairs and gave us a little wave. She had her phone up to her ear. "Breakfast is on the sideboard, sweetie," she said while waiting for whoever she was calling to answer. "Vickie, wonderful news. Stephen found our mages. They're being held in the basement of the old ranger station." She paused, listening. Then she gave us a long-suffering look and rolled her eyes. "Of course I'm sure. If he hadn't heard it, he wouldn't have said it. He heard Fletcher Parks tell the others. Fletcher kept hearing a metallic ping when the storm went through last night and it occurred to him what it was. The old flagpole outside the station still has its cable attached and the wind was knocking it against the pole." She headed toward the kitchen, so her words faded out at that point.

Grandma came in and poured herself a to-go cup of coffee. "Finally, some good news. That'll give town morale a real shot in the arm. You children going downtown?"

"That's the plan, though Aunt Vickie may have other ideas." I turned up the volume on my phone, put it on the dining table, and went to the sideboard. I reached for a plate, then thought better of it. "I have a feeling we'll be needing something to go. Bacon and egg biscuit, it is." Seconds later, my phone buzzed with an incoming text. "Yep, Aunt Vickie. She wants to know if we'd be willing to go with them up to the ranger station for 'veil/ward detection and additional firepower, if needed.' Tell her yes?" I asked Rake.

"Of course. I'm surprised they don't have at least one battlemage in the department."

"Small department equals limited funds," Grandma said. "We're in the sticks. Battlemages go to big cities."

"Think we might be able to find a trout-fishin', deer-huntin' battlemage who yearns to leave the big city and get back to nature?" I asked Rake.

"I know we can look." He took a sip of coffee. "Might be an elf, would that be a problem?"

"Vickie and Mike don't care what kind of ears they got," Grandma told him. "As long as they can count on 'em to stick around."

"We'll find someone," he promised.

I wrapped my biscuit in a napkin and poured my coffee in a to-go cup. "Aunt Vickie said they'd pick us up down at the town square dig site in twenty minutes."

The three of us walked downtown. At the square, a backhoe was digging through the surface dirt and through the thin layer of limestone that covered the ley line crossing. The dirt was being shoveled into bags to be stacked around the pit-to-be. Good idea.

Downtown was a busy place. Like Mom, the townspeople were glad to be doing something to help free themselves. The Witch's Brew had set up a coffee and pastry station for the workers, and with all the holiday decorations it was almost festive, if you didn't know they were filling those bags to protect their lives. When Edwina sent that ley line surge into the sky tonight, it'd be kind of like Old Faithful in Yellowstone, but instead of scalding water, it'd be ley line power, and it'd be way stronger. The people would take shelter in the Hall come sundown.

Edwina was nearby talking with Glendon Kerr. Rake went over to them, giving me time alone with Mom.

I gave her a hug. "You okay?"

"I'm doing something to help him. If Janus has your father, we can't let that surge make it back to the Bishop house." She pressed her lips together. "Vickie called a little while ago. Jimmy got a drone in the air this morning to see what's going on at the Bishop place. The house is gone."

"What?"

"Where the house was is now a field. There are even small trees."

"A pocket dimension. It's Janus's specialty." Janus was definitely working from the Bannerman Island playbook. Rake was right, she was doing a fine job holding it together, and if Edwina could divert the surge tonight, we'd be free of the dome, help could get in, and Janus would have no power to bring his own Frankenstein monster to back to life.

"He has to know we were there last night," I told her. "He's gone to ground."

"With your father."

"We don't know that. So he didn't leave you a severed head this morning. Janus is a wily bastard. Besides, it's not Christmas morning yet. It wouldn't do to get your present early. And speaking of an early present…" I lowered my voice. Until those five mages were back safe and sound, I didn't want to get anyone's hopes up only to possibly have them dashed. I told her what Stephen had found out.

Mom's shoulders sagged in relief, and her smile was genuine. I was glad to be able to give her some good news.

"Vickie and Mike are picking us up here in the next few minutes," I said.

"You and Rake be careful."

"That's always our goal."

"Mother told me some things about last night."

"Oh?"

"She was impressed with Rake's marksmanship. Whatever he aimed for, he hit. She said the two of you worked well together." Mom paused. "She told me when those ghouls were chasing you back into town, every time a shot was fired, Rake made sure his body covered the back of the driver's seat. She said if any of those bullets had made it through, he would have taken them for you."

My lips twitched at the corners. "I didn't know that, but it doesn't surprise me in the least. He's done it before. Many times. He loves me, Mom."

She leaned over and kissed me on the forehead. "I know, and I think your grandmother realizes that, too."

I looked around at our friends and neighbors. Even the children were helping fill the bags. They thought it was fun.

Janus had failed on Bannerman Island. He was determined not to fail tonight.

We were just as determined not to quit.

The Fraser family and the people of Weird Sisters weren't about to roll over while a wannabe god destroyed us all. Yes, Janus had stacked the deck against us and separated us from any additional help. That just meant we would do what we'd always done.

Any trouble that came to our town was dealt with by the town.

We were all family here and we defended our own and eliminated all threats.

Some of our people were what the outside world called

monsters. To us, they were our neighbors, deserving of respect and protection. I had doubts about nearly every plan or precaution we were putting in place, but I had one absolute certainty, and it gave me hope.

When the chips were down, the people of Weird Sisters would always step up.

33

The ranger's station was guarded by six ghouls. Six. Regular ghouls, not the fire-setting kind.

Normally, I'd say this was a prime example of a villain getting sloppy toward the end. Their goal was within their evil grasp, they'd gotten cocky, and they'd stopped sweating the small stuff.

But this was Janus.

Janus hadn't survived all this time as a supernatural archmage archvillain by being careless.

So while the presence of only six ghoul guards looked like we'd finally caught a break, it was probably bad. Very bad.

For us.

I looked at Rake and Rake looked at me.

"Any veils or portals?" he asked.

"Nope. Any drone-exploding wards?" I asked him.

"None."

"Any unpleasant surprises in the building?" Mike asked both of us.

Rake shook his head. "Not one. Just five scared, but mostly angry, human captives."

"We'll take out the ghouls, and you cover us for any nasty magic?" Vickie asked Rake.

"Agreed."

Vickie and Mike deployed their officers to surround the ranger station, and they all had a target. On her signal, six shots were fired, and six ghouls hit the ground. They then moved in, each one drawing a big knife, machete, or hatchet, and separated the heads from the bodies to ensure that the ghouls they'd put down stayed down.

After Rake confirmed there were no traps in the station, Mike and Vickie went in and brought our people out.

Easy-peasy.

"Janus doesn't need them anymore," I murmured as the five earth mages emerged from the station's basement, blinking in the daylight. "Something has changed."

The sun had only put in the briefest of appearances and the clouds had once again closed over us. Below the ranger's station was a deep hollow. It had been clear a few minutes ago. Now it was filling with a shifting fog, a fog that was climbing up the hillside toward us.

Jimmy saw it and that was enough for him. "We need to leave now."

I saw movement inside the mist, and whatever was causing it, there was more than one. "This isn't Janus or any of his ghouls. Rake? What are you getting?"

"Besides thinking Jimmy has a good idea? The same. This isn't Janus's work."

Vickie and Mike started toward us, guns drawn but held low. I raised a hand to stop them from coming closer.

Three hounds the size of yearling bucks stopped just on the other side of the wall of fog. They stood alert, their eyes glittering, waiting for a signal.

I recognized them. Hounds from the Wild Hunt.

I froze. It seemed the prudent thing to do when big dogs you didn't know were only a few feet away. "No one move," I said without looking away from the massive dogs.

Rake's defensive magic flared, and the hounds growled, and I swear the ground vibrated beneath my feet with the force of it.

"Rake, wait."

Judging from the raised hackles on the Celtic Cujos, they were simply reacting to Rake's magic. They had not come here to attack.

"Daughter of Cernunnos."

The words appeared in my head as if spoken from far away.

The hounds pricked up their ears at the words, then turned and trotted back into the fog. As they faded, a horse and rider stopped just on the other side of the shifting mist. Behind him more riders waited.

The Wild Hunt.

I recognized the bearded rider closest to us. His battle ax

was secured in its sling across his broad back. His helmet was gone and he had a cut on his head that looked to have been hastily bandaged. A faint stain of blood had soaked through.

My father was nowhere to be seen.

"He is not here." The ax wielder did not speak, but I knew the words came from him. *"The adversary, the one you know as Janus, has taken him."*

No.

Mom had known.

"Can you hear him?" I quickly whispered to Rake.

"Yes."

"Good."

"We cannot go where the adversary holds him captive. Nor can we part the veil to enter this world. Only Cernunnos can lead us. Without him, we are imprisoned here and unable to help him. He is our Hunt Master. We are bound to him yet follow him willingly. We will not follow Janus. If we refuse, when he comes into his full power, he will use it to force us to serve, and we will lose ourselves to him. Or Janus may simply destroy us. If he succeeds in binding Cernunnos, he could compel him to obey and even turn him against us, or Janus could take his power by force."

Like Janus had done to Tavis Haldane on Widow's Peak.

No.

"Can we help?" I asked.

"Janus uses the First Master's power to hide from sight until his working is complete. Cernunnos's own power is descended from it. You are blood of his blood. Born of two worlds, mortal and immortal. You can see through the weaving the coward Janus is hiding behind. You can ride through it,

leading us. We will free Cernunnos and slay the immortal who would profane and destroy that which we are sworn to protect."

I just had to ask, didn't I?

Lead the Wild Hunt to rescue my father and stop Janus from either taking over or destroying the world.

I was completely in favor of having all of the above done; I was much less sure of my ability to do any of it, especially the whole leading part. It might be a jaunt through the woods for the Wild Hunt, but it sure wasn't for me.

It was as if he heard my thoughts.

"We are not mere men. Janus and the creatures who fawn before him are as vile stains upon this world that need be removed. We are more than equal to the work, and our steel stands ready to serve."

Fancy way to say they were ready, willing, and seriously able to take out the garbage, and didn't mind getting dirty doing it.

"Makenna," Rake said in warning.

I gave him the barest shake of my head.

"I cannot make any pacts for myself or my allies without seeking counsel from the mother of the First Master," I told him.

The fog swirled as the riders shifted nervously.

The ax wielder bowed his head. *"The First Mother possesses great wisdom and can perceive what we cannot. We will yield to her will in this matter. At dusk, we will come for your answer at the place where Cernunnos greeted you and your mother."*

I couldn't keep calling him ax wielder, but in the

supernatural world, names had power and were rarely given except to those you trusted without question—and those with whom you were about to risk your life.

"What is your name?" I asked.

"Helgar."

I inclined my head. "Thank you, your trust honors me. I am Makenna. I will be there at sundown."

With a nod, Helgar turned his mount and disappeared into the fog, the Hunt and the hounds with him.

Oh boy. What did I just do?

34

By late afternoon, our five earth mages were safely ensconced at Nora's inn where she was fussing over them like a mother hen, and I'd sought Edwina's wisdom even though I'd already made my decision. Actually, I'd made it while talking to Helgar.

That left the next few hours for me to come to grips with what I was about to do.

The pit was finished, complete with protective dirtbag bunker.

Edwina wanted confirmation on what Jimmy had seen with his drone, so she'd simply turned into a hawk and flew to the Bishop place. I've seen people turn into non-people plenty of times. Werewolves, in particular, were messy and more than a little ick-inducing. Edwina transforming into a hawk was quite possibly the most awe-inspiring change I'd ever had the honor to witness. She confirmed that Janus was indeed using the power of the First Master to conceal himself and his captive. The trees were his doing, and they had grown considerably since this morning. I guess Janus was testing his control of nature by dabbling in landscaping.

She also confirmed what Helgar had said.

I had a scary thought. I could get in with the Hunt, but would the barrier close after us? "How will Rake, Vickie, Mike, and their guys get in?"

"Passing through with the Hunt will destroy the barrier," Edwina assured me.

"Whew. Scared me there for a minute. I'm extremely fond of backup." I hesitated. I'd learned the hard way not to ask a question you didn't want to hear the answer to. I might not like the answer, but I needed to know.

"All of this that we're doing, will it really stop Janus?"

"Janus was exiled from this world. If he breaks the curse, and I fail to redirect the surge, Janus will not only be able to remain here forever, but he'll soon have the power to shape and remake this world to his liking."

"And if you redirect the surge? What could he still do with the power he's already absorbed?"

"Remaking the world requires more power. Destroying it takes much less."

I knew Janus would gleefully do either one. Or something in between. I didn't want to dwell on any of the possibilities.

"Janus has been absorbing power from my son through the medallion," Edwina continued. "Suspending him over the open ley lines has given Janus more power in less time."

Jeez, like plugging him in to a fast charger.

"Janus wants all the power of nature itself. With it, the curse that bound him and his people will be meaningless."

"Helgar said you perceive that which others do not."

"I do."

"Do you perceive anything about tonight?" I asked quietly. "Will I be able to do this?"

Edwina's smile was warm and confident. "I know that you will make your father and family very proud."

"I'll take that to mean I won't screw up."

And hopefully, not die horribly, either.

"I know that you will do your very best." She placed her hands on either side of my face. "And I know that I am proud of you."

I was now sitting at the bar at the Cauldron which gave me a clear view to the park across the street. I was eating a steak sandwich that I couldn't help but think of as a last meal, and was dressed like a mash-up of a biker, a commando, and an extra from a Mad Max movie. No one was with me. The pub was empty. I'd told my family I needed to be alone.

Aunt Vickie and I wore the same size, and she and Uncle Mike rode motorcycles. Between that and being chief of police, Vickie had fixed me up with some sweet body armor Mike had given her as an anniversary gift. Working at SPI, I'd come to learn that cops and soldiers had some unique ideas as to what was romantic. To top off my ensemble, I had my favorite knife, and my two guns were loaded with silver.

Mom and I had already talked. I told her that she'd come up with the idea that was going to save us all. Grandma had brought us Edwina. Nora, through Stephen, had found our mages, and Vickie had freed them. Since I had Cernunnos's blood in my veins, it was time for me to step up and do my part.

As to Rake, once I'd made my decision, he didn't try to talk me out of it. He even did my hair in a tight goblin battle braid—and gave me the best kiss I'd ever had as incentive to come back in one piece.

I finished my sweet tea and stood.

I looked out the window. It was almost time.

Grandma had always said that the scariest thing I'd ever face in my life was the unknown. Regardless of what the unknown turned out to be, it'd never be as terrifying as what I would come up with in my own head. Sometimes it sucked to have a vivid imagination.

I'd done smarter things in my time. A lot smarter. Actually, this was the dumbest thing I'd ever done, at least as far as preserving my own life was concerned. Most of the ones down the list I'd done on impulse, or the situation was going to Hell in a handbasket too fast to stop and think about the stupid I was about to commit.

I'd had time to think this one through—and I was still going through with it.

Because it was the only thing I could do.

That either meant I was incredibly brave, or unbelievably stupid, or simply suicidal.

I decided to go with the first one. That way, if I didn't live through the night, I'd die with a high opinion of myself.

My father was the Celtic god of life and death, all that was contained in nature.

I was Makenna Anne Fraser. Two days ago, I'd been told

that Cernunnos was my father. I was the seer for SPI from the tiny mountain town of Weird Sisters, North Carolina.

That was all.

It would have to be enough.

Too many of the cabal's mages had gotten away in past confrontations. Vivienne Sagadraco's sister Tiamat had escaped. Viktor Kain had escaped. Ditto for Janus, Isidor Silvanus, Marek Reigory. I was sick and tired of the people who wanted me and my friends dead or worse slipping through SPI's fingers to kill, maim, and torture another day.

Janus had kidnapped and nearly sacrificed my partner. Now he had used me and my mother as bait to trap and imprison my father.

I was through winning the battle only to lose the war.

This had to end tonight.

I glanced at the clock over the bar.

It was 5:11. Six minutes until sundown.

It wasn't full dark, but that time in between.

A dangerous time.

I'd always been able to sense the time when the day was ending and the night beginning. I wonder if I'd gotten that from Cernunnos, too. Calling it sundown was an attempt to describe an event that was much more complex and dangerous. Down through the ages, humans have had a deeply rooted need to be home by sundown. And if by chance they weren't, their feet started moving faster as the light faded, or they urged their horse into a trot or even a gallop. Only in modern times, with its well-lit cities and cars with headlights, did humans begin telling themselves they were safe at night. As long as they could have light at the flip of a switch, it was all good.

But let a storm come up or a transformer blow, and humans' primitive instincts and fears came back. Instant and insistent.

We humans were scared of the dark.

And we had good reason, even if we didn't believe in that reason. Supernatural creatures that hunted in the night didn't care what you did or didn't believe in. If you crossed their path, you were theirs. A small, dark corner of the human brain knew that and knew it well, which was why people kept candles, flashlights, and camp lanterns in their homes. Anything to keep any sudden darkness at bay.

When true darkness came, I felt it. Grandma Fraser made sure her family didn't ignore it.

She knew what was out there.

Tonight, I would hunt the things that were out there.

My family waited in the park. After hugs and whispered words, I stood quietly by the picnic table and waited.

The hounds appeared first.

I love dogs, all dogs, but I have an extra-large soft spot for extra-large dogs.

I removed one of my gloves, sticking it through the hazy barrier that separated me from them. There was the slightest brush of cold air and my hand passed right through. The hound that had approached me earlier came up to me and nuzzled under my outstretched bare hand. Her head was warm.

"Makenna?"

It was Rake.

"Get the Hunt through Janus's barrier and then get out of the way. We'll be right behind you. I'll *be right behind you."*

I nodded and turned back toward the veil as my father's

stallion emerged from the forest. He was taller than even our neighbor's biggest draft horse. He approached and nickered as he put his soft nose in my hand. I shivered with excitement at the contact. He had accepted me.

The Wild Hunt emerged, led by Helgar.

I took the stallion's reins and stepped through the veil. The first step to being confident is to act confident, even if that was the absolute last thing I felt. The stirrups were level with my chest. Dang. Helgar, bless him, dismounted and gave me a leg up. I silently nodded my thanks.

I leaned over the stallion's arched muscular neck. It was like warm, living velvet.

My father's sword was still in its scabbard. A glow came from inside. It reminded me of Lugh's Spear's reaction to Ian. I wrapped my hand around the grip and the glow ran up my arm. I drew the sword. It was a broadsword, but for me, on this night, it was as light as a fencing foil.

It had accepted me, too.

Helgar gave my armor a grin and nod of approval.

The Wild Hunt watched silently and waited.

An introduction seemed to be called for.

"I am Makenna, daughter of Cernunnos."

The archer was the first to speak. "I am Gareth."

I looked to the next one and the next, each telling me his name, and bestowing his trust along with it. I'd never been good with names, but these were burned into my memory. I would never forget them.

I wasn't Cernunnos, but I shared his DNA, or whatever it was Celtic gods had. I didn't kid myself into believing that was the reason the Hunt would follow me.

That may have been part of it, but mostly it was to rescue their leader, their brother in the hunt, their friend. Cernunnos was in the worst kind of danger. They all were. I was taking them to where their leader was—as well as into the lair of the ancient being who had dared to take Cernunnos from them.

Every time I'd encountered Janus, nothing could put a dent in him, let alone stop him in his tracks. Though that wasn't entirely true. Rolf Haagen's ancestral blade Gram had sliced into Janus like hot butter, and Janus had done all that he could to avoid contact with Ian's ancestor's spear.

I had my father's sword, his war horse, and his Wild Hunt, who had sworn to fight by my side. But he'd had all those things as well, and he'd still been taken.

Helgar had mounted, and he and his horse took their place beside me.

"How was my father taken?" I asked him.

"By treachery. Janus took the form of your mother struggling in the hands of ghouls. Cernunnos rode into the trap before we could come to his aid. A barrier more solid than any fortress wall appeared between us and him. More ghouls swarmed him. He fought but was overwhelmed and dragged from his mount. Janus shifted to his true form and fled with his ghouls through a portal, taking Cernunnos with them. His horse was left behind."

Janus didn't need the horse, just my father, once again using my mother as bait.

The kidnapping was nearly identical to when Janus had taken Ian from that bank vault. Though what incentive did Janus have to change his MO? It had worked then, and it had worked now. If it ain't broke, don't fix it.

I turned back to the park. I could see Rake and my family, but could they see me?

I raised a hand.

Rake placed his hand over his heart.

Only he could see me.

"I love you." I mouthed it in case our silent speech no longer worked.

I turned and started through the park at a canter in the direction of the Bishop house. Just before passing into the forest, I glanced back.

The town was gone.

I straightened in the saddle, the great stallion's reins held comfortably in my hands.

I was my father's daughter.

"Let's ride."

Soon even the night forest vanished, opening into a vast expanse of moonlit grassland.

Oh, how I wanted to run.

The stallion instantly responded, the Wild Hunt spreading out on either side of me, their mounts joyfully stretching their legs.

I gave myself over to it.

"We are not in your world or ours," Helgar said in my mind. *"It is an in-between place where time races or slows depending on the desire of the Master of the Wild Hunt."*

The Master wasn't here.

I was.

I leaned low over the stallion's neck urging him to run fast and faster still until the grassland transformed into a starry void which sped by in a blur of night and starlight.

I would never see the night sky the same way again. Mortals gaze up at the sky, seeing stars, white and bright, or color-tinged planets—all small and unreachable against a black canvas. Not this night. The sky was no longer merely black. Purples and blues in all their dark richness, folding and draping in upon themselves like the softest velvets or sleekest silks, ever shifting, always in motion.

The stars and planets were *right there*. I believed I could reach out and touch them, pluck them from the heavens to possess for my own, if I wanted to.

As glorious as this was, I wanted to get to where my father was, free him, and get back to where and when I belonged.

Helgar was on my right flank.

"How long until midnight?" I asked.

"As soon or as late as you wish it to be. We ride beyond time."

"If I want it to be now, would my allies be waiting?"

"Whenever we are there, so they will be. Your father is there, as is the First Master and our adversary who would use the power he yearns to gain to rend all this asunder and destroy us all."

"Is the Hunt ready?"

Helgar flashed his teeth in a vulpine smile, white and sharp. *"Eternally."*

"Then it is midnight."

I slowed the stallion and the Hunt slowed with me. I hadn't realized how fast I was going.

What was the saying? Never drive faster than your guardian angel can fly.

Or in my case, never ride faster than your immortal backup.

Ahead the void abruptly ended. Just beyond was the veil back to my world, and just on the other side of that was Janus's barrier. The veil swirled and eddied, crackling and combusting at each contact with the barrier, sparks and flames separating us from our goal.

Cernunnos had been mortal once, long ago. Cernunnos could pass unharmed through that curtain of consuming fire, leading his Hunt through safely.

So could I. In theory.

My father was the Master of the Wild Hunt.

I was not.

But for tonight, I was.

My flesh burned as I urged the stallion to leap through both veil and barrier. I hoped my scream was more war cry than shriek of pain. I didn't have the time or the ability to care.

Then we were through.

I was alive and unharmed.

And the expression on Janus's face was priceless.

⌒ 35

Janus had only one face now. There was no layering of the faces he had worn over the millennia, just the one he'd had when he'd been born, hatched, or had slithered out from under his evil rock.

Thanks to Cernunnos's blood in my veins and the magic of this night leading the Wild Hunt, I could see the mortal man Janus had been, and got to enjoy the shock on his true face for less than a second before it hardened into steely determination.

I wished Ian could've been here to see it.

Last night this had been a house's basement. Tonight, it was open to the sky and the size of an amphitheater.

Janus had been busy with his new talent.

At the appearance of the Wild Hunt, some of Janus's ghouls ran—or they tried. They'd crossed paths with the Wild Hunt last night and from their reaction, they didn't want a rematch. The Hunt was the ultimate supernatural predator. All other predators paled in comparison, and either deferred to it or got the hell out of its way. Janus's money and promises of all the humans the ghouls could eat only bought so much loyalty when their heads were in danger of being separated from their bodies. Helgar and the Hunt were appallingly efficient in that regard and were delivering as promised.

I wasn't entirely unqualified. I could ride and I'd taken up sword fighting since becoming a SPI agent. When the criminals you were after were hundreds or even thousands of years old, or were elves or goblins from Rake's world, which was like a real-life *Game of Thrones,* it was highly advised to have more than a few arrows in your quiver weapons-wise. I'd taken up archery, too. Rake had been teaching me both.

Fights like this were chaos, and I did what SPI and Ian had trained me to do. Set goals before going in and focus on achieving them once you were there.

Find Dad. Free Dad. Dad kills Janus.

I didn't delude myself into thinking I could do that last one. Having achievable goals also meant knowing your limitations, and my chances of killing a four-thousand-year-old psycho megamage were severely limited.

I drew my father's sword, and between me and my mount, we sliced, diced, stomped, and trampled our way through any ghoul between us and the ley line pit. That had to be where Janus was keeping Cernunnos.

In terms of allies, we were on the friends and family plan. Janus had gone to Rent-A-Thug for his backup. We were fighting for our lives and the lives of those we loved. The ghouls were fighting for their lives and a payday. My money was on us.

I caught fleeting glimpses of Rake, Vickie, Mike, and a werewolf that had to be Jimmy tearing into a knot of ghouls. There were others with them.

The goal, Mac. The goal.

The First Master was no longer in his crystal, but was still suspended over the pit, only now he was on a platform like Frankenstein's monster waiting on the surge from below instead of lightning from above to bring him back to life.

Cernunnos was at the edge of the pit, chained to the First Master's crystal coffin. His chains were anchored inside it. I recognized the green glow. Magic-sapping manacles. One more thing Janus had stolen from the cabal.

I felt the ley line power building and the stallion shied nervously at the tremor beneath his hooves. It vibrated up through my bones until it rattled my teeth. If I hadn't known it was the surge, I would have thought it was an earthquake. A California-level quake. Not the North Carolina kind that might tip over a lawn chair.

The surge had begun.

According to Edwina, it would return here within one minute.

Come on, Edwina.

My father's antlered head turned toward me. Everything had gone into slow motion. I'd had that happen a few times. When you were about to die horribly, your brain tried to help one last time by slowing those soon-to-be-fatal seconds, to give you time to think, somehow, of some way to survive.

What my father did slowed as well. It was the only way I could have seen it in the chaos.

Dad winked at me—and pulled his chains free.

In the two seconds I stared stupidly in shock, he made short work of the six fire ghouls who had been guarding him, tossing them into the ley line pit.

What felt like an explosion deep underground nearly threw me from the saddle. From the direction of town, a column of blinding white light shot into the sky like the business end of a rocket and kept going beyond where the top of the dome would have been.

Janus screamed in rage.

Edwina had done it.

Now it was our turn.

Janus ran to the edge of the pit, the now glowing medallion held high and clutched in both hands. He flung his head back and shouted an incantation into that star-filled night.

What happened next was a nightmare.

The souls that had been captured and imprisoned over untold ages emerged from the medallion as bright pinpoints of light. Pinpoints that elongated and took human shape to swirl in a vortex of raw energy above Janus's head, climbing higher and higher into the night sky. Though released from the medallion, the souls were still captive to Janus's control and command. Alongside those obviously from the far past, I recognized the face of Tavis Haldane and others in modern clothes. The First Master had been encased in that crystal since time primeval. Then Janus had stolen the medallion and had kept adding to the number of stolen souls.

The power of possibly millions of human souls, both mundane and magically gifted, was now about to be harnessed as a weapon.

Edwina had taken away Janus's ability to complete his plan when she'd taken and redirected the surge.

Vengeance was all that mattered now.

Cernunnos stood motionless on the opposite side of the pit, the ley light from below illuminating both him and Janus, and the corpse of the First Master suspended between them.

Janus had to shout across the expanse to be heard above the roar of what looked like a tornado made of souls. "Submit to me or I release them and lay waste to this world!"

"I will not submit." My father's voice was calm and certain, and filled the space with no effort of will. He gazed up at the vortex. "All these you have enslaved, I will free this night."

The light from the pit was dimming.

I realized why. Ley lines were underground energy rivers. The surge had pressurized it, and what Edwina had done was more like blowing up a dam than rerouting a river. The ley lines would fill again from downstream, but for now, the ley lines had drained.

Deprived of its ley line sustenance, the body of the First Master began collapsing in on itself, pieces falling away into the darkening pit and crumbling to dust. The crystal cocoon had been preserving him.

No surge, no ley line power, no preserving crystal.

No more First Master.

I knew from Bannerman Island that Janus's next move would be to open a portal and escape.

Not this time.

I knew what I had to do. The only thing I could do.

Janus controlled the vortex, but that control was balanced on a razor's edge. His attention was focused on maintaining control.

I quickly dismounted. "Janus!"

I'd been going for a distraction. A jumping up and down and waving my arms kind of distraction. That was not what I got. My voice was huge, a voice that could command armies and inspire terror. A voice you obeyed.

From Janus, I only got an annoyed glance.

But that was all I'd wanted—and all my father needed.

For that fraction of a second, Janus's focus faltered, and Cernunnos raised his arms in welcome and the vortex of souls shifted away from Janus and drifted across the pit to my father.

"This just isn't your night," I told Janus.

Cernunnos, the Celtic god of death and now in his full power as the one and only Master of the Wild Hunt, with the grace of the ultimate predator he was, stalked around the edge of the pit toward Janus, the vortex of the dead settling to swirl just above his antlers like a massive crown.

It was long overdue, but Death was finally coming for Janus.

Janus realized the danger, but in his arrogance, believed he could regain control.

He summoned all his power and reached up toward the vortex. The light from the very stars seemed to dim as he drew on his power. The souls did not respond but continued circling above Cernunnos, though what looked like lightning flashed inside as the vortex darkened.

"You are mine!" Janus shouted to the souls.

"Nay, they are their own," Cernunnos said simply. "Captives no longer."

Janus tried to run. Cernunnos was there before him, towering over him, one hand on his shoulder, anchoring him where he stood, the other grasping the medallion and with a sharp jerk breaking the chain that held it around Janus's neck.

"You used my mate and my child to lure me here. But you failed to bind me, and my mate and child are unharmed." He glanced up to where the souls swirled overhead. "I could take your life, destroy your body, and rend your soul as you have done to all of these, but I do not have that right. You took their lives before their time was done. They have earned that right, paid for in full by their suffering. You are theirs, not mine."

Cernunnos drew breath and his voice boomed out over the valley and beyond. "I yield the right to take the body and soul of the mortal known as Janus to those whom he and the First Master have taken from this world. Lives ended without honor and souls imprisoned without cause. He is yours to do with as you will."

Cernunnos released Janus and stepped back.

The vortex of murdered souls descended to accept the gift.

The shrieks and wails of the dead rose beyond even banshee levels as a single scream was torn from Janus's throat as he was drawn upward into the vortex, his booted feet kicking impotently against the combined power of the souls of the ancient dead and recently murdered.

It was over in seconds.

The swirling souls rose into the sky, and then in a burst of pure light, split off like tiny shooting stars on the next leg of their celestial journey.

Cernunnos dropped the now empty medallion to the ground and crushed it beneath the heel of his boot. He gazed around, taking in the razed valley. Our battlefield. He found me with those glorious eyes and inclined his regal head and crown of antlers to me, his daughter, the child of his passion.

He smiled. "I believe that restores the balance."

The moon was full and the sky clear and full of stars.

They were all here, Rake and my family, Gethen and his battlemages, SPI commando commanders Sandra Niles and Roy Benoit and their teams. After rerouting the surge, Edwina had flown over from town as a snowy owl and returned to her form as she touched down.

Cernunnos knew Edwina and bowed to her.

The First Master had been Edwina's son, but his power lived on in each incarnation of Cernunnos. So, in that way, my dad was Edwina's son, giving me a paternal grandmother. I got a dad *and* another grandmother for Christmas.

I handed the stallion's reins back to Cernunnos like I'd borrowed the family car. "He was magnificent."

My father fondly patted the massive neck. "Aye, that he is."

"And a fierce fighter." I paused, giving him a mildly accusing look. "Yet somehow there wasn't a single mark on him when I met Helgar and your Hunt in the park. You used yourself as bait and let Janus catch you."

Cernunnos grinned, and I could swear the horse looked smug. "The lad and I had a plan. Janus was a challenging opponent. When I saw that he had the First Master's medallion, I knew I must free those souls. To do that, I needed to be close. I did not want to risk that my Hunt could also be captured or killed defending me. I separated myself from them to trip the snare Janus had set. I was close to Janus and my Hunt was safe. I could not let them in on my deception, or you and your mother. To succeed, it had to be real to everyone. To stop Janus, I had to be near him."

"Mom's going to be pissed—"

Cernunnos tilted his head in confusion.

"Angry," I clarified.

"Yes, she will be." There was a twinkle in his eyes. "I will accept her beratement. Janus boasted of how he knew you, and what his intentions were once he had me under his thrall." The twinkle turned to a dangerous glare. "This could not come to pass. His long life had to end this night, but I could not have done it without you, my Hunt, and your allies."

"But your Hunt couldn't reach you."

"With you, they could, and they did. I knew Helgar would seek you out." His big hands settled on my shoulders with a gentle strength. "I knew you would lead my Hunt through any barrier Janus would put in your way." He glanced to where my mom was making her way toward us. "You are our daughter. I knew you could do it."

I didn't know what to say, and if I had, I didn't think I could've gotten it past the sudden lump in my throat. So, I reached out and rubbed the stallion's nose and got an affectionate nicker in return.

I smiled. "In the midst of everything, it occurred to me that I didn't even know his name."

"It is Conall." My father put his hand under my chin, raising my eyes to his. "And my name is Ronan."

⤴

There wasn't any piece or part of Janus left to take a proof-of-death photo for Ian, but there were enough witnesses to attest to his messy and definite demise. Ian would believe me and Rake, but every agent in SPI HQ's two commando teams had also had a front row seat to what'd happened. Even without photo proof, it'd be the best Christmas present Ian had ever received. And I could tell him it was from my dad.

Janus was dead and the dome was gone. My family was alive and together—and for me and my parents, it was for the first time ever.

Cernunnos and my mother stood together, a little distance away, talking quietly, the conversation punctuated by kisses. The otherworldly glow around him had dimmed slightly, but it was still there. In that light, he almost looked human, like the mortal man he had once been.

The Celtic god and the mortal woman.

Ronan and Margaret.

My parents.

I had parents.

Even though one of them was a couple hundred years older than the other. Talk about robbing the cradle.

Now they were making out.

My family was safe, and my parents, well…they might want to think about getting a room.

⤴ 36

There were reports from all over the eastern half of the country of a rocket launch or a comet followed minutes later by a meteor shower. NASA reported they had no launches scheduled for the month of December, and certainly none on Christmas. The military issued a brief denial of any launches or activity, which left people free to come up with their own conclusions. As far as the tinfoil hat and conspiracy theory crowd were concerned, denial of such an obvious event by all authorities made for the best Christmas present ever.

Anyone under the age of ten knew exactly what had happened.

Santa had a seriously cool new sleigh.

The light show, and accompanying seismic activity, had been centered in the Nantahala National Forest in

North Carolina. The nearby town of Weird Sisters had had every window blown out in its downtown shopping district. Structural damage wasn't too bad, but local contractors would have plenty of work for the next few months.

Mom told the business owners that rather than having insurance adjustors swarming all over the place, nitpicking over every item on a claim, the cost of all repairs was being covered by the town. Mom didn't say where the windfall had come from, just that the donor wished to remain anonymous. Everyone knew who it was, but no one would say a word to the reporters who would be swarming the town in the coming days.

The people of Weird Sisters knew how to keep secrets.

Edwina had turned out to be Mother Nature and our family's fairy godmother all rolled into one. By the time we got back home, the house had been cleaned, the windows replaced, and rather than smoke, the air smelled of spiced cider. Grandma ran into the kitchen, and this time, instead of an enraged scream came a delighted squeal.

Yes, Grandma Fraser actually squealed. When Rake and I looked in to see what had happened, she was gazing around in wonder. "How?"

There were no broken dishes, glasses, or shattered jars. The kitchen was immaculate.

I opened the fridge, which was now upright. "Uh, Grandma, look."

The holiday meal she would've spent yesterday and into last night preparing was in the fridge, ready to go in the oven.

Edwina stood in the kitchen doorway, a secretive smile on her face. "I have friends who specialize in restoring order to disordered houses."

Mom hadn't come home with us. She was spending the night with Cernunnos.

"He has a place," she had told us at the Bishop house as Dad had leaned down and scooped her onto the saddle in front of him.

Now I was standing out on the front porch, a cup of hot cider in my hands. The jolt I'd gotten from filling my father's stirrups for the night was fading. It'd been good to experience and had helped me save lives, but that kind of power wasn't for me.

I gazed up at the stars. They were nowhere near as bright as they had been when I'd ridden with the Wild Hunt, but they were brighter than before. As a kid, I'd always wondered how Santa Claus could get it all done in only one night. Now I knew. He flew his reindeer and sleigh among the stars between worlds where time itself bowed to his whim. Maybe that particular legend was right, and Santa was like the Master of the Wild Hunt.

Rake came up behind me and slipped his arms around my waist.

"What do you see?" he murmured.

"Much more than I did before, but it's fading."

"Regrets?"

"Absolutely none." I paused. "Okay, maybe a few. But I'll remember what it looked like. That's enough."

"I guess this means you'll be joining Dr. Tierney's Descendants of Demigods and Superheroes Support Group."

I laughed, quietly. Some people in the house were trying to sleep.

Well, except for Gethen and his merry band of battlemages.

Gethen was just inside the front door watching Rake's every move. He'd deployed his team around the perimeter of the house where they were now standing guard, but I was sure the nocturnal goblins were also enjoying the night sky, just as we were.

Rake was right. I'd probably need that support group.

Being descended from the Tuatha Dé Danann and the Fomorians, Ian could telepathically communicate with merfolk. Though Ian was more Aquaman, the Jason Momoa version, not the blond guy with the pompadour who wore his undies outside his clothes. Being the daughter of Cernunnos, I could see through veils and communicate telepathically with dragons—and possibly had a few more gifts that might turn up. And yes, I would consider them gifts.

Ian's ancestor was an Irish king and demigod.

My father was a Celtic god of the hunt, death, fertility, etc. Still alive and kicking hard, thank you very much.

Rake was right. This would earn me a place in Dr. Tierney's group. I knew a couple of the members and liked them. Rolf Haagen, aka the Bionic Viking, who'd blown up a grendel by shoving a grenade down its throat, was always a party waiting to happen.

It could be fun.

Rake and I had both been right about backup waiting just outside the dome. When the dome had come down, Gethen and his team had swarmed in, along with both SPI commando units from New York. Gethen led them all to us within minutes.

Rake had not been amused at how Gethen had found him, but the rest of us had gotten a much-needed laugh.

Turns out Gethen had had Rake microchipped during one of the last times he'd been knocked unconscious.

We'd still been at the Bishop house, and Rake had been catching his breath while sitting on one of the trees that'd fallen during the surge.

Rake had given his security chief a dark look at the revelation. "Where is it?"

"You're sitting on it, sir."

That was another moment I'd remember—every time I saw Rake's bare butt.

Vivienne Sagadraco had checked in with me telepathically. I gave her the abbreviated version of what had happened and promised a full report when I came back from vacation early next week. She encouraged me to take some extra time off to be with my family.

Once Roy and Sandra had been convinced that it was over and everyone was safe, they loaded up their commandos and took the two company jets waiting in Asheville back home to New York to be with their families in time for Christmas morning.

Gethen and his team weren't about to go anywhere. Grandma had insisted that we had plenty of room and that they were staying with us. Naturally, Edwina's mysterious friends had prepped more food than our family could possibly eat. And I had a feeling that food would keep appearing in the kitchen until we were all about to pop.

Out of the corner of my eye, I saw Rake gesture for Gethen to give us some privacy. Gethen hesitated—probably with his patented scowl—but he did as asked.

Rake snuggled in closer. "By the way, while we were waiting for midnight, I talked to Margaret and Agnes about us."

I stiffened. "And how did that go?"

"I told them that I loved you and wanted to marry you, but that you weren't quite there yet. I asked that they consider giving me their permission and blessing when that time came."

"And…?"

"Your mother was ready to say yes right then; but like you, your grandmother isn't quite there yet." His lips twitched in a smile. "I'm a patient man. I'm willing to wait as long as it takes." He remembered something else. "I also talked to Glendon Kerr about buying some land in the area and building a house."

"*That,* Grandma will have a problem with," I told him. "She believes when you visit family, you stay with family."

"This house creaks every time we move," Rake said. "Do you want to have sex here?"

"Build the house. But not too big. A little cabin would be nice. Though I can see Grandma calling it our Love Shack."

I felt Rake take a deep breath. "I also talked to your father about my intentions."

"Ooooh, you didn't?"

"I did."

"And?"

"We have an understanding."

"Care to elaborate?"

"I'd rather not."

"I'll bet. Let me guess. You keep me deliriously happy, or he comes back, kills you horribly, and you become part of the Wild Hunt."

Rake grinned. "Essentially. Though I assured him that would not be necessary as your happiness—delirious and otherwise—is my life goal. And I think he likes me. He was impressed by what I did to him and his Hunt a couple of nights ago. He said he thought about coming back and separating my head from my shoulders, but he realized that I was only protecting you, and you seemed to like me."

"I wish there was a way to get him freed from that curse of riding and hunting for eternity."

"That might actually be possible. That was another thing I talked to him about."

"Edwina said the new Cernunnos has to kill the previous one in single combat," I told him. "Though she said that not all incarnations of Cernunnos are the same, and that Dad's one of the most clever there has ever been."

"Rules *are* made to be broken. First, he needs to find a replacement, then we can work on turning replacement into retirement."

I grinned as I realized something. "He's like the Dread Pirate Roberts. He's merely filling the boots for a while."

"Dread Pirate who?"

I just looked at him. "Please tell me you didn't just ask that question. You've never seen *The Princess Bride*?"

"I've never even heard of it."

"Oh honey, we need to fix that pronto. It's a movie, it's fabulous, and I love it. After we watch it, and I ask how you liked it, the correct answer is 'I loved it.' Though considering where you're from, I'll accept 'it was quaintly enjoyable.'"

Rake grinned. "I think I can manage that."

Later, Rake fell asleep on the couch. I got up for a snack and sat in Grandma's rocker so I wouldn't disturb him and watched him sleep. What to me had seemed like only a few minutes of riding with the Hunt had been nearly seven hours of hell for Rake and my family while they had waited for midnight.

Rake had been there at the Bishop house when I'd led the Hunt through Janus's barrier. Just as he promised.

I must have dozed off. I woke to Grandma covering Rake with a quilt—and not just any quilt, the one she had made with *her* grandmother.

Rake's breathing stayed smooth and even. He was awake. He'd woken up the instant Grandma's foot touched the pine-planked floor at the foot of the stairs.

Grandma needed to do this, and Rake knew it. He wasn't about to give away that he was awake. Grandma wasn't ready to openly show Rake any affection, and he respected that. I silently told him how much she treasured what looked like an old and worn quilt.

The sun was just coming up when Mom came home. I smiled and gave her a little finger wave as she tried to walk across the creaking floor toward the stairs. Rake was still pretending to be asleep.

Mom was beaming. "That'll hold me for a while," she whispered to me.

Grandma stuck her head out of the kitchen. "Margaret?"

"Yes?"

"Your sweater's on backward."

"Thank you, Mother."

Grandma disappeared back into the kitchen. "Just trying to be helpful."

As Mom went upstairs to her room, Rake's shoulders were shaking with silent laughter under the quilt.

Christmas in my family has never been about expensive gifts. It's about family and giving gifts that are meaningful. Thought and love always went into either the buying or the making. Grandma always made us something. I kept each and every gift, even the sweaters and dresses she made when I was little. Grandma did beautiful work and I'd always been proud to wear anything she made. Who knows? I might have children of my own one of these days.

Vickie, Mike, and Nora had joined us to exchange gifts and for lunch. For today, and until his house was repaired, Glendon Kerr was family; and until Rake and I returned to New York, so were Gethen and his five mages.

When Nora came into the house, there was a handsome man at her side wearing a Victorian suit.

Stephen McRae.

I could see him now. I wondered what other abilities may have been awakened by my ride with the Wild Hunt. Well, Dad was the Celtic god of death, and Stephen was a ghost. Though it might be like how I'd seen the stars, this gift might not last, but I would enjoy it while I had it. I gave Stephen a big smile and welcoming nod.

I got a surprised look, then a smile in return.

Stephen was taller than Nora by a head. He had light brown hair and a neatly trimmed beard, and he was just as cute as he could be in his round, wire-rimmed glasses. Apparently if you died with glasses, your ghost needed them, too. Dang. Even when you died you had to keep up with stuff.

Nora was watching us both and gave me a wink and knowing smile.

I knew Grandma had knitted a wool scarf for Rake. I'd

caught her in the kitchen this morning finishing a hat to go with it. Like the scarf, it was black. But the hat was of the softest cashmere. I knew she could whip up a hat in a few hours. Apparently after the past two days, she'd decided that a scarf simply wasn't enough.

I made a fuss over the cashmere when Rake unwrapped it, and she waved it away. "I had some in my stash."

I knew better. Yes, it was in her stash, but she would have been saving it for a really special gift. When I touched the hat, I felt the protective spells Grandma had worked into it.

I knew Rake had, too.

Rake thanked her and gave her a kiss on the cheek.

Grandma blushed a little. "With all those cabal people after you, we can't have you running around completely unprotected. It'd break Makenna's heart if anything happened to you. I'll send gloves when I get 'em finished."

And a sweater. I knew Grandma would be making Rake a Celtic cable sweater. I'd seen her sizing him up for one during breakfast. She never had to ask anyone's size.

Grandma Fraser only made sweaters for people she loved or thought very highly of—or both.

My grandmother approved of Rake.

For Mom and Grandma, Rake gave them each a gleaming blue touchstone on a gold chain. He'd spent a lot of time on each one, infusing the stones with a link from him to them. No need for phone calls, texts, or Zoom meetings. With the touchstone, they could contact Rake instantly.

Mom and Grandma loved the gifts.

Dad had given me and Mom gifts last night outside the ruins of the Bishop house.

He had said, "I believe on this day, it is tradition to give a gift of value—"

"You already have," Mom had told him, glancing at me.

He had taken her hand and slid a heavy gold ring covered with gorgeous Celtic scrollwork on her third finger. On both of his wrists were gleaming, golden cuffs also covered with intricate scrollwork. He removed one and put it on my mother's wrist, then he did the same for me. It should have fallen off, but it gently adjusted to fit me. Warm, like a hug.

Then Dad had given me one of those, too.

He also gave me his hunting knife. "I have used it many times and used it well," he had said. "It is now yours to wield. May it be for you as it was for me."

I must have had the stupidest grin on my face. I now had an heirloom blade for show-and-tell at the my-ancestor-was-an-ancient-god support group. Ian's spear and Rolf's sword had come from ancestors. Mine had been given to me directly from my father's hand.

It had been too cool for words.

I gave him my favorite knife. It wasn't fancy like his, but it was a good knife and I loved it.

Cernunnos slipped it into the sheath at his waist. "I will carry it and treasure it always."

This morning, after exchanging gifts with Mom and Grandma, Rake gave me my gift. I unwrapped it to reveal a flat velvet box with a hinge on the front.

Oh boy. I knew what that meant. Jewelry.

"I don't think I can top what your father gave you, but I'm going to try."

I opened the box.

A necklace, bracelet, and earrings set in gold with a type of green gem I had never seen before.

"They're precious gems from my home world," Rake told me. "I chose them because they perfectly match your eyes."

"When did you have time to—"

"I told my mother what I wanted for you. She had them made." A very slow smile crept over his lips. "I've met your family, now you need to meet mine."

ABOUT THE AUTHOR

Lisa Shearin is the *New York Times* and *USA Today* bestselling author of the SPI Files novels, an urban fantasy series best described as *Men in Black* with supernaturals instead of aliens; the Raine Benares novels, a comedic fantasy adventure series; and the Aurora Donati paranormal thriller series.

Lisa is a greyhound mom, avid tea drinker, vintage teapot and teacup collector, grower of orchids and bonsai, and fountain pen and crochet addict. She lives on a small farm in North Carolina with her husband, a small pack of spoiled-rotten retired racing greyhounds, and enough deer, birds, and woodland creatures to fill a Disney movie.

Website: lisashearin.com
Facebook: facebook.com/LisaShearinAuthor
Twitter: @LisaShearin

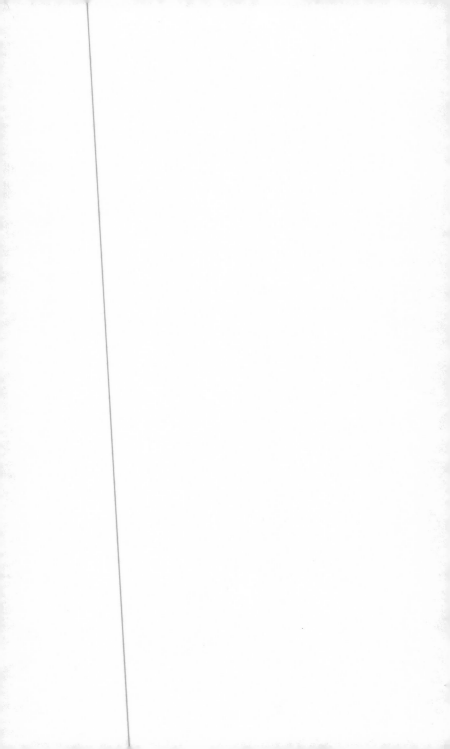

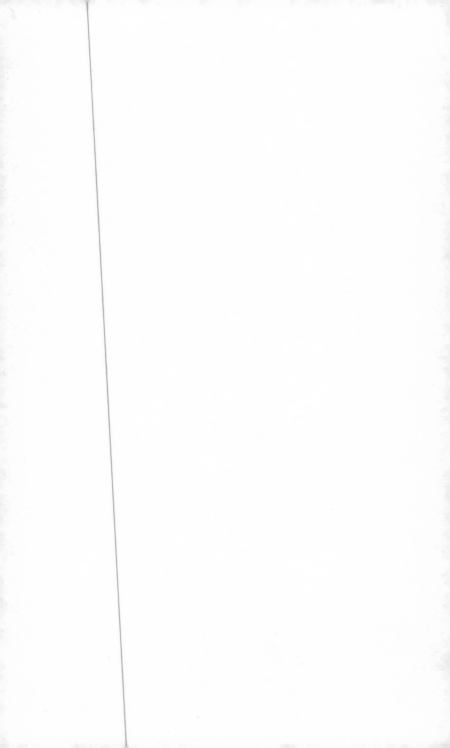

Made in the USA
Coppell, TX
26 November 2021

66500761R00173